Murder Times Three

Murder Times Three

Commissioner Kary Turnell Mysteries

※※※※※※

Mark Okrant

Plaidswede Publishing
Concord, New Hampshire

Murder Times Three: Commissioner Kary Turnell Mysteries

The murder mysteries that follow are fiction. While there is attention to detail in describing the New Hampshire settings in this book, occasionally the author has invented an object for dramatic effect. The events and people described are products of the author's imagination; similarities to actual actions or persons are coincidental.

Printed in the United States of America

ISBN: 978-0-96-268320-6

Published by:
Plaidswede Publishing
P.O. Box 269 Concord, New Hampshire 03302-0269

www.plaidswede.com

Cover photo by Marla Okrant

Cover design by Judy Davison

Price $19.95

Books by Mark Okrant

Judson's Island

A Last Resort

I Knew You When

An Icy Reception

Murder with a View

Sleeping Alongside the Road:
Recollections by Patrons and Owners of Motels

No Vacancy:
The Rise, Demise, and Reprise of America's Motels

Murder at the Grands

Whacked

Death by Lobster

Two If by Sea

One-Track Mind

A Thief in the House

Long Walk, Short Deck

Knock Knock. Who's Dead?

The Remorseful Pawn

Acknowledgements

These three stories in the Commissioner Kary Turnell Mystery Series have been made possible by the support of a number of people:

※※※※※※

Long Walk, Short Deck
Photo by Mark Okrant

Jim Morash, known affectionately as Captain Jim, kindly allowed me full access to the beautiful M/S Mount Washington— the central setting for this Commissioner Kary Turnell investigation. While my wife and I were aboard the historic watercraft, we were hosted by Captain Paul Smith, who filled my head and half of a note pad with wonderful stories about the boat and the gorgeous settings that we passed during our voyage between Weirs Beach and Wolfeboro.

John Scheinman, director of development at Plymouth State University, was my source of information about the Langdon Woods dormitory. Judi Window has been, is, and always will be my go-to person about Manchester. Nick Sackos of Dive Winnipesaukee was a fountain of information about diving gear. Dr. David "Lou" Ferland, retired chief of police with the Portsmouth (N.H.) Police Department, is my go-to guy on matters pertaining to crime scene investigation in these books.

Marla Okrant, my wife of five decades—as always—serves as principal first-round editor, advisor on characters' names, and creator of the books' titles. I truly could not write this series without her multi-faceted input. My two amazingly talented daughters, Robyn and Elisabeth Okrant, offered constant inspiration.

The author wishes to thank George Geers, owner of Plaidswede Publishing, for years of encouragement, patience, and friendship.

※※※※※※

Knock, Knock. Who's Dead?
Photo by Mark Okrant

First and foremost, Judi Window, my longtime dear friend, lifelong resident of the Queen City, and one of the most innovative people I know, inspired me to write Knock. Knock. Who's Dead?

She also introduced me to a cast of incredible people who helped me along the way. John Clayton, executive director of the Manchester Historic Association, provided a wealth of information on the Queen City, and gave me access to the marvelous Millyard Museum. It was a thrill to spend quality time with someone who has had a lifelong impact on the city and state.

Mike Cashion, whose Peddl transportation business was an important element in the story, met with me several times. I also must thank Amy Chhom, real estate broker and entrepreneur, as well as Norri Oberlander, downtown business owner, and Lauren Getts, director of marketing and communications at the Greater Manchester Chamber of Commerce. I've never had a more astute group of advisors.

※※※※※※

The Remorseful Pawn

Photo by Davio DeLuca

Margaret Joyce, president of the Greater Dover Chamber of Commerce, Valerie Rochon, president of the Greater Portsmouth Chamber of Commerce, Michelle Davis, visitor services coordinator at the Greater Portsmouth Chamber of Commerce, and JerriAnne Boggis, executive director at the Black Heritage Trail of New Hampshire have been helpful in researching background about elements of this pair of interesting small cities.

Amos and Mary Desfosses, longtime friends, provided insight about the state university in Durham.

Once again, my thanks to you all.

—*Mark Okrant*

Long Walk, Short Deck

A Commissioner Kary Turnell Murder Mystery

Mark Okrant

Chapter 1

The septuagenarian and his wife boarded the M/S Mount Washington from the dock at Weirs Beach. As the two walked up the short gangplank, no one would have believed that both had entered their eighth decade. Each was of average height and exhibited minimal weight gain over the years. There was an athletic stride to their step and the only clue to their ages was what they playfully termed their "turkey necks." However, on this cool, partly sunny, autumn mid-morning, necks and other wrinkled parts were camouflaged by the light cotton scarves and windbreakers both were wearing.

It came as no surprise to the woman that her husband was immediately recognized by the boat's captain for the day, Quentin Browne. Browne, a tall 50 year old with a head of dark tousled hair, had the perfect personality for a skipper on the Mount, as he and others termed the cruise ship that had plied the waters of Lake Winnipesaukee since the year before the United States entered World War II.

While Browne and the husband had known one another for more than 20 years, the tenor of his greeting was only slightly more enthusiastic than the way he welcomed every passenger who boarded the Mount. Browne waited until the last members of a bus tour group had posed for a compulsory photograph, then the passengers headed into the lowest of three public decks, where hot urns of coffee and water for tea awaited them. Only then did he pull the husband to the side.

Browne couldn't resist chiding his old friend. "I hope you're planning to stay with us for the entire cruise," he laughed. "Please don't make this a working voyage," he added with a firm, friendly squeeze of the husband's shoulder.

"Amen to that," the 70-year-old wife added between sips of a piping hot cup of coffee that her dutiful husband had made for her just the way she liked.

"If I value my marriage... and I most certainly do... this will remain a delightful diversion. As I told you on the phone, Quent, we're here for what the media is calling a staycation, a term I absolutely loathe."

"But an experience you absolutely need," his wife interrupted.

The husband used his right hand to gesture at the Mount's décor. "We'll be on board this classic beauty for two and a half hours, admiring the fall foliage, and staring enviously at the seven- and eight-figure mansions all along the shore. Maybe we'll get lucky and spot a loon or two. But, for my sake, there better not be any unscheduled wildlife on board this morning's sailing."

Unfortunately, among the 200 passengers on board, a handful would be taking part in a drama that was not part of the captain's carefully rehearsed spiel. And, before the Mount would reach its halfway point at the Wolfeboro town docks, an unfortunate out-of-state visitor would meet his demise.

There would be little time for the couple's intended romantic retreat, for this woman was married to Kary Turnell, head of the New Hampshire Task Force for Visitor Safety, master of deductive reasoning, and a peerless crime solver.

Chapter 2

The passengers on board the Mount that morning represented a cross-section of ages. Two young brothers, the O'Neill boys, ages six and eight, began to test their parents' patience within seconds of boarding. Running from bow to stern, they discovered where food and souvenirs could be purchased, and the interior and exterior stairwells could be climbed. Their father, a 45-year-old, dangerously out-of-shape accountant, tried unsuccessfully to catch the boys and contain their sense of adventure. For the first 20 minutes the family was aboard, he found himself apologizing to the growing number of other passengers with whom the boys had collided, nearly tripped or interrupted.

With the male members of the family scurrying elsewhere, Mrs. O'Neill was content to sit in the Captain's Lounge, biding her time until the Mount backed away from its dock. The entire time the boys explored and her husband gave chase, the trim freckle-faced woman sat at a table for four and took an occasional glance out the bow-facing windows. In between sips of her tea, she read a few pages from the murder mystery she kept in her handbag.

Most of the others in the Captain's Lounge were part of a senior citizens bus tour. That large glassed-in space at the bow of the boat provided excellent views of the lake and surrounding landscape. The group's membership, as a reality of nature, was predominantly women. Based on the bantering Mrs. O'Neill overheard, she surmised that a large percentage of these people had traveled together in tour groups previously.

While Kary explored the boat, Nya remained at her table surreptitiously observing several members of the tour group who had separated themselves from the others. As two of the women passed Nya's table, they couldn't resist stopping for a brief chat.

"I hope you won't think me rude," the taller of the two women said while pointing at Nya's enormous, maroon handbag, "but is that a Tumi?"

Before Nya could reply, the shorter woman, heavy-set with hair the color of glacial ice, exclaimed aloud, "Why Mary Lou, sometimes I think you have more brass than a philharmonic orchestra." She focused her gaze on Nya as she continued, "I have to apologize for my friend Mary Lou. She's really a sweetie, but hasn't been able to control her curiosity in the 75 years I've known her."

If Mary Lou was embarrassed, she didn't show it. "Now see here, Cora Lambert, you know I can't resist a beautiful bag, any more than you can keep your eyes off the good-looking men aboard this boat."

Nya could see that reading would need to wait for the time being. So, she placed her book inside the Tumi carry-all and engaged the two women in conversation. She soon learned that Cora Lambert and Mary Lou Silver had been teachers in the New London, Conn., school system. Upon retiring, the two widowed women began a series of travels, most of them by bus within the United States.

When Kary returned to the table, Nya introduced him to the two women as "my retired professor husband." The last thing she wanted to do was pique the curiosity of Cora and May Lou about Kary's present career. Besides, if Kary knew what was good for him, this was to be a day for unwinding, not sleuthing.

"I'm guessing you both are part of the bus tour group we saw boarding back at the Weirs," Kary began to make polite conversation.

"That's correct, Professor," Cora cooed at Kary.

Nya smiled at Cora's response. It was several years since anyone had referred to her husband by his former title. These days, people were more likely to address him as Commissioner or Doctor or, in the case of the people he'd put in prison, something much less flattering.

Mary Lou added, "We see the same faces day in and day out. It gets to be tiresome talking to the identical 50 people."

"Surely, some of these people must have interesting experiences to share," Nya couldn't resist saying.

Before Mary Lou could respond, Cora told the Turnells, "There is one gentleman with us who I'd like to get to know much better. He's a former U.S.

ambassador, and he's gorgeous," she added with a dreamy expression on her face. "We met him at our hotel last night, and, from what I overheard, he's single."

"That is interesting," Nya told her. "Do you know the name of the country where he was posted?"

"It was Kirostanland or something like that," Cora replied, to which Mary Lou shrugged her shoulders.

"Sounds like either Kazakhstan or Kyrgyzstan," Kary replied softly. "So, which one of these people is your former ambassador?"

"Oh, you can't miss him," Cora replied. "He's very tall and beautifully dressed."

Kary recalled a gentleman who matched that description during his own walk through the Mount. There had been something strange about the way he staggered up the staircase between the entry level and second decks, while searching the faces of those onboard. As if on cue, the same man, who Kary ascertained to be at least six feet five with perfectly coiffed gray hair, strode past a nearby stage and across the dance floor where the Turnells and their two new friends were seated.

A longtime news junkie, Kary immediately recognized the man as William H. Marsden III, former ambassador to Kazakhstan during the Obama administration. Marsden was dressed in a three-piece suit with expensive-looking leather wing tips. Kary's investigative sense was aroused, and he deduced that the former ambassador was desperately trying to find a contact who he did not know. Also, despite the late morning hour, it was apparent that Marsden had been drinking.

※※※※※※

While Kary and Nya continued their conversation with Cora and Mary Lou, and Mrs. O'Neill relaxed in the Captain's Lounge, the O'Neill boys and their father made a discovery that would prove valuable. The boys were seeking a hideout to use during their imaginary games, when they spotted two sets of white curtains situated on either side of the boat's second deck dance floor. Before their father could corral them, the boys pulled back the curtain on the port side of the vessel. To their surprise, and the embarrassment of Mr. O'Neill, seated behind the curtain was a member of the crew. Before Mr. O'Neill could apologize and pull his sons away, one of the boys couldn't resist questioning the crewman.

"Why are you in here, mister? That's a pretty small space for a big guy like you."

In spite of his embarrassment, Mr. O'Neill's immediate reaction was similar to his son's. The two small rooms behind the curtains were actually the spaces beneath both outdoor stairwells that lead from the top, open-air deck to the boat's second deck. The crewmember, whose broad shoulders seemed too large for the white uniform coat he wore, looked positively sandwiched into the small space. O'Neill tried not to be obvious while he furtively read the man's nametag: Jackson Kilgore. O'Neill wondered why the man was sitting in such a small space, but said nothing.

Chapter 3

The first hour of the voyage proved uneventful. Nya finally freed herself from the nonstop conversation with the two ladies on the bus tour. As the Mount passed the opulent mansions along the shore of Governors Island, she removed a small, silver Canon Digital Elph camera from her handbag. Kary was amused that his wife still insisted on using such old technology.

"You call yourself a photographer," he laughed. "That old Canon has less than half the number of pixels that your iPad has."

Nya was not amused. "Just answer this. Which one of us is the better photographer—me with this antique, or you with your $1,500 Nikon?"

Kary had to admit that, in terms of photo quality and composition, Nya had him beat.

Now more than half way through the open leg of the two-and-a-half-hour cruise, Kary set off on another tour of the inside of the Mount. From the bridge, the captain announced that the vessel was passing Rattlesnake Island, a long narrow isle whose shores resembled the jaws of a large snake. As they neared Ship and Moose islands just north of the inlet to Alton Bay, Nya stepped out onto the second deck and made her way toward the flagpole at the bow of the Mount.

She jumped about a foot when the Mount's horn sounded and the purser fired a red flare into the air. To pre-empt panic on the part of the 200 passengers aboard, Captain Browne made an announcement over the public address system.

"Ladies and gentlemen, please remain calm. This vessel is in no imminent danger. We have been hailed by a small boat off our starboard bow... that's the right-hand side for you landlubbers." Indeed, the captain's clever use of humor served to assuage the anxieties of all but the most fearful of passengers. He continued, "We will be coming to a full stop as we pass the south shore of Moose Island. At that time, we will either bring the stranded boaters aboard and take them into Wolfeboro harbor, or provide assistance until the New Hampshire Marine Patrol can get them under way on their own."

※※※※※※

Boat passengers are not terribly dissimilar from people driving along the nation's interstate highways. All it takes is a fender bender alongside the road and no one, including the driver, can resist the temptation to see what caused the commotion.

So, following the captain's announcement, nearly everyone rushed to the windows and deck railings on the starboard side of the Mount. A few people were not similarly lured to that side of the boat. It was these passengers who changed the course of events that morning.

Chapter 4

William Marsden III was dealing with a combination of an enduring sense of remorse and the effect of the Glenfiddich single malt whiskey he began consuming the previous evening. As muddled as his mind was feeling, Marsden knew that this would be the perfect opportunity to meet up with the stranger.

The note that was slid beneath Marsden's room door at the motel was the cause of his current condition. The note had been clear. If he wanted to resolve the issue that haunted him from his time in south central Asia, he was to board the MS Mount Washington with the tour group that was staying at the same motel. He was not to discuss his appointed meeting with anyone else. Marsden's contact would recognize him. Only when and where the contact felt the time was right would the two complete their business together. After two years of living with his past mistake, it appeared the suffering was finally about to end.

Sure enough, with nearly everyone standing on the starboard side of the Mount, Marsden made his way past two young men who were slow to join the others. Marsden felt certain that these men had been shadowing him since he boarded the Mount. Nearly tripping over the small stage situated on the second deck, Marsden stood there feeling uncertain of his footing when he heard a voice calling, "Sälem! Körmegeli qan şa boldi," which Marsden immediately recognized as "Hello; long time no see" in the Kazakh language.

Marsden felt a nervous pain in the pit of his stomach. His initial instinct was to turn around and join the others who had crowded along the starboard side of the boat. However, he knew that the only way he would ever deal with the problems of the past was to go toward the voice he'd just heard. Marsden went out the port side door where he joined a man waiting for him on the outside deck. After all this time, he hoped to resolve things peacefully. As he closed the door, he stuck out his hand, in an evident offer of greeting and reconciliation. His offer was met with a cat-like reaction. William Marsden III's cruise was over.

Chapter 5

The Mount lay at full stop alongside the distressed boat. With Nya walking around and taking photographs, Kary's natural curiosity kicked into gear. He positioned himself near the bow, just above where two men were sitting together on the side of a 14-foot bass boat. The open fiberglass craft had three seats and a well for storing a catch of fish. It was powered by a small Mercury outboard motor that was steered by hand.

As Kary peered directly down into the small watercraft, he made two quick observations. The two men appeared a bit too calm for the circumstance of being stalled in the boat lane of a lake as large as Winnipesaukee. Just as curious, it appeared the men had left shore without two items one would expect them to be carrying—oars for propulsion in an emergency and fishing poles. The only item that was observable from Kary's position was a large, green vinyl tarpaulin.

The two men were not the same age. The younger man, who appeared to be in his late twenties or early thirties, had a muscular build and a full head of black hair that was closely cropped. The older man appeared to be in his mid-50s, his gray hair balding substantially. The older man's deep tan and thin, sinewy arms suggested a life of hard work, probably in some primary activity such as farming or fishing. The younger man, who called himself Jim, spoke to Captain Browne in nearly perfect English, with the trace of an accent that Kary placed as southeastern European or south central Asian. At that moment, he wished Nya were with him, as her ear for foreign languages was remarkable.

Suddenly, the older man became agitated about the pace of their progress. When Kary heard him yell at the younger man, he was convinced that his estimate about the men's region of origin was fairly accurate.

What ensued was a complete surprise to Captain Browne. As was expected of him, Browne extended an invitation to the two stranded boaters. He welcomed them to come aboard while he radioed to the Marine Patrol in Glendale. Since the Mount's position was approximately six and one-half nautical miles from the patrol's base station, Browne advised the boaters, who called themselves Bob and Jim Smith, that a rescue boat would take a minimum of half an hour to arrive. Browne gave the Smiths two alternatives: they could come aboard and ride into Wolfeboro while their boat remained in its present location, or the Mount could tow the disabled craft into port. The two men appeared to disagree on the best solution. Finally, after a discussion that was beginning to impact the Mount's schedule and Captain Browne's patience, Jim Smith called to Browne.

"You have been most hospitable, Captain. My father and I are grateful. However, we have already inconvenienced you a great deal. It appears we are in no imminent danger. So, we have decided to remain here with our boat until the Marine Patrol boat has arrived. Hopefully, they will tow us into the dock where we rented this boat."

Browne was not about to argue with the Smiths. He had already spent a good deal of time helping two men who did not wish to be rescued. It was time to head into Wolfeboro.

Kary remained close to Browne throughout the encounter; his analytical instincts had been aroused. These men were visitors to New Hampshire, and Kary was sworn to protect such people. However, he couldn't help but wonder about the circumstances of the encounter.

Kary knew that Browne was anxious to head to the wheelhouse so the Mount could get under way. As the captain placed his foot on the first of 10 steps leading there, Kary called to his old friend.

"Quent, can we talk for a minute?"

"Sure, Kary, but let's go up to the wheelhouse, so I can get this old boat moving."

The wheelhouse was a 15-by-15-foot space that overlooked the bow of the vessel. Windows on all four sides afforded the captain a 270-degree look at the waters of Lake Winnipesaukee, which were as smooth as blue glass.

At the front of the wheelhouse was a set of four windows. A console stretched across the structure. Kary noticed the large number of instruments and recognized a depth finder, compass, anemometer to measure wind speed and direction, and a VHF radio to provide direct contact with the dispatcher serving the lakes region. A wood-crafted ship's wheel dominated the center of the console.

Normally, Kary would have been curious to examine the instruments, but there was news that wouldn't keep.

"So, what's on your mind, Kary?" Before Kary could answer, Browne completed his own thought. "You and I have known one another for a long time; so, I'm reading trouble on that face of yours."

Kary smiled in spite of his concerns. "Tell me you didn't find the 'Smiths' behavior unusual and I'll head right downstairs to finish the cruise."

Browne punched Kary lightly in the arm. "As much I'd like to send you on your way, I have to admit that whole episode was a strange one." Then he paused before completing his response, "Everyone from the governor to the state cops trusts your instincts; who am I to disagree? So, what are you thinking?"

"Just a couple of things," Kary began. "Why rent a bass boat if you aren't going to fish? If all they were going to do was cruise around, there are more comfortable boats they could have selected."

"I don't know, Kary. Maybe the bass boat was their cheapest option; or, maybe it was the only boat available." Browne continued, "What else do you have?"

"Isn't it unusual to turn down an opportunity to get out of the water and go aboard a classic old boat like the Mount?"

"I have to admit that wouldn't be my choice. But, as they say, to each his own."

Kary shook his head. "I may be grasping at straws here, but my instinct tells me we will regret letting those two men stay out there."

"It's a free country, Kary. They were within their rights." Browne looked at his watch. "Besides, the Marine Patrol will be arriving in 20 minutes to tow them. If there's a problem, it will take care of itself."

As Kary was about to leave the wheelhouse, there was a soft knock on the door. Kary took the liberty of opening it and found himself face-to-face with Cora Lambert and May Lou Silver, the two women from the bus tour group who had befriended Nya an hour earlier.

"Oh look, Cora, it's our friend the professor," Mary Lou exclaimed.

"It's very nice to see you two ladies," Kary offered. "I presume you weren't looking for me."

"Yes and no," Cora replied. She seemed upset, a fact that didn't escape Kary's attention.

Kary stepped aside to admit the two women to the wheelhouse. He introduced Cora and Mary Lou to Browne.

"Oh, it's an honor to meet you, Captain. Your boat is beautiful."

Browne was his usual politically correct self. "Welcome aboard, ladies. I presume you didn't climb all of those stairs just to tell me that."

"Is there a problem?" Kary asked.

"Yes, we think so," Cora replied breathlessly. "Ambassador Marsden is missing!"

"Don't you mean that you can't find him?" Browne asked.

"No. I feel certain that he isn't on this boat anymore," Cora replied. "It's impossible to miss him. He's very tall and handsome; beside that, he didn't stop walking around and around once the trip started." As she said this, Cora looked at Kary for his corroboration. He promptly agreed with the two women.

Wanting to avoid a potentially embarrassing situation but needing to get the boat into Wolfeboro, Browne asked Kary if he would agree to help the ladies find the missing ambassador. As the two women left the wheelhouse, Kary remained behind momentarily. The expression on his face betrayed what he was thinking.

"Oh come on, Kary. Don't tell me you think the Smiths kidnapped the ambassador from right under our noses. Jeezus... they were a couple of harmless sightseers, not magicians."

Chapter 6

When Kary returned to the table that he shared with Nya, he found her sitting with her arms across her chest. He could see that he wasn't about to fool his wife by remaining silent.

"Okay, Kary. I've known you too long to disregard your body language. Something's happened; now tell me what it is."

Kary gave Nya a hug. "It may be nothing, but we're looking for Ambassador Marsden. You haven't seen him have you?"

"Come to think of it, not in about a half an hour," she replied. "Do you think something's happened to him?"

Kary replied, "I don't know. Quentin asked me to take a look around the boat. Cora and Mary Lou are searching, too. Would you care to join us?"

Nya was out of her chair before Kary could finish his sentence. "I'll head toward the lower deck and text you if I spot him." Then, she added with a wry smile, "He's not armed and dangerous is he?"

Kary knew full well that Nya was perpetually concerned about his safety, especially after he'd had several close calls with perpetrators during his time as a private investigator. He smiled and kissed Nya on the cheek. "No, my dear, I think we are both perfectly safe out here on the big lake."

Following a search that lasted ten minutes, Kary looked out of the glass door leading to the port side deck. Wolfeboro was coming into view. Unfortunately, the ambassador had not been found.

Before he could return to their table, Kary was approached by one of the Mount's crew members, a young man named Danny Burdette.

"Excuse me, sir," Burdette called to him. "I'm the deck officer for this cruise. You are Commissioner Turnell, am I correct?"

Kary nodded.

"Captain Browne would like to see you in the wheelhouse as soon as possible, sir."

"Please tell him I'll be there in three minutes. I have an urgent phone call to make first."

As Burdette strode away, heading toward the stairwell that lead up to the wheelhouse, Kary hit a single button on his cell phone. At the other end of the line, Sergeant Bob Norton answered on the first ring.

"Commissioner. This is an unexpected surprise. What can I do for you?"

Kary answered Norton's question with one of his own, "Where are you right now?"

By coincidence and good fortune, Norton and his family were spending the day in Wolfeboro, visiting the area's three first-rate attractions, the Wright Museum, the New Hampshire Boat Museum, and the Libby Museum.

"I hate to ask this, Sergeant, but I'm going to need you to meet me on the dock when the Mount Washington comes into port."

"How soon will that be?" Norton asked as he was met with a look of resigned disappointment on his wife's face.

"We should be in port within ten minutes. People will be starting to disembark five minutes after that. Unfortunately, we have a missing passenger."

"How the heck did that happen?" Norton asked. "I take it you'll want me to prevent anyone from leaving until you approve."

"That's why I pay you the big bucks, Sergeant; you don't need me to paint you a picture." Kary then inquired about Lieutenant Bendix's whereabouts, but was told that she was hiking in the White Mountains with her sister.

"We'll have to do without the lieutenant. Fortunately, Nya is on board with me. She has her iPad with her; so she'll need to fill the online research void as best she can."

Kary continued to walk up the stairs toward the wheelhouse while talking to Norton.

"Is there anyone else you want me to contact?" Norton asked.

"Yes, get in touch with Stu Garrison, at the Major Crimes Unit. Tell him to have some MCU people on alert. And warn him that he may need to contact the FBI at a moment's notice. I'll fill him in as soon as I can, probably about thirty minutes from now."

Before Norton could hang up his cell phone, Kary had changed his mind.

"Sergeant, I think it's a good idea for you to call Garrison and ask him to have a couple of people waiting at the docks in Alton Bay, and a couple more at Marine Patrol headquarters in Glendale." Kary had one more thought, "Oh, and Sergeant, tell Garrison that this may all be much ado about nothing. But my gut tells me otherwise."

Sergeant Norton had learned to trust Kary's gut.

Chapter 7

Norton immediately began the phone calls he'd been asked to make. In addition, he called in a favor with Wolfeboro PD, knowing full well that he'd need some help at the docks.

When Kary entered the wheelhouse, there were three other passengers inside. The captain was a master of public relations; so, it didn't surprise Kary that Browne would accede to the wishes of passengers to see the great wooden wheel used to steer the large boat. However, given the urgency of Kary's meeting with Browne, this was an inopportune time to admit two small boys and their father to the area. Before Kary could register his opinion, Browne held his hand up.

"Commissioner Turnell, these are three members of the O'Neill family. I think you may want to listen to what they have to say."

Kary had his doubts that two grammar school students, who appeared to be somewhere between five and eight years of age, would have anything to say that he needed to hear at that moment. After all, he had state and federal law enforcement officials on call, all awaiting his interpretation of what had happened aboard the Mount. It wasn't long before Kary learned he was mistaken.

The boys' father spoke first. He extended his hand to Kary as he introduced himself.

"I understand you are Dr. Turnell, the state's Commissioner of Visitor Safety."

Kary nodded.

"My name is David O'Neill. I'm traveling with my wife and two young sons. My older boy is Davy Jr; he's eight. The younger boy is Timmy, who's six."

Kary remained remarkably patient, given the urgency of the situation.

"It's nice to meet you, Mr. O'Neill, Davy and Timmy. What can I do for you?"

"It's what we can do for you, Mr. Commissioner," Davy blurted out before his father could stop him.

"I apologize for my son, Dr. Turnell. The boys have been running all over the boat and probably had more than their quota of sugar."

Kary crouched down so he was at eye level with the two boys.

"So, Davy and Timmy, what urgent information do you have to share with me?"

"We saw him," Davy spoke first.

"Yeah, we saw him!" Timmy blurted out as his father tried unsuccessfully to control his younger son's energy.

"Who did you see, boys?" Kary asked. Despite his impatience to conclude this interview, he knew that cases had been solved on tips that came from far stranger sources.

"We saw the captain; he was behind the white curtain," both boys said in unison.

Kary was doubting his own judgment for spending valuable time in conversation with the three O'Neills. Still, he persisted questioning the boys.

Pointing toward Browne as he concentrated on steering the ship past a dangerous spot on the route to Wolfeboro harbor, he asked, "You saw Captain Browne behind a white curtain?"

"No!" the boys shouted. "Not that captain; a younger one."

This induced smiles from Kary and Browne.

Mr. O'Neill explained. He told how the boys had been running all over the boat, with him following several steps behind, in an effort to prevent them from tripping anyone and causing an injury.

"At one point, the boys ran over to the white curtain on the left side of the boat."

Kary knew the exact place, as Nya and he had been sitting less than 20 feet from there shortly after the Mount left Weirs Beach.

Browne explained how, to his utter embarrassment, the boys had decided to look behind the curtain. "They were looking for a good place to hide," he said. "Fortunately, I had nearly caught up to them when they pulled back the curtain."

"What was back there?"

At this point, Captain Browne told them, "That's a place where we store odds and ends. Sometimes there's rope, toilet paper or supplies for an event on board. It's a pretty small area. Our deck hands hate it because it's nothing more than a space under the stairs leading from the second deck to the top deck. I can't even count the number of crew members who have nearly knocked themselves cold in there. As a result, no one in my crew goes under there unless it's absolutely necessary."

Once again, Davy had the temerity to contradict what he'd just heard from an adult.

"Well, there was a man sitting under there when we pulled back the curtain," the boy told the three adults.

"My son is telling you the truth, gentleman. There was a member of your crew under there. He was wearing a white coat like your other crewmen, and what looked like a captain's cap."

Browne spoke next. "What! One of my crew hiding under the stairs while we were already under way? I should have him keel-hauled," he couldn't resist teasing. Nautical law and the absence of a keel on the Mount made that an unfeasible scenario. "Boys, what did this captain look like?" Browne asked.

"Well, he looked big, like a football player."

When Kary looked toward Mr. O'Neill for corroboration, he replied, "The boys are right. He was a muscular guy with dark hair that seemed to be cut short... but, remember, he was wearing that cap."

"Is there anything else you can tell us?" Kary asked.

Suddenly, O'Neill slapped the side of his own head. "Of course there is! What was I thinking? I saw his name tag. Let me think a second... I remember ...his name was Jackson Kilgore."

Kary saw Browne's reaction when he heard what O'Neill told them. He waited until the O'Neills left the wheelhouse to question his friend.

"What's wrong, Quent?"

"There's no one on this crew named Jackson Kilgore, at least not anymore."

"What do you mean?"

"Jackson Kilgore was a member of our crew for a season. We didn't realize it at the time, but he was a very sick young man. Unfortunately, Jackson died during the offseason. No one ever turned in his uniform, and we never pursued the matter because the company was having everything redesigned for the next cruise season."

"Then this crew member was an imposter, no doubt. My guess is he's the person who has something in common with Ambassador Marsden."

"What are you thinking, Kary?"

"Elementary, my dear captain. It's apparent that neither the ambassador nor this mysterious crewman is still aboard the Mount."

Browne agreed with Kary's assessment, especially when a quick search of the bowels of the boat turned up neither man.

Chapter 8

Now one half mile from the docks at Wolfeboro, the Mount rounded Seawalls Point. As the boat came into view, Sergeant Norton stood near the outdoor dining area of the Wolfeboro Dockside Grille with two members of the Wolfeboro Police Department. The older of the two men, Dave Arnold, a tall, gray-haired corporal, saw the Mount just before Norton did.

"Here she comes, Bob. I guess you'll want us to come aboard and take names and addresses."

Norton, who had the advantage of working with Commissioner Turnell on two previous cases, had a good idea what Kary's expectations would be.

"Yeah, that's about it, Dave."

"What's it like working on the Visitor Safety Task Force?" Arnold asked.

"It's like nothing I'd ever experienced before." Norton replied.

"I hear your commissioner is something else."

"I'll tell you this, Dave. Commissioner Turnell is ten times smarter than any other boss I've ever had. The guy's mind is uncanny."

"How so?"

"Sometimes it feels like he was in the room when our perps were planning their crimes. He has a kind of sixth sense about what those creeps are thinking. Out of the blue, he'll ask Lieutenant Bendix or me to follow up on some clue. At first, I thought he was just making busy work for me and, frankly, it pissed me off."

"But then... ?" Arnold asked.

"Every time he's done that, I've found information that leads to an arrest. And, to be honest, Dave, I wouldn't have thought to do that stuff in a million years. But, what sets the guy apart from most career cops is the way he builds a case as we go along. He thinks ahead to what a judge and jury will expect. I'm telling you, Dave, when this guy wraps a case, it's over. The perpetrator is as good as on his way to prison."

As if on cue, Norton's cell phone buzzed in his pocket. He walked around the corner and stood under a roof near the restaurant's entryway.

"Sergeant Norton."

Kary was on the other end of the line. Norton wondered whether his boss's ears were burning.

"We're almost there, Sergeant."

"Yeah, I can see you. Have the passengers been alerted that they need to remain on board for a while?"

"The captain is about to make the announcement. Some people won't be very happy about that. But, we'll try to limit their inconvenience."

"So, how is this going to work?" Norton asked.

"We'll split up into three stations. People have been told to queue up just outside the Captain's Lounge on the second public deck. I'll meet with them at the bottom of the stairs in the main salon on the lower public deck."

"Then what happens?" Norton asked.

"You've taken this cruise before, haven't you, Sergeant?"

Norton replied that he had been aboard on several occasions.

"Then you're familiar with the fact that the cruise company employs a photographer who has everyone pose before they board."

"Yes sir; I am."

"I've instructed Captain Browne to have the photographer send a file of all the photos to me."

Norton couldn't help but smile. "You brought a laptop with you on a day cruise, Commissioner?"

"Of course not, Sergeant." Kary pretended to be incredulous. "Nya is with me; and she doesn't go anywhere without her iPad."

Norton knew his boss well enough to realize that Kary's irritation had been feigned. "What was I thinking?" he added with a smile. "But won't it take forever to go through hundreds of haphazard photos."

"I'm way ahead of you, Sergeant. I've instructed the captain to have his photographer alphabetize the file before he sends it."

"I should have expected as much," Norton deadpanned.

Kary went on to explain to Norton that each passenger will pass by a table set up at the bottom of the stairway. The table will be where Nya and her iPad are stationed. Crew members will funnel people up to the table in an orderly fashion. We'll use some of those velvet ropes and stanchions to control the flow. Each passenger will state his or her last and first name, while Nya compares names with pictures. Once she has approved, two other crew members will direct them to the stage situated near the boat's exit ramp. We will have two tables, one on either side of the stage. The two Wolfeboro cops you recruited will handle those tables where they'll collect background information and determine whether the passengers saw anything of significance during the cruise.

"Won't that take hours?" Norton asked.

"Unfortunately, it won't be quick to process a couple hundred people... unless you have a better idea," Kary replied.

Norton was thinking ahead. "Actually, I do. Pass out slips of paper and find as many pens or pencils as you can. While people are queuing up outside the Captain's Lounge have them write their names, addresses, and other contact information on the slips. Then, when they get to the tables, all the officers will need to do is compare information with what's on their operator licenses. This way, we'll only need to detain the few people who have pertinent information to share."

"That's an excellent idea. We'll do just that," Kary told him.

"I do have a question. What will I be doing all of this time?" Norton asked.

"Playing middle linebacker, Sergeant," Kary replied with a bit of humor in his voice.

"Middle linebacker?"

"Yes, if anyone should decide to do a runner without stopping at the officers' tables, it will be your job to change that person's mind."

"Sometimes I feel like I'm being used because I'm beautiful," Norton couldn't resist saying.

"What is it that Carly Simon sang... 'nobody does it better'?"

Chapter 9

As the screening of passengers ensued, Kary and Browne retreated to the wheelhouse.

"This may be my toughest case yet, Quent," Kary announced.

"I knew when I invited Nya and you onboard, I was opening myself up to trouble," Browne replied with a half-smile on his face. "So, what are you thinking?"

"For starters, we have a missing person who may not be a murder victim. I mean, what if Mr. Marsden simply couldn't take life anymore and took a dive into the lake when no one was looking," Kary replied.

"You don't really think that happened, do you?" Browne asked. "My tour guiding isn't that bad, is it?"

The two men enjoyed a brief laugh, despite the dire circumstances.

"I doubt that he jumped, Quent. But, that's one of three possible circumstances."

"And the others are…?" Browne asked.

"Suicide, an accidental fall by an inebriated passenger, or murder," Kary told him.

Browne shook his head. "Right about now, suicide sounds like my favorite choice. Choices two and three will involve more paper work than I'd like to be doing."

Just then, there was a knock on the wheelhouse door. The interruption took both men by surprise.

"What the hell?" Browne said with a start. "No one should be up here now."

Kary opened the door and admitted a short, red-faced man with brown curly hair, who appeared to be in his early forties.

Browne couldn't mask his impatience. "I'm sorry, sir, but you should be downstairs with the other passengers."

The man offered no apology for his actions. He told Kary and Browne that his name was Carl Timms, and he had urgent information to share.

"There are two officers taking statements downstairs," Kary reminded him.

"Yeah, I know. But, I have information that won't wait and I have an appointment to get to… I've gotta get off this boat right away."

"What's the nature of your urgent appointment?" Kary asked.

"I'm not at liberty to say," Timms replied.

"Well then, you need to ..." Kary began.

"Look, I came up here because I think I saw something that will help you."

Kary's sixth sense was activated. No announcement was made about the purpose of the background checks that were proceeding two decks below the wheelhouse. So, what information could this man have and why was he in such a rush to leave the Mount?

Using the same calm demeanor that had served him so well in numerous cases, including several when his life was in peril, Kary asked Timms to share his information.

"I saw two men. They were similar in appearance. Early twenties, tall, muscular, with dark hair that was close cropped."

Kary considered Timms' description for a moment. The men he was describing sounded like younger versions of the two men who were stranded on the lake. Also, the description was remarkably similar to the crewmember who had been identified as Jackson Kilgore.

"Is there anything else you can tell us about those two men?" Kary asked.

"Yes, as a matter of fact. The two of them seemed to be following that tall guy wearing the suit. Wherever he went, they followed him. And, there was one other thing," he added.

"What was that, Mr. Timms?"

"I overheard them talking while they were watching the tall guy."

"Could you tell what they were saying?" Browne asked.

"No. They were speaking a foreign language. I don't know what it was, but it sure wasn't English. It wasn't French or Spanish, either."

"One last question, did you see them at the time we were stopped assisting that stranded boat?"

"They were still near the stage on the dance floor, not far from where the tall guy was standing. When I went outside to see what was happening with that small boat, they were still inside watching the tall guy."

Browne quickly called downstairs to ask the cops to detain the two men Timms had described. He returned with a look of dejection as he informed Kary that the process downstairs was complete and at least half the passengers had left the Mount.

Kary quickly informed Sergeant Norton about the situation and asked him to find the men in Wolfeboro. Next, Kary told Timms that the line downstairs had dissipated, and reminded him to share his contact information with one of the officers.

Once Timms left, Browne asked, "What do you make of all that?"

"That just added a major kink in the proceedings." He pulled a small pad and pen from his pocket and wrote as he talked. "We have a missing former ambassador, another missing man who palmed himself off as a crew member, and now two mystery men speaking an unfamiliar language..."

"And let's not forget the two stranded men in the bass boat who, for some reason, refused our hospitality and decided to wait for the Marine Patrol to pick them up," Browne added.

"I'll bet you an ice cream cone when we get back to the Weirs," Kary told Browne.

"Okay, what's the bet?"

"I owe you two scoops of your favorite flavor if those two men are still on the lake when the Marine Patrol arrives."

Not long after Browne agreed to the wager, he received a message on the VHF radio in the wheelhouse. After hearing the message, he turned to Kary and said, "I should know not to bet with you."

"What did the Marine Patrol have to say?" Kary smiled as he asked, while knowing full well what the message had been.

"There was no boat in the area matching the description I gave them. Not so much as a trace. One of the patrolmen stopped several boaters in the area and asked if they'd seen the bass boat. No one had noticed anything."

"That's discouraging," Kary replied, "but not necessarily a game changer."

"You're right!" Browne exclaimed. "I wrote down the call numbers from the bow of their boat. I've sent it to the patrol guys; so, it should be a piece of cake to pick them up when they return it."

Kary was much more skeptical than Browne. One small compensation was the Ben and Jerry's ice cream cone he'd be enjoying later, compliments of his friend Captain Browne.

As Kary started to leave the wheelhouse, Browne called to him. "All I can say is good luck with this one, Kary. You may or may not have a murdered tourist on your hands. And, let's see, any one of five people could have done the deed."

As Kary stepped out of the wheelhouse, he turned and replied, "Or, all of them."

Chapter 10

Five minutes after Kary joined Nya and the two officers in the main salon of the Mount, Norton made his way breathlessly onto the boat. He was sweating profusely.

Kary couldn't resist chiding his team member. "You look like someone who's just run a marathon, Sergeant."

"I was all the way down South Main Street when I heard the boat's horn sound," he replied. It wasn't long before the ultra-fit officer was breathing normally. "I knew you wouldn't want me left behind, so I ran like a bat out of hell to get here."

"That was a commendable act on your part," Kary told him. "However, you needn't have bothered because Nya, you, and I will be staying here for the time being."

Nya overheard what Kary said. "So, we're going to have a pleasant lunch in Wolfeboro," she chided her husband.

"Not exactly, my dear," he replied. "The three of us and these two officers," he added while pointing to the two Wolfeboro police who had assisted with the passenger interviews, "will find a quiet place to debrief... hopefully over a sandwich and a cold drink."

"Will the Mount be returning to Weirs Beach right now?" Nya asked.

"In about ten minutes. Wolfeboro PD has been kind enough to loan us one of their detectives. He's doing an inventory of the space under the stairs as we speak. He'll bag any evidence and take photographs."

By this time, it was evident that Norton wasn't able to find the two mysterious men that the passenger named Timms had identified. Kary was too preoccupied to show concern for that news. "They'll turn up" was all he said.

※※※※※※

Before the group of five sat down for lunch in the outside seating provided by the Downtown Grille Café, Kary had already written an agenda in the small spiral-bound notebook he carried. He removed the notebook from his pocket and looked at the list he had made: 1) who is Marsden(?); 2) origin and destination of two "stranded" boaters; 3) motive, means, and opportunity of the mysterious crewman; 4) who were the two passengers stalking Marsden(?); and 5) other possible witnesses.

Just as Kary presented this list to the other four diners, his cell phone rang. It was apparent from the way he'd answered the phone that the caller was Quentin Browne, who, by now, was piloting the Mount back to Weirs Beach.

"What's happening, Quent?"

"Well, you know how the Marine Patrol told us that the bass boat was no longer in the area when they arrived?" Browne asked.

"Of course; it cost you the price of a two-scoop ice cream cone."

"Well, apparently they kept searching the area and found something within yards of where we originally stopped to help them," Browne's voice betrayed his concern.

Kary had a premonition about what Browne was going to tell him. "So, what did they find?"

"They found the crewman's jacket and cap that the so-called Jackson Kilgore was wearing. What the hell is that supposed to tell us?" he exclaimed.

Kary was still deep in thought when he returned to the lunch table. This did not go unnoticed by the others at the table.

"Tell us what's going on, Kary" Nya said, as the others stared at the commissioner.

Kary shared the news about the retrieved items of clothing with the others.

"So, what's that mean, Commissioner?" Norton asked.

"I'll be damned if I know, Sergeant," he replied.

Hearing this, Corporal Arnold couldn't resist chiding Norton under his breath. "I thought you said the commissioner's mind is uncanny, Bob. So how come he doesn't know what's going on?"

Before Norton could reply to the corporal's dig, Nya looked across at Arnold and said quietly, "I'll bet you a lobster dinner he soon will, Corporal."

Arnold thought it best to keep quiet. But, Kary wasn't troubled for long.

"Let's take a half hour to review the items on my list. Then, we'll be in a better position to determine our next actions."

Chapter 11

Before Kary and the others could begin their debriefing, Kary's cell phone rang a second time. He recognized the name on caller ID and signaled to the others at the table to take five.

On the other end of the line was Stu Garrison, now a major and the director of the state's excellent Major Crimes Unit. MCU and his Visitor Safety Task Force had worked together on two previous murder cases. The two men had a great deal of mutual respect that was evolving into a friendship.

"Tell me what's happened, Kary. Sergeant Norton told me you have a missing passenger from the Mount Washington, now presumed dead, I suspect."

Kary took five minutes to brief Garrison about what had happened up until that moment.

"Jeezus, Kary. You seem to have a knack for attracting strange cases. Most of our work is pretty cut and dry... a woman shoots her husband and is holed up in a sleazy cabin someplace. We surround the joint, talk her into giving up her weapon. She surrenders and gives up her gun... end of story. But, not you. Your bad guys ride trains, hide bodies at golf courses, and disappear into Lake Winnipesaukee. You'd better be careful or you'll develop a reputation for grandstanding."

In truth, Garrison had the highest respect for Kary's investigative skills, and the commissioner's willingness to deflect credit to other law enforcement personnel who were part of his criminal investigations. Kary exuded respect for other members of the state's law enforcement family, and was widely respected for it.

"I'm just lucky, I guess, Stu. There's one thing that concerns me about this case... just like all of the others so far."

"What's that?" Garrison asked.

"Because we're dealing with out-of-state visitors, I feel like the governor has me on a stop watch. The last thing he expects is for the state's reputation as a safe and beautiful destination to be tarnished."

"I understand your concern, Kary. And, this time your apparent victim is a former U.S. ambassador."

"Thanks for pouring peroxide on an open wound, Stu," Kary replied.

"What are friends for, Kary?" Garrison couldn't resist saying before closing the connection.

※※※※※※

Kary rejoined the others at the outside table just as their food was arriving. As he sat, Kary told Nya and Norton that Garrison had sent his regards. While he picked at his lunch, Kary reminded the others about the tasks that lay ahead.

He began with Nya. "Since Lieutenant Bendix is unavailable for another 24 hours, I need you to use your iPad to find information about Ambassador Marsden. Did he have any posts other than Kazakhstan? Were there any problems during his watch… that sort of thing?"

Before Kary could move onto the next issue, Nya replied, "His name has been troubling me since we met Cora and Mary Lou on the Mount. There's something peculiar about the ambassador, but I can't remember what it is?"

Always a much quicker eater than Kary, Nya had finished her lunch well ahead of him. So she excused herself from the others. "I'm going to find a quiet comfortable place to do some research on my iPad. I also want to check the photos I took during our trip over here." Nya stood up and excused herself while Kary, Norton and the two Wolfeboro officers continued their meeting.

Not wishing to keep Corporal Arnold and his partner from returning to their normal shift as patrolman, Kary told them, "I don't have any jurisdiction over you two men, but there is something you can do that will help the sergeant and me immensely."

"We're happy to help," Arnold replied. In truth, he would have liked nothing better than to be assigned to work with the intense but resourceful commissioner and Norton, who was highly regarded among uniform personnel in the state.

"I appreciate your willingness to serve," Kary replied. ""I'm hoping a couple of enterprising local cops like you can solve a puzzle for me."

Both officers were curious.

"While we were onboard the Mount, a passenger named Carl Timms approached us. He seemed a bit overzealous to me. Timms was also in a hell-fire rush to leave the Mount and head to some emergency meeting, presumably here in Wolfeboro."

"So, you'd like us to find out who Timms is and where he was really headed," Arnold replied.

"Exactly."

To which Norton added, "And, knowing the commissioner, he'd like that information ASAP."

The two officers rose and promised to find what they could as soon as their police department duties allowed. Kary shook hands and tipped his fedora at the two men as they departed.

"What's next?" Norton asked Kary.

"There's some information that we need to find urgently, and other stuff we'll be able to find in the next couple of days."

"I presume you're talking about the IDs of those two stranded boaters you've been describing."

"Absolutely. We can't allow that trail to turn cold, or we'll never see those two men again."

"Is there something you want me to do on that front?" Norton asked.

"No. I have Garrison and the MCU on that trail. MCU and the Harbor Patrol have accepted the responsibility for locating the two boaters, hopefully by the end of daylight today."

Kary had to admire his young colleague's demeanor. Norton had the tracking instincts and keenness of a wolf. While he seemed impetuous at times, once the sergeant was on the trail of a suspect, the offender's days of freedom were limited.

"You and I have worked well together for nearly a year now, Sergeant. So, I've saved the two toughest parts of this investigation for the two of us." Kary could read the glint of pride in Norton's eyes as he said this. Looking at the time on his cell phone, Kary continued, "We have about an hour until the Mount returns. Before we board the boat for home, I'd like to spend the time looking at motive, means, and opportunity."

Norton pondered for several seconds before offering a theory. "If we can presume that the mystery crewman was responsible for the ambassador's disappearance..."

"I think we can safely do that," Kary interrupted.

"Assuming that's true, then I'd be willing to rule out a random act in this instance."

Kary was impressed with Norton's growth as an investigator during the time the two had worked together. So, he felt certain a quick challenge wouldn't unsettle the young sergeant.

"Why rule out a random act?" Kary asked.

Norton smiled across as Kary. He knew Kary wanted him to support such an assertion. "Well, Commissioner, I'd say that a guy who disguises himself as a crewman and then hides in a space that would only fit a Hobbit, has planned his actions rather carefully."

Kary smiled at Norton. "You do make a good point, Sergeant. Although, I suppose there's a defense attorney out there somewhere who will argue for manslaughter."

Norton threw his head back and laughed, "...or self defense," he countered.

"Of course, based on the information we have, we're still presuming that the disguised crewman committed a crime. As of right now, solid evidence is still unavailable."

"Not anymore!" Nya enthusiastically called to the two men as she entered the outdoor eating space.

"Did you find something, Nya?"

"I sure have. Remember that junky old camera you were making fun of a couple of hours ago?" Nya smiled broadly at Kary.

"Yes, the one with the tiny amount of pixels."

"Well, take a look at these, mister hotshot photographer," she replied.

Standing between Kary and Norton, Nya opened her iPad to the photos app. Calling up the first picture then using her thumb and forefinger to enlarge it, she said, "How's this for photographic clarity?"

Amazingly, Nya had captured a sequence of four pictures showing a violent interaction between the mystery crewman and the tall, inebriated former ambassador. In the first picture, the ambassador had just exited through the doorway amidships on the port side of the Mount. His hand was extended and the crewman had grabbed the ambassador's arm. In the second picture, the crewman had wrestled the ambassador over to the chain link fence and was beginning to lift his right leg over the steel railing. The crewman was facing toward Nya's camera, so his image was clear. In the third, he had just delivered a hard punch to the ambassador's left cheek. In the final shot of the sequence, the crewman had climbed over the railing and freed the ambassador's desperate grasp, as the two men were beginning their plunge into Lake Winnipesaukee.

Norton let out one of his characteristic shrill whistles.

Kary hugged Nya's shoulders. "Not only did your little Canon camera perform admirably, but how in the world did you remain so calm under such trying circumstances? I'd never have been able to hold the camera still."

"I had no clue what was on those photos. All I tried to do was take a photo of the Mount from a bow perspective. If I'd known what those pictures showed, I'd have shown them to you an hour ago."

Kary placed his hand on Norton's shoulder. "That takes care of any claim of self-defense, wouldn't you agree, Sergeant?"

Chapter 12

Just as Kary and Norton were about to resume their evaluation of the mystery crewman's means and opportunity, Kary's cell phone rang. On the other end of the line was MCU director, Stu Garrison. Kary could tell from the background noise that Garrison was calling from a helicopter.

"What's the news from the ground, Kary?"

"I take it you decided to get up this way as soon as possible," Kary replied.

"With evidence showing that this is a homicide, I figured it was best not to wait," Garrison replied.

"Your timing is impeccable." Kary then told Garrison how a fortuitous set of four photographs taken by Nya show that the former ambassador had been a victim of assassination.

"Tell Nya for me that she did great!" Garrison continued, "This whole situation is about as bizarre as it gets. Why would the guy risk his life to pull Ambassador Marsden into the drink? From what you're describing, the disguised crewman was in complete physical control. Why didn't he just throw Marsden overboard? Chances are he would have drowned, especially if he was as inebriated as you described."

"Those are good questions, Stu. I wish I had answers for you."

"So, should we ask the Marine Patrol to do an underwater search of the area?" Garrison asked.

"Not just yet," Kary replied. "I'm hoping the body or bodies will surface in the next day or two. But, if they don't, we won't have much choice." Next, Kary proceeded to tell Garrison that he wanted MCU to supervise the Marine Patrol and local law enforcement in a thorough search of the area between Alton Bay and Glendale, along the south shore of Lake Winnipesaukee.

"I take it we're looking for the two men who flagged down the Mount late this morning," Garrison replied.

"That's right. We want to find them and their boat. Something tells me there will be forensic evidence your people need to look at."

"I have your description of the men and the ID number from the bass boat. Is there anything I need to tell the search group?"

"Not that I need to tell you this, Stu, but the people in the field should proceed with caution. I didn't see any weapons in their boat while they were next to the Mount; but I can't guarantee there weren't any."

Garrison told Kary that the chopper's ETA at Laconia Airport was in five minutes. He and his sergeant were to be met by a state police cruiser. From there, he would meet with his search group in West Alton, which was equidistant between the east and west bounds of the area where they would be looking.

※※※※※※

As Kary closed his cell phone, he noticed that it was now 1:30, 15 minutes before the Mount was scheduled to make a return trip to Weirs Beach. He looked out into Wolfeboro Bay just as the boat was docking. Kary had amazing powers of concentration. He had been so engrossed in his conversation with Garrison that the sounding of the Mount's horn went completely unnoticed.

Before Kary and Nya headed to the dock to re-board the Mount for its return trip to the Weirs, Kary asked Norton to meet him at the Visitor Safety Task Force office the next morning.

"We didn't get the chance to discuss a possible motive," Norton called to Kary as he stepped onto the Mount.

"I have 75 minutes to think about that, Sergeant." Kary was alluding to the length of the return trip to Weirs Beach. "Hopefully, Lieutenant Bendix will have returned from her mini-vacation by morning. She'll have a lot of research to do that should enlighten us."

Chapter 13

For the first 15 minutes of their return trip, Kary stood on the port side second-level deck. He hoped that by standing near the very spot where Ambassador Marsden had been thrown overboard, he might have a brainstorm. All he could come up with were solid ideas about the mystery crewman's means and opportunity. The motive for his act escaped Kary for the time being.

Nya had been married to Kary for four decades. For several years, she assisted him as a co-investigator. So, she knew that Kary needed his space to work out details of the investigation. She also knew that he wouldn't hesitate to seek her counsel when the time was right.

Kary opened the port side door and walked back into the main salon on the second deck. He immediately asked Nya to join him in front of the white curtain where the mystery crewman had been hiding earlier that day.

"I'd be grateful for a second set of eyes," he told her. Before they peered into the small space, Nya had something to show Kary.

"I took a few pictures of the men in the bass boat," she told him. "I didn't bother to show these to you, because this rude little red-faced man kept cutting in front of me to take a closer look. I was pretty sure they were all ruined." Nya placed her hand on Kary's arm as she added, "Beside that, you're such a photography connoisseur, I didn't want to give you the opportunity to tease me about these."

In fact, two of the three pictures Nya had taken of the men and their seemingly stranded boat were useless. In one, the subject matter was completely out of focus. In the second, the smaller man's head blocked any view of the boat. However, the third photo provided a clear look at the two men that Garrison and his search party were pursuing at that moment. Kary asked Nya to use the linking wire she always carried to send the photo directly to Garrison.

Kary put his arms around Nya and kissed her cheek gently. "That's the second time today your photos contributed enormously to this case. Looks like I may need to buy you a real camera for our future daytrips."

Then, as he was about to open the white curtain, an idea struck Kary.

"May I see those three photos again for a second?"

When Nya handed Kary the camera, he looked very carefully at the photo that showed a man's head blocking her view of the bass boat.

"Is there something the matter, sweetheart?" Nya asked.

"It may be nothing, but that looks like the back of Carl Timms' head. He's the man who told us about two young guys stalking the ambassador, just before the Mount had to stop."

"Does that mean something?" Nya asked.

"It may turn out to be nothing at all. But, if that is Carl Timms, then his statement about what was happening inside the Mount becomes questionable."

"Wasn't that just before the ambassador went missing?" Nya asked.

"It was indeed, my dear."

Now Kary's resolve to interview Carl Timms a second time was stronger than ever.

Chapter 14

As Kary and Nya prepared to look inside the space behind the white curtain Nya asked, "My pictures showing the ambassador being thrown overboard don't leave much doubt about means and opportunity; but what are your thoughts about a motive?"

Kary repeated what he'd said to Nya earlier. "We would be nowhere if you hadn't been out there taking pictures with your dinky camera. As to motive, we're a long way from establishing that. Presumably the suspect and the ambassador share some kind of history. Had the guy simply thrown the ambassador overboard, I'd be willing to dismiss motive from the equation. But, this guy had a fairly elaborate disguise, and had even found a way to hide in plain sight."

"Do you expect to find anything of interest behind this curtain?" Nya asked.

"It's a long shot, but I haven't seen the Wolfeboro detective's report yet." Kary pulled two pairs of investigative gloves and shoe covers from his jacket pocket.

"Here; put these on. Norton gave them to me in Wolfeboro. We don't want to disturb anything until the MCU's forensics guys meet the boat at Weirs Beach."

Once both of them were ready, Kary carefully reached high up on the curtains to pull them apart. In this way, he hoped to avoid disturbing any prints that may have left behind.

Once inside, Kary closed the curtains so no one would disturb them. With a number of passengers having disembarked at Wolfeboro, there were fewer people on board. Also, the appearance of bright sunshine had lured most of the remaining passengers onto the Mount's top deck.

Kary looked for anything that might have been missed by the detective. The low ceiling made forward progress inside the space nearly impossible. The combination of limited lighting and Kary's poor close-up vision convinced him to back out of the space.

"Hold on, Kary. I see something interesting over there in the corner."

What Nya spotted appeared to be a tattered, tightly rolled, canvas of some type. It was covered with dust from being flung into the corner of the crawl space. For that reason, it was undiscovered during the Wolfeboro detective's quick search. With considerable difficulty, Nya reached into the back of the crawl space on her hands and knees, finally retrieving the grimy object.

Once the canvas was unrolled, it proved to be an old duffle bag. Inside, she found a thick, black hose that was about eighteen inches in length. Nya photographed the hose, then placed it into an evidence bag she had retrieved from Kary.

Kary helped Nya back to her feet, as she handed the evidence bag to him.

"Do you know what this is?" she asked.

Kary shook his head. "Maybe Quent Browne will know."

Fifteen minutes later, Browne took a quick look at the contents of the sealed, transparent bag then shook his head. "That looks like some kind of oxygen hose; but I'm not sure, Kary."

Kary asked Browne, "Do you usually store oxygen tanks onboard?"

"Hell no. Having oxygen tanks onboard for anything but medical reasons is a potential hazard; and the Marine Patrol tends to frown on that sort of thing."

"So, we're clueless about what that hose is and how it ended up in the crawl space under the stairs."

Browne responded with a shrug of his shoulders.

"This is becoming more and more interesting," Kary offered. "The suspect must have stayed in the crawl space waiting for just the right moment."

"Does that mean he knew the Mount was going to stop at that exact moment?" Nya asked.

"He may not have known the exact moment, but he must have known there was a window of time when he could act."

"But, once we came to a stop, how could he know the ambassador wouldn't be just as curious as the other passengers?" Browne asked.

"I'm not sure how that played out... not yet, anyway. Nya and I couldn't help noticing the ambassador as he lurched back and forth during the trip."

Nya added, "He never stopped walking. It certainly appeared that he was looking to meet up with someone."

"Yes, the someone who was about to murder him," Kary added.

"If he suspected that he was in danger, why board the Mount in the first place?" Browne asked. "And, if he was being threatened, why not simply go to the authorities?"

"There's much more than meets the eye here, Quent; but I can assure you we'll determine what the killer's motive was. And once we do, we'll find him."

Chapter 15

Following a late night phone call between Kary and a very frustrated Stu Garrison, Kary asked the head of MCU to join a meeting with his team the next morning, in the Visitor Safety Task Force offices on Capitol Street.

Kary was happy to see Lieutenant Mary Bendix, who looked refreshed from a weekend away from law enforcement. Bendix was a bright career law enforcement officer. Now in her early fifties, she was an absolute whiz at finding information on the Internet. She was so attached to her Mac Pro that Norton couldn't resist asking whether she had taken the laptop with her on vacation.

"As the commissioner and you are well aware, there was no coverage out in the boondocks. So, no, my baby stayed home this time," she added while massaging the cover of her Mac.

Once Garrison entered the room, Kary asked him to bring the task force up to speed on his investigative efforts. "Three other sets of ears should prove helpful," he said to Garrison.

For Bendix's benefit, Garrison began by briefly reiterating what had transpired aboard the Mount on the previous day. Bendix couldn't resist chiding Kary. "So, this is your idea of a nice day away from the office with the Mrs." That elicited a smile from everyone.

Garrison wore a glum expression while telling the others how he had quickly assembled a team of searchers comprised of several members of the MCU, two Marine Patrol officers, and two members of the Gilford PD.

"We met at West Alton and split into four teams of two. Two teams searched the shoreline and, using binoculars, looked to see if the bass boat with call numbers NH-94 96-AB was out on the lake. The other two teams were prepared to intercept anyone attempting to bring the boat to shore."

"I take it you came up empty," Norton stated the obvious.

"No one found anything. As you know, when the Marine Patrol guys arrived on the scene where Captain Browne reported the boat's breakdown, there was no boat to be rescued. Those guys are pros; so they searched the waters within a quarter mile of the reported breakdown. Finding nothing, they interviewed other boaters in the area. No one saw anything. We've held off doing an underwater search because, by this time, there's no rescue to be made."

"Are you confident that you've covered the entire ground between the Bay and Glendale?" Kary asked.

"Apparently not," Garrison replied. "We checked with state Motor Vehicles to find out who owns the boat with call numbers NH-94 96-AB. It turns out to be a small boat rental place in West Alton. Unfortunately, the owner had some kind of family emergency. So, the place was locked up tight when my men arrived; but there was a note on the door."

"What did the note say?" Norton asked him.

" It mentioned the family emergency, told people to tie their boats carefully to the dock, and leave any paperwork, keys, etc. in an envelope that was taped to the door."

"That's either a strange coincidence or very suspicious," Kary added.

Garrison told them, "As we speak, I have two members of my team waiting for the place to open. If that gets us nowhere, we're prepared to interview every boat rental place all the way to the town docks in Alton."

"Why do that?" Norton asked Garrison.

"Just in case those guys decided to bury the boat in plain sight by leaving it at a different dock where it wouldn't be noticed for a day or so." Garrison continued, "Also, because it was getting dark yesterday, we weren't able to complete a full water-to-land search of the area. I've gotta believe that one or both of those efforts will be successful. Otherwise, we'll need to be sending out divers. And that's the last thing I want to do."

※※※※※※

At this point, Kary stood up and walked over to his white board. He wrote several lines on the board:

Opportunity: stalled boat

Means: Ambassador contacted (threatened?) by disguised passenger

Motive: ???

Turning to the others, he asked, "Comments?"

Bendix, who was still being brought up to speed, said, "So, you have a mystery guy who disguised himself as a crew member, hid in a crawl space, waited until the time was right, then drowned a former ambassador."

"That's the size of it, Lieutenant," Kary replied. "What are your thoughts?"

"This whole thing appears to be motivated by revenge, Commissioner. What's especially troubling is the suspect was able to set up a rather uncomplicated hit on a former U.S. government official."

"What do you mean by uncomplicated?" Norton asked.

"I mean, it came off like clockwork… even the getaway."

"What does this tell you?" Kary asked.

"This thing was premeditated. It was well planned. It might even have been a professional hit of some kind."

Garrison asked the others, "Are you thinking that the two boaters we're looking for are professional hit men?"

"It's a definite possibility," Norton replied.

Kary interrupted the conversation. "I'm not quite ready to look at this as a KBG or Mafia retaliation. And, I certainly hope that's not the case."

As Kary always encouraged his task force members to do, Norton was prepared to challenge him. "I don't see how you can dismiss organized crime from all of this. You have the smooth take out of a U.S. official; and the two boaters must have been sent there as a decoy." Norton continued before any of the others could challenge him, "And what about the two mystery guys you told me were on the Mount. Haven't we learned that all of these people had foreign accents, probably from eastern Europe or south central Asia. There has to be a connection."

"You make a strong case, Sergeant," Kary replied. "But, there's one other character in all of this who muddies the waters, if you'll pardon the pun."

Bendix looked at her notes before saying, "I presume you're talking about this Mr. Carl Timms."

"That's right. Until I'm sure who he is, why he felt a need to involve himself, and where he hurried off to, I'm not ready to focus completely on organized crime."

Chapter 16

Stu Garrison's cell phone buzzed. He looked at caller ID and announced that this was the call he had been awaiting. Garrison turned on the speaker so Kary and the others could listen.

"What do you have for me, Sergeant?" Garrison asked. "I have Commissioner Turnell and his task force here with me on speakerphone."

The voice over the phone betrayed neither disappointment nor elation.

"We finally were able to talk with the manager at Parker Marine in Alton. He verified that the bass boat with registration NH-94 96-AB is theirs."

"I assume you showed the manager the photo of the two boaters that Ms. Turnell took," Garrison replied.

"Yeah. It helped a lot to have that photo. Kudos to Ms. Turnell."

"So, did the manager recognize the two men?" Garrison asked.

"This is where things got a little sticky."

Garrison was visibly annoyed by what was transpiring. "What the heck does that mean, Sergeant?"

"Well, sir, the manager was not the one who rented the boat to the two men. It was one of his clerks, and he's been out on a service call since early this morning."

"Surely, the manager must have paper work that will identify at least one of the two men," Garrison replied, while becoming more testy by the minute.

"I'm afraid that's not the case, sir."

"Explain, Sergeant."

"The boat was rented over the phone by a parish priest from Manchester," the sergeant replied.

Garrison looked over at Kary and the others who simply shrugged.

"Let me get this straight," Garrison demanded, "the boat was rented over the phone by a parish priest from Manchester. But, the priest was not one of the boaters... am I correct?"

"That's a roger, sir. The priest paid with his credit card and told the clerk who booked the rental that a man named Bob would pick up the boat when Parker's opened at 9 a.m. yesterday morning. He and a friend were going to use it that morning and return the boat by 1 p.m."

Garrison wrote down the name of the priest, then asked the sergeant, "Is the bass boat there right now?"

Garrison, Kary, and the others could hear the frustration in the sergeant's voice as he responded, "No, sir. The manager says no one has seen the boat since it left there yesterday morning."

Garrison's exasperation was evident. "So, just to get this straight: the boat is unaccounted for, and our only link to the boaters is a priest."

"That's correct. The man who rented the boat is Father Czodak at the St. Anne-St. Augustin Parish in Manchester."

Hearing this, Kary looked across the table at Norton and said, "It looks like you're going to be taking a quick road trip, Sergeant."

Once he had ended the phone call, Garrison stood and told the others he was going to take a walk so he could think. Garrison was clearly peeved. Even

Norton, as gutsy as he was, knew it would be unwise to speak to him.

Norton stood and told Kary and Bendix that he was going to call ahead to St Anne-St. Augustin. If Father Czodak was there, Norton intended to meet with the priest as soon as possible.

Now Kary was alone in the office with Lieutenant Bendix. He intended to put her computer research skills to work as soon as possible.

"I'm glad you were able to get some R&R, Lieutenant, but we really missed you yesterday," Kary told her.

"I'm not so certain, Commissioner. It sounds like Mrs. Turnell did a great job yesterday."

"Nya was fantastic in the limited time she had," Kary agreed. "But, she isn't the Rembrandt on a computer that you are."

"That's a lovely compliment, Commissioner. But, I prefer to be compared with Frida Kahlo or Georgia O'Keeffe," she replied with a wry smile.

"Understandable," Kary appreciated Bendix's clever retort. "Now, I need you to apply those Kahlo-like skills to find everything you can about our late ambassador, William H. Marsden III."

"Is there anything in particular I should be looking for?" she asked.

"I don't need to know anything before his posting in Astana. My instincts tell me that something happened while he was representing the U.S. in Kazakhstan. The obvious things to look for are politically related; but he may have been involved in something of a more personal nature."

"What if everything I find is in Kazakh?"

"You're a resourceful woman, Lieutenant. I'm sure you'll find a way to ferret out the information we need. You won't allow a little issue like a very complex language to stand in your way."

Bendix smiled and shook her head at Kary's sardonic vote of confidence, then headed down the hall to the small office she shared with Norton, with her Mac in hand.

※※※※※※

Fifteen minutes after Bendix left Kary's office, his phone buzzed. His administrative assistant, Jayne Window, was on the line.

"You have a visitor, Commissioner," she told him.

At this stage during a criminal investigation, Kary did not like to be disturbed. He sighed, then asked, "Who is it, Jayne? This isn't the best time."

"It's a tall, dark-haired gentleman wearing a naval uniform," she replied. "He says he has information that is vital to your case."

Kary could hear the humor in Window's voice. The gentleman could only be Captain Quentin Browne from the Mount Washington.

"Send the officer in, Jayne. By all means."

Kary rose from his desk as Browne entered the office. The two old friends shook hands warmly before Kary motioned Browne toward a captain's chair.

"This is a surprise, Quent. I figured you'd be preparing for the morning cruise."

Browne had an impish glow in his eyes. "You screwed up my cruise yesterday. I knew when I saw you on board, something crazy was going to happen. And it did in spades."

As Browne said this, he handed a thick manila envelope across the desk to Kary.

"What's this?" Kary asked, his face showing puzzlement.

"Those are the fully developed photos of every passenger who came on board yesterday. I figured if we look at them together, we can narrow things down to a few interesting people. Then I can use their charge cards to find them for you."

"This is great stuff, Quent. Of course it's the least you can do for screwing up my getaway with Nya."

The two men enjoyed a good laugh, then sat side by side and began sorting through the high-quality photographs that were taken by the Mount's staff photographer. Most of the photos were in alphabetical order. However, because Kary knew few of the passengers by name, it was necessary to go through all of them.

Chapter 17

Norton was en route to Manchester in the DTF staff car that the drug enforcement agency made available to the Visitor Task Force. He stopped briefly at the state welcome center in Hooksett to grab a large black coffee to go. When he returned to the cruiser, he used the Bluetooth connection to dial a telephone number that Jayne Window had provided for him.

The phone on the other end rang twice before being answered by a voice that clearly belonged to an elderly man. Norton asked to speak to Father Czodak. The line went silent for at least a minute before a younger, deeper voice was heard.

"Father Czodak."

Norton was concentrating on the road and the pronunciation of the priest's name, and nearly missed taking the road toward the Everett Turnpike. Norton zipped into the left hand lane while explaining who he was, then asked the priest if he would be available to talk to him in a half hour. Czodak replied in the affirmative and told Norton how to find the St. Anne-St. Augustin church building on Beech Street.

When Norton pulled up to the church, he was immediately impressed by its multiple arched entries, and the very tall copper-gilded steeple, topped by a simple cross. Norton put on his blue lights and pulled the cruiser part way onto the sidewalk. Approaching the middle of three arches, he was met by an elderly parishioner, who Norton presumed was the first man he spoke with on the telephone 20 minutes earlier. Without so much as a hello, the elderly man instructed Norton to follow him into the church.

Father Czodak was a big man who stood nearly a head taller than Norton. Norton told himself that he was glad this was a conversation, not a wrestling match. The priest led Norton through the sanctuary before opening a thick, carved wooden door to his office.

Once the two men were seated, Czodak asked Norton what had brought him all the way down to Manchester from Concord.

Norton replied that his research partner, Lieutenant Bendix, had done some research on line. She had found out that this church reached out to immigrant groups of all nationalities, including Kazakhs.

"That's true," Czodak replied. "Is one of my flock in trouble?"

Norton explained that there had been an incident on Lake Winnipesaukee involving two men who are believed to have eastern European or south central Asian accents.

The priest smiled. "That's like saying an American is from North Carolina or maybe Nebraska."

Norton quickly felt at ease with the priest. "I realize that's a pretty big stretch. But there's one large difference," he smiled.

"What's that, Sergeant?"

"The people from North Carolina and Nebraska didn't rent a bass boat with your credit card, and these two men did."

"Well, then, it appears you have me there, Sergeant."

"I do my best," Norton replied while pulling a photograph from the breast pocket of his uniform. As he prepared to hand the photograph to Father Czodak, Norton told the priest that the two men had identified themselves as Jim and Bob Smith.

The priest looked at the photograph and shook his head. "This makes me very unhappy, Sergeant. Sometimes I can be too trusting. These two men are part of our parish's English as a second language class. I speak some Kazakh, so I have been meeting with these men myself."

"What can you tell me about them?" Norton asked.

"They use their English names, Jim and Bob. But their last name is Czechezny. They're hard-working men who entered the country legally and are trying to earn their citizenship so they can send for their families."

"I'm afraid they may have put all that in jeopardy," Norton told him.

"That's why I can't believe they would have done anything illegal," Czodak replied.

"What did Jim and Bob tell you they were going to do with the boat?"

"They said that a friend from Kazakhstan had contacted them and needed help with something."

Norton asked, "Did they tell you the nature of this 'help'?"

"Not really, only that their friend is a diver and would need transportation back to land."

"Did they tell you the friend's name?"

"I'm sorry, Sergeant. I never asked. This didn't seem like anything but a short errand." He paused before asking, "Are you able to tell me what this is about?"

"I can't tell you much, Father. However, your friends Jim and Bob may be accessories to a murder."

"Oh, my goodness," Czodak replied. "Does this have anything to do with the U.S. ambassador who went missing on Lake Winnipesaukee?"

"It does, and that's all I'm able to tell you right now."

"This is terrible, just terrible. I'm telling you, Sergeant, the Czecheznys are good men. I suspect that they naively got into something while trying to help a countryman."

Chapter 18

Kary and Captain Browne had just begun to examine the photographs taken by the Mount's staff photographer, when Kary's intercom sounded. Jayne Window was on the line.

"Commissioner, there's a man named D'Agostino on the line. He claims he has information that will help you with the missing ambassador."

Since the news team on WMUR-TV had been carrying the story of Ambassador Marsden's disappearance, Kary knew full well that publicity seekers and cranks of all shapes and sizes could be calling. Kary trusted Window's savvy as a screener, so he answered the call.

Kary answered the phone, "This is Commissioner Turnell. My administrative assistant tells me that you may have pertinent information about the case I'm investigating."

The caller sounded a bit shaky, as though he wasn't in the habit of calling the authorities. Kary assured the man that any information could or would be helpful, and to just tell his story as clearly and concisely as possible. He then set his phone on speaker.

"Okay." The man paused, still unsure how to share his information. "My name is Sam D'Agostino. I rent a house on Moose Island every summer."

Browne quickly scribbled a note on a piece of paper, which he showed to Kary: "Moose Island is opposite where the ambassador disappeared. I know D'Agostino. He's good folks."

Now Kary was anxious to hear what D'Agostino had to tell him.

"I was sitting out on the rocks on Moose Island, getting ready to fish, when the Mount came to a full stop. I've never seen that happen before. So, I focused my binoculars on the port side of the Mount. That's when I saw it."

"What did you see, sir?" Kary asked.

"A tall guy came walking out onto the narrow second deck. It looked like another guy wearing a white uniform jacket and officer's cap was waiting for him out there."

"What happened next?"

"Once the tall guy had stepped outside, the other guy—he looked pretty beefy, by the way—pushed and pulled until both of them went over the railing into the water. They were submerged for quite a while, two minutes or more."

"This is very helpful, Mr. D'Agostino. Did you see anything else?"

"Yes. The tall man never resurfaced. But, the dark haired guy popped up. He didn't have his cap or white jacket anymore. But, I'm certain he had on diving gear."

"How could you tell that?"

"I'm a diver myself. So, I recognized what I was seeing."

"And, what was that?

"The guy who surfaced was wearing a pony bottle; and I'm pretty sure I saw a regulator. I couldn't see if he had a mask or fins, but that kit would allow him to stay submerged for at least ten minutes… until the Mount shoved off."

"And is that what he did?" Kary asked.

"He stayed under for about ten minutes. The last time I saw him, he was climbing into that bass boat. I think it was the same one that flagged down the Mount."

"Can you tell me why you waited so long to tell someone about this?" Kary asked.

"I know that was pretty stupid of me… I… I… guess I was reluctant to get involved. But, after hearing the story on WMUR, I knew it was important to tell someone what I'd seen. It took a while for me to be directed to you."

Kary thanked D'Agostino for his candor, then instructed him to stay on the line so Jayne Window could get his contact information.

Browne assured Kary that he could trust D'Agostino's information.

"This puts those two boaters right in the middle of a murder," Kary told him. "I can't wait to hear what Norton and Bendix find out. Meanwhile, let's get a good look at those photographs.

Sitting side by side, the two men used the surface of a small conference table in Kary's office to sort them. Browne recognized most of the people in the photographs, while only a dozen were familiar to Kary. He smiled when he saw the pictures of Cora and May Lou, but otherwise looked through the stack without changing expression.

Finally, Browne saw the picture of Carl Timms. "Here's that strange little man who accused those two young guys of stalking Marsden."

"I want to have a long talk with that gentleman," Kary replied while setting Timms' photograph aside. "I'm hoping that Corporal Arnold and his partner from Wolfeboro PD will have some news about him soon."

They continued to look through the stack of photographs, eliminating most from further scrutiny. Browne spotted the photograph of the two men who had aroused Timms' suspicions. He handed the photo to Kary.

"This has to be the two men Timms told us about. We're almost through the entire stack and these are the only two young males traveling together," Kary told Browne.

"Yeah, and they appear to be about the right size, with short dark hair," Browne agreed.

Browne looked at the names at the back of the photograph. "Alen and Arman Iskakov," he read aloud.

"Those aren't your everyday New Hampshire names;" Kary replied, "but it may be a bit of a reach to say those young men are from Kazakhstan."

Browne stood up and entered a number into his cell phone. After a few minutes, he returned to the conference table. "I just talked with Carol in the cruise office. I had her check to see how these two men paid for their tickets. They paid with a Visa card; and you'll never guess their local address."

Kary admitted that he had no idea. "Don't keep me in suspense."

"Their address is listed as room 112, Langdon Woods."

Kary smiled broadly at the irony. "So, they're students at my old university. People do say it's a small world."

"What are you going to do?" Browne asked.

"I'm going to make a phone call to my old friend on the university police force and arrange a meeting with those two men this afternoon."

Browne looked at his watch. "Holy cow! I need to get back to Weirs Beach for the afternoon cruise. It looks like we have only a few photos left, so I'll hang around until we finish.

It was when they reached the penultimate photograph in the pile that they struck pay dirt. Comparing the man in the photograph with the backdrop shared by all other passengers, they were able to identify several distinguishing characteristics. The man appeared to be tall, at least six feet, with a muscular torso, and black hair that he wore closely cropped. Of note, he was not wearing the crewman's uniform that the O'Neills had described.

Kary was the first to notice something on the ground behind where the man was standing. "That looks to me like a large duffle bag of some sort."

"Makes sense," Browne replied. "He probably had the white coat and hat in there."

"That's a pretty big duffle," Kary noted. "It appears he was carrying a lot more than a hat and jacket."

Browne replied, "He was probably storing it in the crawl space when the O'Neill boys discovered him."

Kary shuddered to think what might have happened if the O'Neills had seen everything the man was carrying.

"What's the name on his photograph?" Kary asked.

Browne held up the photo so Kary could read it. "You tell me; I can't read this."

The name on the back of the photograph was Öledi Qasaqana.

Chapter 19

Five minutes after Browne left Kary's office, Bendix returned with her ubiquitous laptop. There was a satisfied expression on her face that did not escape Kary.

"I take it you've been successful," Kary said matter-of-factly. "It amazes me how fast you can find things on that flat box. It would take me hours; and I probably wouldn't come up with half of what you do."

Bendix felt comfortable with Kary and couldn't resist the opening he'd just given her. "It's a generation thing, Commissioner. I'm getting pretty long in the tooth for the new technology. So, you certainly shouldn't be blamed because there was no wireless service on the Mayflower."

The pair shared a laugh before Kary asked, "What can you tell me about Ambassador Marsden?"

"This hasn't been the easiest research I've ever done. I was able to find information on line from a paper that I presume was written in Kazakh. Of course, I couldn't understand anything. I found photographs of what apparently was a horrific car crash. Next to those were photos of Marsden and a young woman."

"Was that all you found?" Kary asked.

Bendix looked at her boss with an expression of feigned indignation. "Of course not. I was able to read the date at the top of the newspaper, and I used that to find a copy of Izvestia."

"Isn't that in Russian?" Kary asked.

"Yes, and my Russian is a little rusty; so I kept digging," Bendix replied. "That's when I remembered that the Moscow Times is online, and in English."

"Very impressive, Lieutenant. So, tell me what you've learned."

"Apparently, Ambassador Marsden was a very good diplomat by day, but something of a bad boy at night," Bendix replied.

"Interesting. Now what exactly does that tell us?"

"According to the Moscow Times and the Guardian, which I also accessed, Marsden was ultimately recalled for repeated instances of DUI, at least one of which resulted in the death of the young woman pictured in the Kazakh newspaper. From best

I can tell, she died on a bridge over a river called the Ishim."

"The reference to his drunkenness is consistent with the brief exposure I had to Marsden. He appeared to be well over the legal limit to drive while he was on the Mount," Kary replied. "Okay, let's keep this information on our radar. Meanwhile, we need to interview a couple of students at the university in Plymouth."

"Are those the two mystery men from the Mount who you were discussing earlier?"

"They are. Speaking of mystery men, have you heard from Sergeant Norton recently?"

"Yes, he's dropping off the cruiser and is anxious to talk with us about his visit with the priest in Manchester."

"Hopefully, he'll know something more about the two boaters who've vanished. I don't think it's a stretch to say that the link between these Kazakhs and the murder of the former ambassador is more than circumstantial."

Chapter 20

As Norton entered Kary's office, the expression on his face was anything but cheerful.

"Did you learn anything from the priest, Sergeant?" Kary asked.

"Yes, but not as much as I was hoping. The priest was able to identify the two men as the Czecheznys, a father and son who prefer to be called Jim and Bob."

"The names Jim and Bob are consistent with what they told Captain Browne when he tried to assist them," Kary said before adding, "only, they called themselves the Smiths."

"I'm sure no one was buying that," Norton replied.

"At the time, no one cared very much about their last names. Browne just wanted to help them."

Kary encouraged Norton to continue his story.

"It turns out the two men are members of an English course the priest teaches. He says they're good men who are hoping to stay in New Hampshire and bring their families from Kazakhstan to join them."

Bendix couldn't resist adding, "They aren't doing that cause much good."

Norton continued, "The two men were contacted by another man, a friend or relative from Kazakhstan. All they told the priest was they needed to borrow a small boat with a motor and help this other guy with a job he was doing. Neither man owns a credit card, so Father Czodak, who seems like a do-gooder, told them he would rent a boat for them at a friend's business in the Alton Bay area."

"Has Father Czodak heard from the Czecheznys since the time of the incident?"

"No, and he seems genuinely concerned about them," Norton replied. "Czodak also claims not to know the person who they were helping, but presumes he must live somewhere in the Alton Bay area."

"Well, this isn't quite as much information as I was hoping you'd get, but it does help," Kary told him.

"So, what's next, Commissioner?" Bendix asked.

"We're all going back to college," Kary replied. "There's a nice new dormitory on the Plymouth campus I'm dying to visit."

Chapter 21

Kary, Bendix and Norton drove north on I93 in the DTF cruiser until they reached exit 25. They took the exit ramp and drove west past the university's athletic complex. Soon they saw the tall clock tower of Rounds Hall in the distance. As they crossed the Pemigewasset River on the DiCenzo Bridge, Kary had a sense of familiarity that comes with having lived in a place for decades.

His concentration was broken by a question from Bendix, "How many years did you teach at Plymouth?"

"More than thirty-five years." Kary directed Norton to bear right at a roundabout and head north up Route 3 for about a quarter of a mile. After a left turn and then a quick right, they found themselves in front of a new "green" dormitory. The sign on the structure read 'Langdon Woods'. Norton pulled over next to a waiting campus police car and lowered the window on Kary's side of the car.

A young campus police officer informed them that they were expected, and could leave their car where it was parked. He then accompanied them into a long, narrow lobby where two tall, dark-haired male students were waiting for them. The two students introduced themselves as Alen and Arman Iskakov, fraternal twins from Kazakhstan. Introducing himself, Bendix and Norton to the men, Kary's instincts told him that these two young men would prove to be innocent of any wrong doing.

"We're confused about why we are here," Alen told them.

"We know you were aboard the Mount Washington cruise boat several days ago," Kary began.

The two men nodded in unison.

"As it turns out, I was on that same cruise."

This made the pair smile.

"I'm certain you're aware that there was an incident aboard the boat while we were traveling to Wolfeboro."

"Yes. How could we forget? Those two men were stranded in a small boat," Arman replied.

"I'd like you to tell me what you saw that day," Kary asked.

"To tell you the truth, we almost didn't notice the small boat," Arman added.

Kary found this statement interesting. "Why is that?"

"I'm afraid we were a little star-struck... is that the expression you use?" Arman replied.

"Star-struck? I'm not following you," Kary said.

"The man who made it possible for us to study in your country was aboard the boat. It was a surprise for us."

"Who was this man?" Kary asked.

"His name is William Marsden, and he was U.S. Ambassador to Kazakhstan until two years ago. He made it possible for us to be given a student visa to come here to study."

Kary looked at Bendix and Norton, who seemed favorably impressed with the boys' story.

Bendix asked, "Did you have any interaction with Mr. Marsden?"

The two looked at one another sheepishly. "No, we behaved like two school boys tailing a famous movie star. We followed him as he walked around the boat. But, neither of us could call up the courage to say anything to him."

"When was the last time you saw the ambassador?" Norton asked.

"A minute or two after the boat stopped next to the smaller one. We lacked the courage to talk with the ambassador who, by the way, appeared to be very unsteady on his feet. So, we went outside with everyone else to see what was going on," Arman said.

"That was a very curious thing," Alen added.

"What was curious?" Bendix asked him.

"We pushed our way to the front of the Mount so we could see better what was going on," Alen replied in his heavy accent. "We were completely surprised when we heard one of the men speaking in our own language... in Kazakh."

This was a piece of information that Kary and the others did not expect.

"Could you understand anything that was being said?" Kary asked.

"There was much noise from surrounding people and speeding boats, but we heard a few words."

"Can you tell us what those words meant?" Kary continued.

"Yes. They referred to someone else as a bastard. The bastard's name was Taras. I'm certain of it."

"Would Taras be his first or last name?"

"Taras is usually a first name in Kazakh. I'm sorry but I didn't hear a last name."

The two men asked if they could be excused to attend a two o'clock seminar that they couldn't afford to miss. Before allowing them to leave, Kary pulled a photograph from a leather folder he was carrying. It was the photo of the man they were certain was the disguised crewman. Narrowing things to this man had not been difficult, as only two photographs had not been matched by Nya to the remaining passengers aboard the Mount—the ambassador's and this one.

"Do either of you recognize this man?" he asked.

At first, the two men stared at the photograph without expression. But when Kary turned it over and revealed the name on back, they broke into laughter.

"Is something funny about the writing on back of the photo?" Norton asked.

The men apologized before Alen added, "Yes, this is not the name of a man." Pointing to the wording, Öledi Qasaqana, he said, This means, 'Die murderer.'"

Kary and the others thanked the two men and encouraged them to go to class. As the three members of the Visitor Safety Task Force headed south in the cruiser, Kary turned toward Bendix and Norton and asked, "Any doubts now that this is a case of premeditated murder?"

Chapter 22

On the return trip from Plymouth, Kary and the others reviewed where their efforts had taken them. As each of them took a turn in laying out what she or he knew, Bendix compiled a list on her laptop, much as Kary always did on his office white board. When they were finished, she read the list aloud.

1. A man, presumably of Kazakh nationality, boarded the Mount Washington with the expressed intention of murdering former U.S. Ambassador to Kazakhstan, William Marsden III
2. Marsden came aboard and was inebriated; he appeared to be wandering around looking for someone or something
3. The presumed perpetrator took refuge under the stairs where he changed into a crewman's jacket and cap; apparently, he stored his duffle in that space
4. Approximately one hour into the cruise, the Mount was flagged down by two men in a bass boat; they informed Captain Browne that they had a problem with the boat's motor
5. Two passengers aboard the Mount identified the stranded men as Kazakhs
6. While people were standing on the starboard side of the boat watching the activities, the perpetrator—dressed as a crewmember—lured Marsden onto the port side deck and pulled him over the boat's railing into the lake
7. According to an eyewitness account, the suspect reemerged, but Marsden did not; Marsden has not been seen again
8. The two boaters insisted on remaining behind; when Marine Patrol arrived, they had disappeared; it is believed that the suspect was on board.
9. The bass boat was rented for the two men by their parish priest; none of the three men has been seen since
10. Based on two college students' testimony, the presumed perpetrator and the two boaters were Kazakh nationals
11. Apparently, Marsden was involved in one or more fatal car accidents while he was serving in Kazakhstan

When Bendix finished reading the list, Norton asked, "What's next, Commissioner?"

"There's now very little doubt that this was a revenge killing. What little information we have about Marsden's service record in Astana indicates that he was a diligent administrator. So, I'm thinking whatever he did was during nonworking hours." While Norton drove, Kary turned to Bendix and asked if she could tap into the State Department's website, to see if there was anything in Marsden's official record about disciplinary action.

"I'm way ahead of you, Commissioner. I researched Marsden's record on the way up here."

Kary smiled. "I should have known you'd do that. So, what did you find?"

"Absolutely nothing. There are numerous mentions of his work on state meetings, grants-in-aid, etc. But, there is no mention of his extracurricular activities in the official record," she replied.

"Isn't that just like the government?" Kary told them. "It was well known at the time of his termination from service that Marsden had a drinking problem. The fact that it's not mentioned anywhere in the official records may be telling us something." He paused before adding, "When we catch our suspect, I expect the truth to come out."

Kary looked over to Norton. "Sergeant, when we get back to the office, will you please make some calls around to diving shops in the vicinity of Wolfeboro and the Weirs? See if anyone rented minimalist diving equipment to a man matching the description of our suspect."

Norton nodded.

A thought occurred to Kary. "Before you do that, call your priest contact, and ask him to meet with you."

"Do you think he'll be willing to do that, Commissioner?" Bendix asked.

"He won't want to. But, if the Sergeant here were to allow it to slip that we definitely regard his two parishioners as accessories to a murder, I'm thinking the Father will be happy to help us."

Kary cautioned the others, "I'd really love to catch this guy ourselves. But, that may not be the case."

"Are you thinking of calling in the FBI?" Bendix asked.

"We have enough evidence to show that the murder of a former U.S. official has been committed. Apparently it was the act of a foreign national. I'll update Stu Garrison at MCU as soon as we're back at the office. Protocol dictates that he needs to notify the FBI at their branch in Chelsea."

Chapter 23

Norton dialed the number for the St. Anne-St. Augustin church in Manchester. The same elderly parishioner who Norton met earlier answered the telephone. Apparently, Father Czodak had informed the older man to expect Norton to call, as he brought the priest to the phone in less than one minute.

"Sergeant Norton, I was just getting ready to call you."

Norton was skeptical, but said nothing.

"I've just talked with Bob Czechezny. Jim and he are willing to talk with you, but they are scared," Czodak told him.

"Have you explained to them that police here are different than in their part of the world?"

Father Czodak paused before replying, "It's not you that they are afraid of, Sergeant."

Norton asked the priest where and when he could meet with the two men. They agreed that the best course of action was for Norton to return to the church, and meet with the men there.

Meanwhile, Kary was on the telephone in his office, talking with Stu Garrison of MCU. Garrison supported Kary's assessment that a foreign national had murdered a former member of the federal government. However, he raised concerns that this may have had a more sinister motive.

"We can't rule out that this was purely a political assassination, Kary."

"I'm not buying that, Stu. And if we can take this guy alive, I think I can prove it to you. But, first we have to find him."

"How's that going?" Garrison asked.

"We're making steady progress; but I think the proverbial dam is about to break," Kary replied.

"Well, regardless of which of our hypotheses is correct, I'm sure you realize that I need to call in the FBI." Garrison paused before adding, "Although, I'm not certain who they'll be able to send up here."

Garrison reminded Kary that, due to a federal government shut down, the FBI, like everyone else, was short of staff. "It appears that not even the FBI is totally immune to sick outs."

※※※※※※

A thought occurred to Kary. He asked Bendix to come to his office with her laptop.

"Lieutenant, you have all of the photos that Nya took while we were on the Mount, am I correct?"

Bendix nodded.

"Let's take a look at the ones that show the actual assault on Marsden. I've only looked at them on Nya's little camera. It should help to see them in a larger format."

While Bendix was making the necessary arrangements, Garrison called Kary. "I've spoken to the folks in Chelsea. They'll be sending someone up here in the morning tomorrow." They chatted a few minutes while Bendix went to find a needed wire. "One more thing, the FBI tells me that only three people from Kazakhstan have entered the U.S. during the past month." Kary asked whether they had names to share.

"Not yet. They got those numbers from the U.S. Customs database. With everyone shorthanded, that's the best they could do for now."

Kary thanked Garrison and sat back awaiting Bendix's return.

Several minutes later, Bendix had connected her laptop to a large flat screen television in Kary's office. When she was done, Bendix looked at Kary and said, "Your wish is my command, Commissioner."

Bendix forwarded through Nya's photographs until she found the photos Kary asked about.

Kary looked at the first photo, then the second. When he found what he was looking for, he asked Bendix to zoom in on the picture.

"That's it!" he cried.

While the blown-up version of the photo was slightly grainy, the quality was sufficient for their purposes. As Kary and Bendix huddled closer to the television screen, Kary pointed to the legs of the two men. There was a stunning revelation."

"The guy shoving the ambassador overboard is wearing a diver's wetsuit," Bendix exclaimed.

Next, Kary asked her to zoom toward the upper torso of the perpetrator.

"What do you suppose that is, Commissioner?" she asked.

"The way the guy's crew jacket is bulging at the shoulders and neck, he must be wearing a miniature diving tank." Then Kary looked closer. "Look, there's a hose and a dial of some kind sticking out of the top of his jacket!"

Now Bendix was skeptical. "How could he be onboard without anyone noticing?"

"Ordinarily, that wouldn't make sense," Kary told her. "But, think about the circumstances. The Mount was at full stop. It was only natural that everyone would huddle over to the starboard side to look and listen to what was going on."

"Everyone except the ambassador, the killer and Nya, Bendix reminded him.

"And, possibly one other person," Kary told her.

Bendix was puzzled.

"You and I haven't talked much about him, but there was that little, red-faced guy with the curly hair named Carl Timms, whose behavior was suspicious. I'm still waiting to talk with him."

Kary and Bendix reviewed the photographs several times to be certain they hadn't missed anything. Finally, Bendix said to Kary, "Assuming he didn't bring diving equipment with him from Kazakhstan, we should contact local dive shops. Hopefully, someone remembers him."

Chapter 24

Norton retraced his steps from the earlier meeting he had with Father Czodak. Just as he had earlier, Norton pulled part way onto the sidewalk in front of the church's main entrance. This time, the priest himself greeted Norton at the front of the building.

The two men exchanged a brief handshake, then proceeded into the building without talking. Once inside, Czodak told Norton that the Czecheznys were waiting for him in the priest's office.

As Norton and Czodak entered the small room, both Czecheznys stood up and removed the ball caps they had been wearing. Norton's first impression was that there was a strong family resemblance between the two men. Each man was approximately six feet tall, with close-cropped hair and muscular builds. The younger man, Jim, spoke for the pair, as his English was nearly flawless. His father, Bob, sat silently but watched Norton's face warily for any sign of difficulty.

The priest started to explain the Czecheznys' position, but Norton quickly raised his left hand to silence him.

"You're welcome to remain here, Father, but I need to hear from these two men right now."

The priest nodded and indicated to Norton to proceed with his questioning.

"I have a number of questions for you gentlemen," he began while looking back and forth at the two men. "Let's begin at the beginning. Why did you ask Father Czodak to rent a small boat for you?"

"My cousin… my father's nephew," Jim began while looking across at the older man, "recently came to this country. He told us he was going to be diving for something valuable and called upon us to help him."

Norton pondered what the younger man had just told him. "Did he tell you what he was diving for?"

Jim and Bob Czechezny shook their heads in unison. "No, and we did not ask."

At this point Bob said something to his son in Kazakh. When he finished speaking, Jim told Norton, "My father says, he is family; it was our duty to help him."

"We have been told that your relative's first name might be Taras. Is that correct?"

The two men looked at one another. This time, it was Bob who replied in Kazakh, "Ïä."

"He said, yes," the priest informed him.

Norton continued his questioning. "What else did Taras tell you?"

"He said to be in the place where the big boat passes. We were told to find a buoy numbered seventy-eight, drift one hundred yards toward the big bay..."

"Alton Bay?" Norton questioned.

"Ïä," the older Czechezny replied.

"Then what?"

"We were told to shut off the engine and remove one of the wires hidden under it. Then we were to flag down the big boat with our jackets."

"Were there any other instructions," Norton asked.

"We were to place a large... how do you say... tarp on the rear seat, unfold it, then move to the front of the boat. Taras told us that the big boat would stop to help, but we were not to accept."

Now Norton fixed a very serious expression on his face. "Did either of you know what Taras was really planning to do?"

Both men swore that they knew nothing. "Shortly after the big boat had sailed away, we felt the back of our small boat dip; then we saw the tarp rise noticeably," Jim told Norton, then added, "Once he settled himself in our boat, Taras called 'jurw,' which means 'go.'"

"We rode toward the big bay for about 10 minutes. Once we entered that place, Taras sat up, folded the tarp, then told us to head toward shore. Soon, we reached an area that he called Pumpkin Point, where he had us pull in toward shore. But, when we got there, he made us leave the boat."

"He told you to leave... what happened next?" Norton asked.

"He told us not to talk to anyone for two days, or..." Jim paused.

His father continued in broken English, "He say he kill our family." Both men wept openly at this point.

At this point, Father Czodak asked to speak privately with Norton outside of the office.

"You know these men, Father. How much of their story should I believe?"

"All of it, Sergeant. These are good people. They are here trying to live the American dream. Neither of them would do anything to jeopardize their chances. Frankly, what they've done today is remarkably brave. They had no idea what their cousin had done, but broke their promise and called me 10 hours before they were supposed to. At first, they refused to let me go to pick them up because they feared for their family's safety. But, they finally relented when I said the police wanted to talk with them in connection with the ambassador's possible murder."

Czodak looked at Norton, and placed his hand on the Sergeant's arm, "On my oath as a priest, those men had no idea what Taras had done until I told them." Next, Czodak told Norton, "I've never met this cousin of theirs but, based upon their description of his qualities as a person, the ambassador must have done something terrible for him to do what he did. Whatever the ambassador did, Jim and Bob have never said anything to me about it."

Before parting ways with Norton, Czodak told him, "I'm not supposed to tell you this, but Taras' last name is Abdulov."

At last, the Task Force knew the identity of the man they were chasing.

Chapter 25

Kary and Bendix wanted to talk with someone who had experience about diving. Kary told her, "I know a guy named Nick at Dive Winnipesaukee in Wolfeboro."

"Sounds good to me, but I didn't know you were into diving, Commissioner."

"I'm not. The biggest body of water I'm comfortable in is a Jacuzzi. I met Nick at a conference last year, and he told me to call him if ever necessary."

Bendix found Dive Winnipesaukee's telephone number on line and Kary dialed. Nick answered on the second ring and recalled meeting Kary.

"As I remember, you're some kind of an investigator, aren't you, Kary? In fact, I see your name all the time associated with that visitor safety task force. And, to think, I knew you when."

Kary smiled, but got right down to business. He explained that someone had smuggled diving gear on board the Mount and is believed to have used it to murder a fellow passenger.

"Sounds like something right out of James Bond," Nick replied. "I tell you what, if you can send me the guy's picture, I'll tell you if he rented here. But I have my doubts."

A few minutes later, the picture of Taras Abdulov arrived on Nick's business computer. Nick excused himself for a few minutes.

When he returned to the phone, Nick told Kary, "No one here recognizes him; and I'm not surprised, really."

"Why?" Kary asked.

"Even if your killer was using a small breathing apparatus, he still would need to drive over an hour to bring it to the Mount. If it were me, I'd get my gear as close to the dock at Weirs Beach as possible."

"And where would that be?" Kary asked.

"There's a shop called Fathom Divers. It's on Lake Street in Weirs Beach

...no more than three miles from where the Mount docks. The owner's name is Davy. Tell him I sent you."

By the time Nick hung up the phone, Bendix had Fathom Divers' telephone number for Kary. The call was answered on the first ring.

"Fathom Divers; this is Davy."

Kary explained to Davy what he was looking for, then asked if he would look at Taras Abdulov's photo. Bendix quickly sent the two photos that Nya had taken of the assault, plus a photo of the hose Nya and he had found on the Mount.

Davy's reaction to the first photo was instantaneous.

"Shit, yeah, I recognize that dude. He rented a pony bottle and a regulator with all the necessary hoses."

"Has he returned them yet?"

"Hell no, he hasn't. And, he owes me for two days' worth of late fees."

Next, Kary asked if he had an address for the wayward diver. Kary heard a drawer open and some paperwork being sorted.

"Yes, sir. Here is his application. Guy's name is Jackson Kilgore. Showed me a New Hampshire driver's license… oh, shoot!" Kary heard Davy say.

"What's going on, Davy?"

"Someone's going to get fired is what's happening. The young kid who checked Kilgore in didn't look at the date on the license. It expired years ago, and the picture on the license looks different from the guy I saw."

Kary suppressed his disappointment, not that he expected Abdulov to provide an accurate address.

Kary had one further question for Davy. "One last thing; take a look at the two photos I sent you. Tell me what you see."

Davy scanned the photos then replied, "The first photo shows your guy is wearing a wetsuit. In the second, I can see what can only be the pony bottle he rented from us. The hose from his regulator is sticking out from his coat. If he had a larger unit like an Aluminum 80, he wouldn't have been able to hide it under that coat of his. The pic of the hose looks exactly like the extra one we made him take." Davy paused before adding, "I hope you catch that asshole."

Chapter 26

In Kary's experience, people who commit major crimes are diligent about planning the steps leading up to and completing their acts. Many of these same criminals are far more lackadaisical about the actions that follow the commission of their crimes, resulting in their capture.

For Taras Abdulov, aka Jackson Kilgore, his mistake was misjudging the Czecheznys' intestinal fortitude. He was confident that his threat would prevent the pair from talking to anyone about him for at least two days... plenty of time for him to escape into Canada.

After leaving the Czecheznys on the shore of Alton Bay, Abdulov waited until dark while he motored along the shoreline looking for an abandoned summer cabin. He found the perfect candidate on the east side of the bay, around a bend from where he'd left his cousins. He tied the bass boat at the dock just downslope from the cabin. After determining that there was no food in the cabin, he walked up Echo Point Road until he came to a small mom and pop grocery store. This is where he made his second mistake.

When Abdulov entered the small store, he was greeted by a very pretty 16-year-old store clerk. Instead of minimizing contact, he engaged the young woman with flirtatious talk, even inviting her back to the cabin where he was hiding temporarily. Therefore, when authorities arrived hours later, she not only recognized the mysterious, dark-haired foreigner, but told them where to find him.

The searchers' big break came while the Marine Patrol was making a sweep of area waterways in search of the missing bass boat. In the fading daylight, they recognized the distinctive shape of the boat's bow from 200 yards away. On closer inspection, they matched the registration number on the boat's bow, NH-94 96-AB, with that of the missing boat. Wisely, they made an immediate call to the Major Crimes Unit.

Within minutes, the dispatcher at MCU contacted Garrison, who was having dinner mere miles down the road at Patrick's Pub in Gilford. Joining him were Kary, Norton and Tim Ponds, the agent who had arrived from the Chelsea FBI office.

Garrison quickly advised the Marine Patrol officers to keep their distance, remaining out of sight until Kary, Garrison and the two others could rendezvous with them at Pumpkin Point.

The four men rode in the DTF car, with Norton behind the wheel. Norton used the vehicle's blue lights and siren to alert traffic of their presence. As they covered the 10-mile stretch along Route 11, there was complete silence in the car. Once they were within a mile from Pumpkin Point, Norton shut off both warning devices.

As agreed, the two Marine Patrol officers were waiting for their arrival.

Garrison asked the two men, "Do you see any activity across the way?"

One of the officers responded, "He hasn't come out toward the boat, but I think he's in the cabin. He turned on a light about fifteen minutes ago, and it's still on." Next, the Marine Patrol officer looked at the others and asked, "How do you want to play this, gentlemen. We can only take two of you safely in our boat."

It was Kary who responded first. "I won't do you much good if he wants to make a stand." Next, Kary looked over at the FBI representative. He appraised Ponds to be over 50, small boned, and no taller than five feet six inches tall. Looking at Garrison, he said, "I think our best option is for you and Sergeant Norton to go with the Marine Patrol. Meanwhile, Agent Ponds and I will use the GPS in the car to drive around to the other side."

One of the Marine Patrol officers advised Kary, "You won't need GPS. I grew up around here. So I know those roads like the back of my hand. I'll ride with you gentlemen."

Ponds replied, "That leaves room for me in their boat. I think it's best if I join them."

Before Garrison, Ponds and Norton could climb into the boat, Kary advised, "Look, we don't know whether this guy has picked up a gun in the past couple of days, so no one goes anywhere without a protective vest."

Norton started to protest, "And if he doesn't have a gun, those damned things are a major hindrance." However, Kary left him no option.

Once the three men reached the other shore, it was agreed that Garrison would approach the cabin from the shoreline side, while Ponds remained with the bass boat Abdulov had stolen. Meanwhile, Norton would approach from the Echo Point Road side of the cabin. Kary and the Marine Patrol officer would time their arrival just minutes after the men exited the patrol boat.

With their watches synchronized, Garrison pounded on the door connecting the cabin to a back porch. Norton noticed that the front door had been left slightly ajar, so he used Garrison's distraction to enter the cabin. As Abdulov exited a small bathroom five paces from where Norton stood, he froze.

"Police!" Norton said. In a remarkably calm voice, he added, "The cabin is surrounded. Mr. Abdulov. I'm here to place you under arrest."

Abdulov was not armed. However, at the same moment Norton first saw him, he spotted a Glock sitting on the back of a ragged-looking easy chair—equidistant between the two men. Abdulov was a tall man whose powerful build attested to a life of hard labor. Norton could see that he was assessing his situation and guessed correctly that Abdulov determined that the best route to escape was by overpowering Norton, then grabbing the Glock and taking his chances with the men outside. After all, only this single police officer, who was at least several inches shorter than him, stood in Abdulov's path to freedom.

He charged at Norton, and surprised the sergeant with a remarkably quick left hook to the head. What Abdulov could not have known is that the man in his path had a remarkably muscular physique with forearms the size of most men's calves. More to the point, Norton held high degree black belts in two martial arts disciplines.

Abdulov attempted to follow his left hook with a right cross. It was the last move he would make. Standing on the back porch, Garrison was astounded by the loud crashing sound that he heard inside the cabin. He would later compare it to a small explosion. Concerned that Norton might be in trouble, Garrison forced his way through the back door with his service revolver at the ready. He need not have hurried. There, unconscious and sprawled on an old wooden coffee table, lay Abdulov, courtesy of Sergeant Norton.

Minutes later, when Kary and Ponds rushed through the front door, the commissioner was concerned at the sight of blood oozing from a gash in Norton's cheek.

"Are you okay, Sergeant?"

"Yes, Commissioner, no thanks to you."

"Me? How is this my fault?"

Norton replied dryly as a wiped the streak of blood from his face, "You made me wear that protective vest, which slowed me down just enough to get this."

Chapter 27

Taras Abdulov spent the night in a Concord lockup. The next morning, he was to be interrogated by Garrison, Ponds and Kary. As things transpired, no interrogation was necessary. The young Kazakh refused the presence of a lawyer and spoke freely to his captors about his actions.

Abdulov told them that he had been raised in one of Kazakhstan's finest families. "If you check my records, you'll see that I have not even crossed the street where I should not."

He said his life was like a dream until 40 months earlier. At that moment, he bowed his head and appeared to be wiping tears from his eyes. "On my 25th birthday, my wife and I were celebrating. We had walked hand-in-hand through the park and onto a bridge, when a large car appeared out of nowhere. The way it was—how do you say—swerving, you could tell the driver was not acting normally."

Again, Abdulov became noticeably emotional but forced himself to continue. The men could see that he needed to tell his story.

"I leaped out of the path of the car and thought I'd saved my Katarina. But, the driver swerved again and hit her so hard. Her body flew through the air many meters, and her head hit hard against the pavement. Somehow she survived, but she never regained consciousness."

"Did you see the driver?" Garrison asked.

"Oh, yes, I saw him and I knew who he was instantly. He was an important American… the man you call Ambassador Marsden."

"What was his reaction?" Ponds asked him.

"Reaction… reaction… he had no reaction. He got out of his car, glanced at her blood-covered body, then was taken away."

"By the police?" Kary wanted to know.

"No, not the police. An American embassy car took your ambassador away, and I didn't see him again. He didn't even have the decency to send flowers or apologize to our family."

"When did you decide to avenge your wife?" Kary asked.

"Not immediately. At first, there was newspaper coverage in my country and in some European newspapers. When he left his ambassador job, I was relieved, because I was sure the American government was punishing him. For nearly two years, I searched through different American government records. I looked for information on his punishment. But, there was nothing. He was able to come home and resume his very pleasant life, while the anguish my young children and I felt was ignored. I finally decided to do something about it," Abdulov told them.

"How did you decide where to punish Mr. Marsden?" Ponds asked him.

"I saved my money then waited to receive a visitor's visa. I read that Marsden was living in this part of America. All I needed to do was find a suitable place to end his life. The solution came to me by chance."

"Go on," Garrison said.

"I wanted to find a place where I could end his life and remove any evidence without being captured. I looked through a number of those small travel booklets they have at... what do you call them... rest areas? I narrowed my choices to the Mount Washington and the Lost River. That's when I found the cruise uniform."

While Garrison and Ponds didn't immediately understand what Abdulov was saying, Kary knew what he meant. Abdulov told them that he was shopping for a disguise, when he walked into a second-hand store in Meredith. While his pronunciation wasn't clear, Kary knew that the Etcetera Shoppe in that lakeside town bought used items on consignment.

Abdulov went on to tell them that he saw a cap and coat that appeared to be from a cruise vessel. When he questioned the store clerk, she told him that those items had belonged to a young man who once worked on the Mount Washington. Abdulov felt that this must be a sign. After he bought the two items, he found a name tag and an old drivers license in the jacket's inside pocket. It was then that he decided to call himself Jackson Kilgore.

"My mistake was not using that name when the photographer asked," Abdulov.

"No," Kary replied, "your mistake was taking revenge the way you did. Also, what kind of man involves his uncle and cousin the way you did? They will be fortunate not to serve time in prison for their part in this."

Before being led away, Abdulov begged the three men not to charge the Czecheznys. He assured them that he used his family shamelessly, then dumped them off on the shore and threatened their family if they talked.

Chapter 28

Once Abdulov signed his confession, Ponds arranged for him to be transported to Chelsea to await trial. Garrison congratulated Kary and his team for another job well done; however, something was clearly bothering Kary.

"What's the problem, Commissioner? You act as though we didn't get our guy," Norton asked him.

As Kary, Bendix and Norton walked toward the cafeteria in the State House, he told them, "I'm not excusing Abdulov for what he did. Nor can I feel a sense of victory, given the circumstances that motivated his actions."

They walked into the State House before he added, "I still have a problem with that guy Carl Timms. Something about his role in this is nagging at me. I can still see him getting into my face, saying that he saw something that will help our investigation."

Kary paused before saying to Norton, "Apparently, Arnold and his partner came up empty."

Norton replied, "It wasn't for a lack of trying, Commissioner. Timms left behind a false address. The guy seems to have vanished into thin air."

"Everything about that guy was just too contrived. Can you two see if you'll have any luck finding him? I'm not sure why, but I still think it may be important."

※※※※※※

Very little information on the internet escapes the research talents of Lieutenant Mary Bendix. Three hours after lunch that day, she knocked on Kary's door with Norton by her side.

Norton placed his hand on Bendix's shoulder as he proudly announced, "We've got him, Commissioner… that is… the lieutenant did."

Kary was anxious to hear their news. "How did that happen?"

"I did a search of all online newspapers within a 200-mile radius. I entered his name in the archives of the Lowell Sun and several pieces popped up."

"What did you learn?"

"It appears Mr. Timms is a wealthy man who made his money in plastics back in the 1990s. He was also mentioned, just in passing, in two pieces about his opposition to some of the city's open housing practices."

"Interesting. So, Timms has a bit of a problem with people who are less fortunate—like minorities and immigrants—gaining a foothold in Lowell."

"It's stronger than that. Here is a photograph showing a group of people protesting the Dream Act of 2017. And, look who's in the front row."

"His hair and short stature are unmistakable," Kary said. "Let's bring him in. But, before you do, I want to ask Garrison and FBI agent Ponds to join us."

The following day, Carl Timms met with Kary, Garrison, Ponds, Bendix and Norton in the larger DTF conference room.

By agreement, Kary assumed the role of spokesperson. He began by telling Timms that the Visitor Safety Task Force had a difficult time locating him.

Timms immediately came across as self-important.

"Why is that, Commissioner? I'm in the phone book," he added with a laugh.

"Perhaps it was because you gave a false address to the officer who interviewed you on the Mount Washington," Kary replied.

Timms remained silent, all the while eyeing the five with an expression much like a wolf in a sheep pen.

"I'm not liking the temperature in this room, Commissioner. Why wasn't I advised of my rights? I would have brought legal counsel with me this morning."

Garrison was quick to respond. "There was no need for either of those things, Mr. Timms. We only advise people of their rights when they're in the process of being arrested. And, since you are here for questioning, the presence of a lawyer isn't necessary, nor, for that matter, is it permitted. We will, however, be taping this session for the record."

Timms rose suddenly, "Well then, if I'm not under arrest, I suppose I have the right to… "

"Sit down, Timms!" Norton barked at him.

The other four officials were momentarily taken aback by Norton's outburst, although they shouldn't have been surprised that the mercurial sergeant was the first to lose his patience. Kary quickly decided that the best course of action was to go on the offensive with his suspicions.

"I was very disturbed by your actions aboard the Mount last week, Mr. Timms."

"Disturbed… why disturbed? I did what any good citizen of this country would do. I pointed out the suspicious actions of several… aliens."

This time it was Bendix who raised an eyebrow. "Aliens… Mr. Timms… which of those people was from Mars?"

"You people can make light of a situation if you want, but I think what I did was patriotic. I spotted those two guys with the strange accents stalking the tall guy who, as we now know, disappeared mere moments later."

"Yes, and we've caught the murderer. No thanks to you," Kary said sternly.

"No thanks to me; how dare you..."

"This is why I dare—as you've termed it," Kary replied angrily. "Because of your xenophobia, you immediately suspected two young men who happened to be from a part of the world you find unacceptable as a source of U.S. immigrants. Furthermore, you tied up state and federal resources while we went on a wild goose chase... a pursuit of your making. Worse yet, your so called evidence was all a lie."

"What do mean it was a lie. I saw those men stalking the ambassador, looking at him suspiciously, and sharing secrets in their foreign language."

Kary had Timms right where he wanted him. "Thank you for repeating that for the tape, Mr. Timms. The facts are these: you were not inside the Mount when the ambassador went missing, like you said you were. You were standing near the bow on the starboard side, no doubt critically appraising the stranded boaters' accents."

"That's not true. How dare you accuse me of lying?" Timms shouted.

At that juncture, Kary removed a blown up copy of the picture Nya had taken of the people viewing the bass boat and its occupants.

"Do you deny that the man in the middle of the picture is you, Mr. Timms? I warn you not to lie to us."

Timms knew that his deception had been caught, but he was unrepentant.

"Okay, so that's me. And, yes, I was outside when I said those two foreigners were stalking the ambassador. It was a small fabrication that means nothing. You have nothing on me. I didn't kill anyone."

Ponds was quick to pounce on that statement. "I don't know what turned you into a xenophobe, Mr. Timms. And, frankly, I don't care whether you and your ilk want to march around with placards. But, when you use your hate to slow down the process of a federal and state murder investigation, that means serious trouble."

"What do you mean?" Timms asked. His arrogant demeanor had been pierced. Now his voice had grown weak.

Kary handed a sheet of paper across the table to Timms while paraphrasing its contents. "You are in violation of Title 18 of the U.S. Code of Laws, specifically section 1001. This section declares when someone willfully falsifies, conceals or covers up a fact up by means of any trick, scheme, or device, you may be imprisoned for not more than five years. However, if said action involves international or domestic terrorism, which it does in this case, you may be imprisoned for up to eight years."

Timms knew he was caught. He began to weep openly. "I never meant to do anything like that. Honestly"

Timms was instructed to call his lawyer. In the mean time he would be placed under house arrest in one of the DTF's offices. The five law enforcement officers huddled after their meeting with Timms.

"How does behavior like Timms' get started?" Norton asked the others.

Ponds was first to reply. "It's been my experience that people like Timms are looking for a greater public voice—frequently through politics. Their entire motivation is a lust for power."

Bendix contributed, "I've done a lot of reading about this. People like Timms know just what buttons to push on their followers. They play on the fears of a group for whom life hasn't been easy, and are now looking for change. It's easy to scapegoat minorities like immigrants."

Kary had been thinking about Timms for weeks. "Unfortunately, in this case, Abdulov played right into the hands of the haters. He's an immigrant who involved other innocent immigrants in the commission of a felony. When the news of this case spreads, and that's already begun, it will stoke the fears of people who are being misled by Timms and his kind. In that sense, Abdolov's crime to society will be far greater than his vengeful act toward William Marsden."

Norton listened before adding, "It's amazing how the actions of someone in another part of the world can have far-reaching consequences in another."

At that point, Kary looked at Bendix with a smile before replying, "You're correct, Sergeant. And thanks to people with research skills like the lieutenant's, there are no more secrets."

※※※※※※

Several days after Taras Abdulov's arrest, the body of Ambassador Marsden was found floating several hundred yards from where he had been dragged overboard. Miraculously, a button from the jacket Abdulov had been wearing was found in his clenched left hand.

Following his trial, the young Kazakhstani was convicted in federal court of murder in the first degree. The presiding judge weighed the circumstances of a carefully planned and executed murder versus the grief Abdulov had suffered due to the irresponsible actions of his victim. Ultimately, he handed down a life sentence with possibility of parole after serving 25 years.

It was determined that the Czecheznys had acted out of ignorance. Although they aided and abetted their cousin to commit a heinous act, Kary and Norton spoke in favor of the two men at their arraignment. The presiding judge ultimately agreed to suspend any jail time, but assigned the pair to 500 hours of community service each.

Carl Timms did not receive any jail time. With his lawyer present, he agreed to apologize to the Iskakov brothers and to the Czecheznys in person and in writing. He further agreed to an interview on WMUR and WBZ, in which he recanted his xenophobic ways. As of this writing, Timms has not been involved in any public activities where hate is spewed toward minorities of any kind.

Knock Knock. Who's Dead?

A Commissioner Kary Turnell Murder Mystery

Mark Okrant

Prologue

If the sexagenarian's corpse were able, it would demand to know what he'd done to deserve this predicament. Here was the John Doe lying lifeless in Manchester's Cat Alley, with the two dimensional feline characters depicted on the passage way's brick walls staring down dispassionately. There had been a single mortal visitor an hour after the body's unceremonious arrival here. That was at about three o'clock in the morning. An inebriated street person had taken the same shortcut between Franklin and Elm that hundreds of others used while on their way to experience life along the Queen City's main thoroughfare during work hours.

There was no reason for the late night denizen to be deterred by the lifeless one—no idle conversation, not even spare change for a cup of coffee at the Red Arrow. No, John Doe would need to lie for several more hours in the cool spring night air before receiving the attention he deserved. But, once that came, the stranger would be treated with a level of attention fortunately needed by very few. Only then would the set of events leading to his shameless abandonment in the iconic alley be uncovered.

Chapter 1

Wednesday, May 12, 8:00 a.m.

Kary Turnell sat in his overpriced, tan leather recliner. Tension was having its usual effect upon his tired neck and lower back muscles. He had taken a couple of extra-strength Tylenol, and was sitting upright while waiting for his meds to work. Kary had scheduled this particular day away from the New Hampshire Visitor Safety Task Force's office. He hoped to catch up on some pleasure reading, as Nya had purchased a copy of Stephen King's latest tome for him. His cell phone rang unexpectedly.

"The best laid plans of mice and men," Kary sighed, paraphrasing Robert Burns. Kary smiled, despite the interruption. Glancing at caller ID, he recognized the telephone number as belonging to Jayne Ingolls, his administrative assistant, and one of Kary's favorite people in state government.

With a bit of effort, he managed to sound enthusiastic about the call.

"Jayne; how are you on my day off?" he couldn't resist a little sarcasm, given the circumstances.

"I just know you're thrilled to hear from me, Commissioner."

Kary began to feel his stomach knotting. It didn't take brilliant deduction on his part to realize that this call would mean the end of the leisurely morning he planned.

"I'm sorry, Commissioner, but you and your team have been summoned."

Ingolls proceeded to tell Kary that a body had been found early that morning down an alley, just off of Elm Street in Manchester.

"Which state did our latest victim hail from?" he asked. Given the fact that Kary and his two colleagues, Lieutenant Mary Bendix and Sergeant Bob Norton, were only called into the field when victims were visitors from outside New Hampshire, it was a logical query. Only, this time it wasn't necessarily accurate.

Ingolls paused before responding, "I'm afraid the local officers aren't sure."

Were it anyone other than Ingolls on the line, Kary may have used a different tone of voice. However, he was careful not to fall prey to one of the admin's infamous pranks.

His response was so composed that she nearly burst out laughing. "What do you mean, they're not sure, Jayne?"

Ingolls restrained herself, as the moment hardly warranted levity on her part. "As I was about to say, Commissioner; there was no ID on the victim's body."

"If that's the case, why is the VTF being summoned?" he replied.

The three members of the Visitors Safety Task Force had earned a reputation for successful investigations during a mere matter of months. Moreover, other law enforcement agencies respected them because they were not shy about sharing the credit. As a result, their presence was generally appreciated, and they were widely referred to simply as the VTF.

"My understanding is the governor himself requested that Stu Garrison's team and yours be involved in this. That's really all that I can tell you."

If Kary was nonplussed by this news, he wasn't about to share that with Ingolls or anyone else—with the possible exception of his wife and lifelong confidant, Nya. Before ending the call, he calmly instructed Ingolls to notify Bendix to meet him at the office in a half hour.

"And, please tell Sergeant Norton to head down to Manchester, ASAP."

Remaining in his recliner briefly, Kary pondered what all of this meant. The governor wasn't in the habit of sending teams into the field. It certainly made sense to dispatch the state police's major crimes unit, not to mention the FBI. But, why include Kary and his team, especially before knowing whether the recent victim was an out-of-state resident?

"I suppose it doesn't matter," he muttered. "So much for a quiet day at home with Stephen King." And, as soon as those words had passed his lips, Kary was on his cell with Captain Stu Garrison, lead investigator with the state's Major Crimes Unit.

Chapter 2

When Stu Garrison saw the name on his iPhone, he couldn't help but smile.

"Hello, Kary. And, how are you on this wonderful spring day?" Garrison couldn't resist taking a verbal jab at his good friend.

"I was having a peach of a morning until about five minutes ago, Stu. So, what the heck is going on down there in Manchester? Don't tell me this case is so tough that three law enforcement agencies can't solve it without the VTF." Kary's mood lifted briefly as he joked with his friend and frequent investigative partner.

"Apparently that's what the governor thinks." Garrison replied, "And you can be sure that at least two other law enforcement agencies completely support his decision."

"So, what you're telling me is that someone in Manchester isn't thrilled with our impending arrival."

"You might say that," Garrison replied with a mirthless chuckle.

"Exactly who are you talking about, Stu?"

"Have you crossed paths with Paul Ambrose before?"

"I can't say I've had the pleasure," Kary replied.

Now the laughter emanating from the other end was for real. "I wouldn't exactly describe my past dealings with Detective Sergeant Ambrose in those terms," Garrison said.

"So, what's the issue?"

"This is a situation with which you are eminently familiar," Garrison told him.

"I don't follow."

"Just like your Lieutenant Bendix, the law enforcement system has not been particularly fair." Garrison gathered his thoughts before continuing. "There is a woman police officer down here named Stella Gillespie... Sgt. Stella Gillespie to be precise. It's pretty common knowledge that Gillespie thinks she should have made detective a long time ago. No doubt Ambrose knows how she and a few others feel. So, when you pair being promoted to detective in controversial circumstances with the sudden presence of MCU, the FBI, and now VTF tramping on his turf, you have one very unhappy city cop."

"Terrific," Kary deadpanned. "This sounds like another episode of the Peter Principle. Is there any particular way I should handle this?"

"If it were me, I'd have Lieutenant Bendix serve as your liaison with Manchester PD," Garrison told him. "She's adept at dealing with touchy cops."

After about 20 seconds of silence, Garrison took the hint.

"Let me guess. You've sent Sergeant Norton to the crime scene... am I correct?"

"You're a mind-reader, Stu. In fact he should be arriving in 10 minutes."

Garrison sighed audibly. "If only I could disappear. So, Norton, who drips testosterone, is going to be the first member of your team who interacts with the detective sergeant. Hopefully there won't be any more bloodshed in that downtown alley."

Kary smiled as he closed the connection with Garrison. However, the more the commissioner thought about it, the circumstances didn't seem to add up to a clean investigation.

Chapter 3

Tuesday, May 11, 2:30 p.m.

The drive from Connecticut to Manchester had taken nearly three hours. After making a brief pit stop south of the city, the driver obeyed his GPS and used exit 6 to get off I-293. As Waze directed him, he headed east and crossed the Amoskeag Bridge. Next, he took a ramp onto Canal Street before taking a left turn onto West Merrimack, then drove up the steep hill until he saw a sign for Franklin Street. Looking in both directions, he elected to take a right onto Franklin before pulling his 2012 two-door, dark green Nissan Altima over to the curb. Rather than use his debit card, the driver pulled coins from a roll of quarters to obtain a parking pass for two hours.

He returned to the car and sat in the driver's seat, while placing his paper parking ticket on the dash. Sitting behind the steering wheel, the man looked both ways along the sidewalk. Ascertaining that there was no one in the vicinity, he reached into his pants pocket to feel that the large wad of $10 bills was still there. Next, he removed the wallet, car key and cell phone from his pants pockets, placed them inside a small canvas bag with the roll of quarters, and shoved them into a special hiding cavity that he'd created beneath the front passenger seat.

Before exiting from the car, the driver reached behind him and grabbed his navy blue blazer and canvas Jack Wolfskin half knapsack from the back seat. He put on the blazer and checked to see if the contents were inside his bag. Satisfied, he pulled one of the straps over his shoulder, then reached across the seat and locked only the passenger side door, before walking up Merrimack toward Elm Street.

As he walked, the man could almost hear his elderly mother's admonition, "My darling, why you continue to leave your car unlocked while you're walking around in cities without any identification or credit cards, escapes me. I have to tell you, Jack, one of these days you'll be sorry that you keep doing this."

Jack should have listened to his mother.

Chapter 4

Wednesday, May 12, 9:00 a.m.

At approximately the same time that Mary Bendix was entering the office suite of the Visitor Safety Task Force in Concord, Bob Norton arrived at the crime scene in Cat Alley. Kary greeted Bendix cordially just as Norton was about to experience something quite different. When Kary informed Bendix who Norton would be assisting until the full task force arrived in Manchester, Bendix shook her head.

For years, before being appointed to the New Hampshire Drug Task Force and later, the VTF, Mary Bendix had been passed over for promotion after promotion to lieutenant. She refused to allow such unfair treatment to impact her job performance. As a result, Bendix had a well-earned reputation as an outstanding member of the law enforcement family. On one occasion, several years earlier, she had been asked to counsel a young woman patrol officer who was not dealing well with the same poor treatment that Bendix had received. That young police officer was Stella Gillespie. So, if anyone was aware of the anger that Manchester's Sergeant Gillespie was harboring, it was Mary Bendix.

Bendix couldn't resist admonishing Kary for sending Norton to meet with Ambrose and Gillespie without her along to serve as a referee.

"This may not go down in the annals as your shrewdest move, Commissioner."

Chapter 5

Donnie Batchelder, a 15-year veteran in the Manchester PD, was the first officer on the scene. He was flagged down by a jogger taking a mind-clearing, early morning run along Elm Street, when the man spotted a rather large inert object lying in Cat Alley. Figuring he must have seen a street person spending the night protected from the wind, the jogger was conflicted over whether to call someone or to mind his own business. It was when Batchelder came slowly cruising past in his police car that the jogger decided to summon the officer.

Batchelder's actions were textbook. He asked the jogger to remain nearby while calling headquarters to report what he had found. Next, he cordoned off both entry points to Cat Alley and carefully searched the area for anything that seemed out of place.

Ten minutes later, Sgt. Stella Gillespie pulled up in her cruiser. Batchelder was pleased to see Gillespie. While she could be caustic, he knew that she was a by-the-book cop. So, as long as he did his job properly, she would respect him. In Batchelder's mind, no patrol officer could ask for anything more from his superiors.

"Mornin', Donnie," she greeted him. "So, what do we have here?"

"Hi, Sarge. We have ourselves a dead body. Guy looks like he's been here for at least a couple of hours. But, of course, that's not my call."

"Above my pay grade, too, Donnie. Did you see any signs of a struggle?"

"There's no visible blood trace. He's just lying there peacefully, face up."

"You can do me a favor, Donnie." Pointing over to the jogger who was jumping up and down to maintain his heart rate, "Do a preliminary interview of the guy who stopped you, get his information, and send him on his way. Then, just continue your route. I'll assume supervision here until that idiot, Ambrose, arrives with the rest of the cavalry."

Ambrose, to whom Gillespie referred, was the same Detective Sgt. Paul Ambrose, a 20-year member of Manchester PD who was selected as a detective rather than her. Batchelder knew that there was no love lost between Gillespie and Ambrose, and was just as happy to be leaving before the detective sergeant arrived. As a veteran of the force, Batchelder knew that Ambrose would be accompanied by one of the assistant deputy medical examiners from the Office of the Chief Medical Examiner in Concord. Most likely, it would be Dr. Bill Harris, a highly qualified medical professional who lived down the road in Hooksett.

Stella Gillespie was born and brought up in Manchester. After graduating from West High School, she enrolled in the Law Enforcement Administration program at NHTI, in Concord. Over the years, she had worked hard and proven herself to be an excellent cop. When she finally was promoted to the rank of sergeant at the age of 37, Gillespie began to set her eyes on becoming a detective. Most fellow members of the department rank-and-file believed it was a promotion she deserved.

During recent years, Gillespie found herself working on occasion with Dr. Harris. The pair had developed an excellent working relationship, as she was a counterbalance to the amateurishness of Ambrose. Now, anticipating the arrival of Ambrose, she gritted her teeth.

"If the ME's office suspects this was a homicide, the good Lord only knows what other idiots will be coming down here from Concord," she said aloud.

Gillespie was in for a pleasant surprise.

Chapter 6

Tuesday, May 11, 2:50 p.m.

As he arrived on Elm Street, Jack was feeling pangs of hunger. Never a fan of big lunches, he would kill for a halfway decent cup of coffee and a piece of pastry. While walking north on the west side of Elm Street, Jack's nostrils became captivated.

"Wow, something smells really good!" he told himself. Looking to his left, he spotted the open doorway to Lala's, a small storefront establishment specializing in Hungarian pastry. With two people in line to pay for their food, Jack scanned a nearby glass case where he spotted a delicious-looking coffee cake. Soon he was seated at a table in front of Lala's, where he made short work of what would prove to be his first, and only, meal of the day.

As Jack continued his walk along Elm, he passed a narrow alleyway whose walls were covered with art depicting cats in various forms. He stood on the sidewalk without entering the alley, admiring the unusual sight.

"We call that Cat Alley," said a voice behind him. "I'll bet you've never seen anything like it."

Jack had to admit he hadn't. He also had never seen anything like the strange vehicle the man was leaning against—at least not in the United States.

Parked in front of a storefront called The Bookery was what looked like a rickshaw with a bicycle welded to the front. The rickshaw portion was painted white with a bright red trim. It looked as though it could accommodate two, or possibly three passengers.

"Is that thing yours?" Jack asked the fit young man who had initiated a conversation. After a few minutes of chatting, Jack learned that the driver's name was Mickey, that he'd used some grant money to start his carbon-free transportation service called 'Peddl' and that he was relaxing between customers. That's when Jack decided to become Peddl's next rider.

After a quick discussion of company rules, Mickey left the curb on Elm and headed south, passing the city's Veteran's Park. As he peddled the vehicle, Mickey acted as a guide, pointing out some of the city's highlights. He took a left onto Central Street, passing George's, the iconic men's clothing store, then took a left onto Barrister Lane, and another on Merrimack Street. As they finished circumnavigating the park, Jack complimented Mickey on his safe driving.

Now headed north on Elm, they went through a traffic light at the intersection of Elm and Hanover, traveling past several bars and restaurants. Jack soon discovered that his driver was something of a local celebrity. All along the way, people called out, "Hey Peddl" or "You go, Mickey." Some even stepped out into the road to offer both Mickey and Jack high-fives. As the vehicle passed 1000 Elm Street, Mickey pointed out the Brady Sullivan Plaza building, and immediately entered the middle turn lane. While heading down Spring Street's sharply sloping hill, they could see the massive brick Millyard complex, with the sun reflecting off of the turbulent Merrimack River and the Notre Dame Bridge beyond.

For the next few minutes, Mickey remained silent as he concentrated on controlling the speed of his rapidly descending pedal vehicle. He rang the bell mounted on the handlebars to remind a jaywalker that this was not the appropriate time to take a leisurely stroll across Spring Street.

"Assholes!" the jaywalker yelled at the pair as they passed.

As the vehicle reached the Wall Street Tower and parking facility, Mickey could relax momentarily.

"It's interesting how that dude breaking the law somehow thinks we're assholes." Then looking back at his customer, Mickey noticed for the first time that the older man was wearing a blue blazer with a matching baseball style cap.

"What's that insignia on your cap?" he asked.

Jack removed the cap and held it so Mickey could read the front. "It says 'UConn Women's Basketball', he said proudly. "Where I come from, just about everyone is a fan... a lot like the following the Patriots have up this way. What I mean is, they're the biggest thing Connecticut has going for itself sports-wise."

Before Jack could place the cap back on top of his head, Mickey observed that the man was completely bald.

Chapter 7

When Norton arrived at the small passageway known as Cat Alley, he was greeted by Garrison and one member of his MCU team. Behind them, he could see that the medical examiner had placed a small white tent over the area where Norton presumed the body was found. Standing near the tent's main flap was a tall, powerfully built, middle age, female African-American police sergeant.

The sight of Gillespie standing there with her arms folded reminded Norton of those bronze statues situated outside of sports arenas, positioned there to celebrate great former athletes.

Manchester, like all U.S. cities had its issues with crime—to both property and person. Now, as Norton viewed Gillespie for the first time, he was satisfied that law enforcement in the city was in good hands.

"She looks as tough as nails," he told himself.

Never much of a poker player, the look on Norton's face was not lost on Garrison.

"You haven't met Sergeant Gillespie, yet, have you?"

"I haven't had the pleasure. But, based on appearances alone, I'm surprised there's any crime here."

In reality, Sgt. Stella Gillespie was the female counterpart of Norton; although, at nearly six feet in height, she was several inches taller. Extremely fit, with a muscular frame and no-nonsense demeanor, she was someone who street criminals avoided at all costs. Gillespie's single enduring concern was that she would remain in the patrol division forever, despite her outstanding performance in the field. Therefore, when Ambrose was promoted to detective rather than her, it took Gillespie a long time to get over it. Standing there in Cat Alley, she was a cop with an attitude.

Garrison took Norton over to Gillespie to introduce the pair. To the surprise of each, the handshake received from the other was more powerful than any experienced in quite some time.

Norton smiled at Gillespie. "I can see you're no shrinking violet, Sergeant."

In response, she told Norton, "That wasn't too bad either, Sergeant. I just hope that isn't all you've got."

Garrison told himself that these two would either get along famously or kill one another.

Thirty minutes passed before Dr. Harris pulled up the flap from the evidence tent and exited. No introductions were necessary, as Harris had worked cases with Garrison, Gillespie, and Norton previously.

Garrison noticed that Gillespie was acting as the representative of Manchester PD, and couldn't help commenting.

"Sergeant, where is Detective Sgt. Ambrose? Shouldn't he be here by now?"

"I'm afraid you're stuck with me, Captain Garrison. Ambrose is indisposed and the other detectives are dealing with cases right now. But, I won't disappoint you."

Garrison was aware that Gillespie had proven herself to be an excellent field investigator. Besides that, he'd always suspected that nepotism or some other unseen force led to Ambrose being promoted after the prior detective had retired.

If Gillespie was nervous about substituting for Ambrose, it didn't show. Standing in front of Harris, she asked, "What can you tell us about time and means of death?"

Harris frowned, then looked down at a small spiral bound notepad he was carrying.

"This isn't an easy one; I can tell you that."

"Explain, doc," Norton said.

"Let's start with the external examination. There is no evidence that your victim was either shot or stabbed, as I don't see any puncture type wounds. However, there's enough here to rule out death by natural causes or suicide, for that matter."

Gillespie and Norton asked in unison, "So, what does the evidence show?"

"Patience please, people. I was about to say that the victim has two glaring wounds. First, there is a very rough bruise around the base of his neck."

"Strangulation then?" Garrison asked.

Harris held up his hand to signal they should allow him to continue. "This bruise is on the back of his neck, which would indicate he was roughly pushed or pulled to the place where his head was smashed against a very hard object."

"What kind of object, doc... maybe the pavement in this alley?" Norton questioned.

Harris shook his head. "I can assure you that this alley was not the scene of the assault. We'll get the full field forensics report in a day or so, but based on what I've seen, there is absolutely no evidence of blood or release of other body fluids one would expect to find at a murder scene."

"But you are saying that this was a murder, right? So, what's the estimated time of death?" Norton asked.

"You three are more demanding than my wife is when I get home from work late," he smiled. "I'll know more once we've done a full autopsy, but my strong conclusion is that your victim died of hemorrhaging produced by blunt force trauma to the frontal lobe, likely the result of a hard blow or push delivered from behind. Since he was not killed here, the time of death is tough to estimate. I'm surmising he was killed inside a building near here. His body was probably stored near the murder scene, possibly wrapped in a blanket or stuffed in a big trash bag to avoid discovery, then moved out here once foot traffic in the area was at a minimum. This makes it tough to rely on body temperature to gauge the amount of time that transpired between the event and arrival here."

"So, if you eager beavers will allow, I'll reserve judgment on time of death for now, but there is one more thing I can share with you: we found a strange substance pressed into the wound on the front of the skull. Once our lab identifies it, we may know more about the actual scene of the crime."

Before parting company, Harris promised the others he would deliver his preliminary report as soon as it could be approved by the state medical examiner in Concord. "And, of course, you'll have the full autopsy as soon as that's available. I presume I'm sending copies to your captain, Sergeant Gillespie. Captain Garrison will receive one, as will Commissioner Turnell. Am I correct?"

All three nodded in approval. When Garrison joined his MCU colleague off to the side, Gillespie called to Norton.

"Say, Bob, is it all right if I call you by your first name?" Given Gillespie's reputation as a hard ass, Norton was surprised by her accommodating tone of voice. "You're one of the three VTF hotshots I've been hearing about, aren't you?"

With rapport apparently established, Norton replied, "I don't know anything about hotshots, Stella, but we're off to a pretty good start."

"You work with a former mentor of mine, Mary Bendix," Gillespie told him.

Norton nodded. "Then you should stick around. She and the commissioner will be here soon."

"Your commissioner… he's the dude that walks around wearing one of those fancy dress hats… that's him I saw in the newspaper, isn't it?"

"It's a fedora. And that dude, as you called him, is without a doubt the smartest criminal investigator I've ever met. If you don't believe me, ask Mary when she gets here."

Chapter 8

Kary headed directly to the alley, while Bendix dealt with some issues on her iPad. By the time Kary arrived, activity in the alley had subsided. Photos of the scene had been taken by someone from Manchester PD as well as an officer on Garrison's MCU staff. The jogger had been questioned, and Harris' assistant had bagged the victim's body, which was on its way to the morgue in Concord Hospital, adjacent to the state medical examiner's office.

By this time, there was an additional presence at the scene—Detective Sgt. Paul Ambrose. Based on information supplied by Garrison and others, Kary's expectations of Ambrose were low. Despite the fact that the detective sergeant had been in his present position for less than a year, he proved to be full of braggadocio.

"City cops see these kinds of cases all the time," he told Kary and his colleagues, while Gillespie stood nearby looking apoplectic. "I'll bet you dollars to donuts that this is some local down-on-his-luck dude who was the victim of a robbery gone bad." Puffing out his chest, he added, "We don't need the Major Crimes Unit to solve this one." Then, looking at Kary, he added, "And I'm telling you, Commissioner, calling out your Visitor Safety Task Force was a complete waste of your time, 'cause that dude ain't no tourist."

Preempting what was certain to be a severe tongue lashing from Norton, Kary replied to Ambrose, "With all due respect, Detective Sergeant, you haven't seen any of the evidence as yet. So, it would be premature on anyone's part to concern ourselves with jurisdiction in this case. I'm not about to tell you how to handle your investigation. However, we've been charged by the governor to conduct our own."

Overhearing this conversation, Gillespie had a sudden urge to kiss Kary. For nearly a year, she was powerless to watch Ambrose bungle his way through a job he'd received as part of the good old boy network. With no basis in fact, Ambrose would follow up on his pie-in-the sky theory. However, this time, he would be under the watchful eye of MCU Captain Garrison, with oversight by the FBI, neither of whom would be fooled by his bluster. Meanwhile, until it was learned otherwise, Kary and his team would proceed under the assumption that the victim was from out of state and deserving of their full attention.

Chapter 9

An hour later, Kary, Bendix, and Norton huddled inside The Bookery, a popular establishment known as a good place to find a current book as well as an excellent cup of coffee or tea. Pulling two small tables together, the three were preparing to review what they knew about the John Doe and the circumstances of his death. Bendix and Norton were seated facing the entry to the store, while Kary's back was to it.

"Well, look who's here!" Bendix exclaimed as she stood up behind the table.

Norton smiled at Gillespie. "That's right, you two know each other."

Bendix hugged Gillespie, then turned to Kary and said, "Commissioner, this is Sgt. Stella Gillespie. She is truly one of Manchester PD's finest."

Kary stood up and removed his prized fedora. Offering his hand, the handshake he received sent shockwaves up his arm and shoulder.

"It's a pleasure to meet you, Commissioner. Of course, I already know Mary here, and I think your sergeant and I have similar attitudes toward law enforcement."

Kary's intuition told him that this meeting had not been accidental.

"I'm sensing that you have something on your mind, Sergeant," he told her.

Gillespie blushed. "I guess you're as smart as everyone says, Commissioner. Either that, or I'm being way too obvious."

"Come on, Stella, spill," Bendix told her.

"Please hear me out, sir," she said to Kary. "I've been on the force here in Manchester for 15 years. During the past three, I've applied for every detective opening. I think you'll find that my field record is excellent, and my scores on every department exam have been among the best. Yet, up until now, I've been bypassed."

As Kary searched for a way to say the right thing, Gillespie continued.

"I don't know whether I'll ever make detective, but I do know when an opportunity to make a difference presents itself. My instinct tells me that there is something unusual about that John Doe we found next door in Cat Alley. I also know that the first 48 hours in a murder investigation are critical. And, if our detective sergeant intends to look in the direction he talked about, some murdering SOB is going to get away."

"So, what are you proposing, Stella?" Bendix asked.

"I know I can't be a detective... at least, not right now. But, I sure as hell can provide you three with a lot of assistance. None of you is from Manchester. I am; and I know this wonderful little city inside and out. You all can use me. I can help you find people and places way faster than you'll be able to do. So, please, let me help. If I need to work 20-hour days, I'll do it. I just want to be part of this investigation."

Bendix and Norton looked at Kary. He looked at all three of them, with the expression on his face betraying nothing. Finally, he told Gillespie, "I can't have a person on my team working 20-hour shifts. I'm sorry, Sergeant." Then, turning to Bendix, he said, "Contact the governor's office. You know who to involve in this. Let's find a way to assign Sergeant Gillespie to our team for 72 hours. That should be enough time to find out exactly what's happened here."

Gillespie's hug literally took Kary's breath away. For three days, the VTF would have a fourth member.

Chapter 10

Before proceeding further, Kary outlined a plan of investigation for the three others.

"This is certainly the strangest case I've ever worked on... with the VTF or without. First and foremost, we need to determine whether the victim qualifies as one of our investigations."

"Ambrose is convinced that the vic is a local guy. So he wants us to step aside and let him do his job," Norton reminded the others.

Gillespie couldn't resist a rejoinder. "That dumbass couldn't find a poop in a dog park, unless he stepped in it."

"While I wouldn't express things quite as colorfully as the good sergeant has, I don't trust his instinct at all," Kary replied. As he said this, Bendix and Norton nodded their heads in agreement.

Kary continued, "If we're going to proceed using the assumption that the vic was visiting from out of town, we'll need to cover a lot of ground in a hurry. First, let's brainstorm. What are the reasons that a man, presumably traveling alone, has chosen to visit Manchester?

"Commissioner, this place is changing so fast. There's so much new development, most of it tied to hi-tech," Gillespie told him. "And, some of the main movers and shakers in Manchester are women," she added with a smile.

Bendix couldn't resist adding, "That's right, gentlemen; and the city even has its first woman mayor."

With that, Gillespie and Bendix exchanged a high five.

Norton had just finished talking briefly on the phone to his wife, who was updating him about a sick child. "What are those two so excited about, Commissioner?"

Kary didn't respond. Instead he brought the discussion back into focus.

"My gut tells me that the victim's presence here is somehow intertwined with the development of the city itself."

"His gut?" Gillespie whispered to Norton.

Norton felt the need to tell Gillespie that it wasn't smart to question the commissioner's gut feelings. "Don't question the man in the fedora, Stella. He has a sixth sense for figuring these situations out."

Gillespie's mock sense of horror was not lost on Kary, who couldn't resist chuckling at her reaction.

Bendix was first to reply. "I know you live here, Stella, but all of us—even the commissioner—are too young to know this city's entire story. So, I Googled Manchester's history." She reflected a minute before continuing. "For years, the area known as the Millyard was one of the nation's leading textile manufacturing centers. Many of the families living here today are descended from the original mill workers; a lot of them immigrated from Quebec."

Gillespie added to Bendix' narrative. "My grandmomma told me that everything came to a screeching halt in the mid-1930s, when the Amoskeag Mills closed for the final time. She told me the city was dying. It was saved by a bunch of city bigwigs who were determined to stop foreclosure on the mill properties."

Bendix confirmed Gillespie's story, before adding, "Then, years later, Pandora Industries came in and employed tens of thousands of workers who knitted sweaters with machines."

Kary told the others how the city found itself enmeshed in the national debate over urban renewal during the 1960s.

Gillespie concurred. "My momma's family was scared they were going to be moved out of Manchester during the late sixties. Poor folks and minorities like my family were sent packing in a bunch of cities all over the U.S., just so downtowns could look pretty for wealthy white people and out-of-town visitors."

"That was a big problem in cities like Philadelphia, New Haven, and Hartford." Kary told them. "Fortunately, Manchester opted for a rival urban planning philosophy called 'urban redevelopment'. With urban redevelopment, programs were designed that were future oriented, not just pretty show places. That made it possible for community residents' voices to be heard, not ignored."

While Gillespie was enjoying her three new law enforcement colleagues, they could see she was growing increasingly impatient.

"This is all pretty interesting, but why are you people spending time talking about this stuff. Shouldn't we be out finding a killer?"

Kary appreciated Gillespie's energy, but she needed to be acculturated to the way the VTF investigated.

"We ARE investigating, Sergeant; but this needs to be done carefully. Otherwise, we won't be any more successful than your colleague, Mr. Ambrose."

Gillespie muttered something about Ambrose under her breath. Kary and the others chose to ignore that.

As one who knew about Gillespie's trials and tribulations, Bendix was willing to be patient with her.

"This is your bailiwick, Stella," Bendix prodded her. "Why do you think our vic came to Manchester?"

"Shoot. There's loads of reasons that man could have come here. He might just be visiting as a tourist. We have a ton of attractions to see."

"Good. And we'll need to take a look at as many of those as possible," Kary replied. "Why else could he have been visiting?"

"Manchester has been having lots of growth in hi-tech; I read in the *Union Leader* that it's fast becoming one of the most innovative cities in the U.S.," Bendix told the others.

Norton added, "Right, and let's not forget about medical tourism... people travel worldwide to get health care for themselves, or to visit family and friends who are patients. Two top-end facilities come to mind—Elliot Hospital, particularly for cancer treatment, and Catholic Medical Center for heart issues."

The others were silent for a minute, so Kary told them, "This is a good list of the most obvious reasons the victim may have been visiting. Let's keep thinking about others. In the meantime, we have a lot of ground to cover in a very short period of time." Looking at Bendix and Gillespie, he asked, "What are the quickest ways to cover that ground?"

Gillespie offered, "When I'm chasing down some dude, I look for help from two places."

"What are those, Sergeant?" Kary asked.

"The local media and transportation," she replied.

"Explain."

"There are only a few ways to get into downtown Manchester—driving yourself, renting a car at the airport, or taking a taxi, Uber, or Lyft from there; and then there's the Concord Trailways bus."

"That's helpful. And what about the media?" Kary asked.

"The folks at WMUR-TV and the *Union Leader* newspaper are always helpful," she replied.

"This is good work everyone. Of course, you all realize that there is one scenario we haven't discussed," Kary said with a mirthless smile on his face.

"What's that, Commissioner?" Norton asked.

"He could be here for VFR," Kary replied.

"What the heck is VFR, Commissioner?" Gillespie asked.

Bendix responded for Kary. "It means visiting friends and relatives."

Gillespie groaned audibly. "You mean, that dude might have come here just to visit his momma or somebody... then, how will we find out who he is?"

"There's no need to panic, Bendix immediately offered. A thought occurred to her, "No matter why he came to Manchester, we're going to need an artist's sketch ASAP. Unfortunately, the last I knew, sketch work has been increasingly difficult to come by."

Kary agreed about the importance of getting a sketch out to the public.

"That sketch has to be in the media and online within the next few hours. And, each of us needs to have a printout to email or take with us as we contact all of those attractions, industry folks, and hospitals… not to mention downtown shops and restaurants."

He contrived a plan for their investigation on the spot. "This case is going to necessitate a lot of shoe leather in a short period of time. Let's split up responsibilities. I'm going to call Stu Garrison at MCU. I know he's stuck babysitting Detective Sergeant Ambrose, but I'm going to ask him for some additional person-power. If that doesn't work, I'll call the governor personally," Kary told the others. "He sent us here without evidence of the victim's state of residence. So, I have no problem asking him for additional resources."

It was agreed that Bendix would take responsibility to contact the hospitals, to determine whether someone had seen a person matching the victim's description. Much of that process would be initiated with phone calls, supported by one or two visits. Norton and Gillespie would work together to canvas the city's visitor attractions, a list that would prove formidable. With some gentle prodding from Kary, the VTF's administrative assistant, Jayne Ingolls, volunteered to contact the various transportation operations. Meanwhile, Kary elected to focus on technology businesses and services housed in the Millyard.

※※※※※※

The first and most essential step in the process was completed in a surprisingly quick amount of time. By good fortune, the nephew of Bill Harris, assistant deputy medical examiner, was visiting his uncle while the victim's body was being delivered to the morgue in Concord. Harris knew that his nephew, Doug Plant, was a talented art major, specializing in figure drawing at the state university in Plymouth. Harris asked young Plant if he had ever attempted to draw the facial features of a cadaver. When Plant replied that he was interested in the challenge, Harris decided to take a chance. After a brief conversation with Kary, Harris asked Plant to produce two sketches—one showing the victim from the front, with both his shaven head and light colored eyes exposed. The second also would depict the victim from the front, but this time wearing the UConn women's basketball cap found among his possessions.

Less than two hours later, the two sketches were in the hands of Kary and his team. Recognizing the importance of the matter, people from the electronic media and internet enthusiasts were eager to help. After hours of tedious, unproductive fieldwork, soon there would be a significant lead.

Chapter 11

Jack was enjoying his tour of downtown Manchester. The weather had turned warm and sunny, with a steady breeze blowing in their faces from the direction of the Merrimack River. As they approached Arms Park, Mickey Calhoun explained to Jack how the river's raw power had been responsible for the city's growth from an important Abnaki fishing site into one of the country's leading textile producers.

"Tell me more about how those incredible brick buildings are being used," Jack asked.

"This is New Hampshire's hi-tech center. There are over thirty firms situated here. We have everything from robotics, to customer engagement, to universities, to cloud-based employee software. Also, Dean Kamen's company, DEKA, is housed here."

"Kamen... he's the guy who invented that two-wheeled transportation thing, isn't he?"

"Yup, the Segway was developed right here in Manchester. And Mr. Kamen is a major reason for the city's continuing growth."

"I'd like to learn more about all of this. Maybe I'll take a walk through this Millyard of yours after our ride. Besides, I have a bone to pick with someone who works there."

Calhoun was too busy looking out at the impressive current in the Merrimack, as he steered the Peddl along the Arms Park's brick pavement. So, Jack's comment failed to engender a response.

Jack called to Calhoun, "Hey, Mickey, show me something really interesting... you know, a real source of pride for Manchester."

"That'll be easy, Jack. Bear with me for another minute."

As they made their way along the red brick pathway, Mickey called back to Jack, "We're almost there; it's just ahead."

Calhoun parked the Peddl vehicle adjacent to a large rectangular sign. Several feet away was a bronze statue seated on a green park bench.

"Who's the guy seated on the bench?" Jack asked.

"This is the one, the only, Ralph Baer."

"I give up. Who the heck is Ralph Baer?"

"Read the sign, Jack. Ralph Baer was a great inventor. Among his many ideas, he designed the first home video game console."

"Oh, that's just wonderful," he chided. "So, we can thank this guy for the countless hours that the last three generations have spent with their butts in soft chairs and their minds on a small screen, instead of communing with nature, playing ball and having meaningful discussions… is that right?"

"I'm afraid so, Jack. This is that guy."

Jack let out a sound that sounded like a harrumph, before asking Calhoun to take him deeper into the Millyard complex. After several minutes, Jack called to Calhoun.

"Mickey, stop! This is where I need to get off. I want to stop by and talk with a few folks in these firms. Then there's someone I need to find."

"Listen, Jack. I can come back for you. I have a pickup to make on Elm, but I can be here in about a half hour, if you want."

"No, Mickey, that won't be necessary."

But Mickey hated the idea of Jack walking up the hill at the end of a long day. Reaching into his pocket, the younger man handed Jack a slip of paper with his contact information on it.

"Take this, Jack. If you need me to come back, just send a text message to that number," he said while pointing at the slip of paper.

Jack offered Calhoun his hand. "Listen, Mickey, you've been terrific. I loved riding in the Peddl, and you're one heck of an ambassador for this city." Then, he reached into his pants pocket. However, instead of pulling out a wallet, Jack retrieved a large wad of bills surrounded by a green elastic band. He peeled off two twenties and pressed them into Calhoun's hand.

"It's been a pleasure, young man."

"Forty dollars is a lot of money for a 10-block ride, Jack. Please remember what I said. I'm happy to come back for you. Hell, you've already paid me enough to… "

However, Jack was no longer listening. He'd begun his walk toward the first Millyard building. With one last effort, Calhoun called to him, "I hope you find your friend."

In a voice that was barely audible, Jack replied, "Who said I'm looking for a friend?"

As soon as Calhoun was out of view, Jack tossed away the slip of paper with Mickey's contact information, then headed toward the entry of the nearest Millyard building. Before entering, he reached into his knapsack, replacing the ball cap on his head with an expensive looking man's wig.

Chapter 12

Wednesday, May 12, 11:30 a.m.

Kary, Bendix, Norton and Gillespie exited The Bookery and walked south a few yards along Elm. Before they parted company to begin their respective tasks, Kary wanted the entire team together in Cat Alley, at the spot where the victim's body had been found.

Kary asked Gillespie to explain the origin of Cat Alley. Once she had concluded, he told the team that all of those depictions of cats were symbolic of the city as a whole.

"My sense is that, at one time, Cat Alley was little more than a passageway between the factory buildings and Elm Street. Its evolution into what it is today is a metaphor of Manchester itself."

"I'm not sure I follow what you're saying," Norton told him.

"Years ago, this city was dying along with its heavy industry. Today, thanks to a flourishing arts and culture experience, not to mention technology, the city is thriving. Manchester is a prime example of the creative economy at work. We need to remember this because, by understanding how Manchester's creative economy works, we'll be able to ascertain why the victim came here. I feel that's going to help us to figure out where and why he was killed. And, more importantly, by whom."

"That's the biggest crock of shit I've ever listened to in all my years as a police officer." It was the unmistakable voice of Detective Sgt. Paul Ambrose.

A large man, whose booming tenor rebounded off the sides of the buildings that formed the alleyway, Ambrose couldn't resist asserting what he, alone, deemed his superiority.

"The four of you are getting on my nerves. I'm trying to lead an investigation and you're spouting nonsense. What's it going to take to get this through those thick skulls of yours? You are way out of your jurisdiction. The guy who was found dead here this morning is either a local lowlife or some transient deadbeat."

Knowing that Captain Garrison of the MCU was riding along with him, Ambrose was determined to put on a show. So, he began by attacking the VTF members individually, starting with Gillespie.

"I have to laugh," he began by pointing at her. "You've deputized my sergeant here as your local contact. She's been on the force for more than a decade and still hasn't made detective. My guess is she never will."

Norton saw Gillespie's body tense. To prevent her from physically attacking Ambrose—something he secretly would like to see her do—Norton quickly put his arm across her shoulders.

Kary was Ambrose's next target. Pointing at the commissioner's hat, he bellowed, "And what's with you and that stupid hat, old man… you don't really think you have what it takes to out-think Paul Ambrose?" As he said this, the detective was pounding himself on the chest.

Garrison had heard enough out of Ambrose. He signaled to Kary to move his team out of the alley. Once the VTF was out of range, Garrison physically cornered the Manchester detective.

"What the hell was that, Ambrose?" Garrison didn't wait for his response before continuing to dress him down. "This isn't some stupid kids' game. We have a murder to solve, and you're fortunate that your chief has given you this assignment." Once again, before Ambrose could respond, Garrison continued. "Insulting your own sergeant is your business, but it's damned poor form. However, you just affronted one of the great criminal minds this state has ever seen. And, so what if he's chosen a fedora for his brand. Exactly how does that hurt you?"

Ambrose was too dumb to remain silent after Garrison's stern words.

"Those damned uppity Concord people burn my hide, Captain Garrison. Who do they think they are, coming in here and countering my investigation?" he asked rhetorically. "And did you see the look on that Sergeant Norton's face? In another minute I was going to pound that bastard."

Although he knew it was best not to respond to such a threat, Garrison couldn't resist.

"I would have loved to see that, Detective Sergeant."

※※※※※※

Ten minutes after his team members had gone their respective ways, Kary's iPhone buzzed in his breast pocket. Answering the call, he saw that Assistant Medical Examiner Bill Harris was FaceTiming him. Harris informed Kary that he also had Stu Garrison on the line. Garrison and Kary would not be able to talk to one another, but would be seeing and hearing Harris at the same time. Harris promised that the next time he contacted them, both men would be able to talk with one another.

"Kary and Stu, I'm calling you from the morgue here in Concord."

Garrison couldn't resist chiding his longtime associate, Harris.

"Wow, you guys have finished the autopsy already? This must be some kind of record!"

Harris was well aware that Garrison knew the autopsy would not be completed in two hours, if not days. "You're a regular comedian, Stu."

Kary's interest was piqued. "What's the purpose of this call, Bill?"

"We finished the ID sketch of the victim. I'm sending copies of two versions to both of you, and one to Detective Ambrose."

Kary and Harris heard Garrison mutter something at the mention of Ambrose; both wisely remained silent.

"I'm calling you on FaceTime because I know you'll want to see the vic's personal effects, ASAP."

Both men thanked Harris for his diligence.

As the camera on Harris' phone depicted about 10 items spread along the top of a steel surgical table, Harris selected each item and held it up so it could be seen clearly. Once he was finished, he asked the two investigators whether they needed to see anything a second time.

"I don't," Kary replied. "But, let's discuss what we've just seen, or rather, what we haven't seen."

"Sure. You lead off, Kary."

"Let's begin with the vic's clothing. It's obvious that Ambrose's theory—if you want to call it that—about the man being a vagrant is way off base. Do you agree with me, Stu?" Harris relayed Kary's question to Garrison.

Garrison agreed. "The guy was well dressed, that's for sure. I see an Oxford shirt, gray wool or flannel slacks, a blue blazer. Hell, even his socks and underwear look like they're in good shape. I'm not sure that the guy was wealthy, but it certainly doesn't seem that he was destitute."

Kary continued his observation. "What impresses me most is how little he was carrying in his pockets. How much money did he have wrapped in that elastic band?"

"Four hundred and fifty dollars, all in U.S. currency."

"This almost seems ritualistic. Like he habitually carried five hundred bucks with him. If that's the case, it's probable he spent some money along the way."

"We should have a partial answer once we empty the contents of his stomach," Harris replied.

Kary continued, "What has me stumped is the absence of a wallet and any identification. Hell… where are his car keys?"

"Once Harris told Garrison what Kary had said, the MCU head added, "You know what else is missing?" Garrison asked, "There's no cell phone."

"Yeah, even my kids carry cell phones, and they're in elementary school," Harris told them.

"All of this makes it impossible to ID our vic. No car, no wallet with driver's license and no phone. So much for being able to ping the guy's phone to find out where he's been and who he's talked with," Garrison muttered.

Harris had an epiphany. "Could this be a robbery gone bad?"

Garrison was ready to respond in the affirmative, but Kary wasn't so sure.

"So, someone robs and murders this guy, but leaves a wad of cash behind..."

"Yeah, that doesn't make any sense," Harris admitted.

"What makes even less sense is finding a dead body lacking both any ID and an apparent way of getting around the city. How in hell did he get to Manchester, and why was he here?" Garrison sounded exasperated.

"By the way, Bill, what's that blue canvas looking thing on the table?" Kary asked.

"It's a small knapsack that was with the body when we found it in Cat Alley."

"Was there anything inside?"

"I asked my assistant to take out any contents. There was only the UConn cap. By the way, there was also only one thing inside the blazer."

"What was that?" Kary asked.

"He had this DEKA brochure in the inside breast pocket," Harris replied.

"I suppose that's a start," Kary told the two men. "I'll check that out. I'm on my way over to the Millyard in a few minutes. Meanwhile, I know you'll show Stu any fingerprints we can use to ID this guy."

"My lab will deal with the fingerprints. In the meantime, at least I know one thing," Garrison told them.

"What's that, Stu?"

"This is definitely a case for the VTF. So Bill, tell Kary that he and his team are now officially on the clock. I can't wait to see that jerk Ambrose's face when I tell him," Garrison smiled.

"Bill, ask Stu if there's any way he can hold off telling Ambrose?" Kary asked.

"Yeah... but, why?"

"Because, he's not in our way if he's tilting at windmills. Let him go and do his thing for another few hours. After Bill shares the same information with him that we've just received, I'll bet dollars to donuts that he doesn't alter the course of his investigation."

Garrison smiled at the shrewdness of Kary's idea. "Tell Kary I can only promise him two hours. Any longer than that and I'll get my ass in a sling."

Chapter 13

With the two drawings produced by Bill Harris' nephew having been distributed, Kary's team of investigators was working non-stop. Norton and Gillespie had a daunting task. As they considered the number of possible, if not probable, attractions the victim may have visited, Gillespie was visibly deflated.

"Come on, Stella. What's with the glum face?"

"You don't live down here, Bob. So, you have no idea how many places that dude could have visited."

In truth, Norton and the other VTF members were required to familiarize themselves with data from each of the state's administrative departments. So, he was aware that the Merrimack Valley tourism region produced more rooms and meals tax revenue than any of the other regions, including the White Mountains and Lakes.

"I'm sure it's a long list," he agreed.

"Long... long? It's freakin' ridiculous! Even if we limit ourselves to the 10 most popular, we could be at this all week." Handing him a sheet of paper, Gillespie said, "Some people think that this is just a big, old, former mill town with nothing for visitors to do. Well, I'm here to tell you that there's plenty. There's the Currier Museum, the Amoskeag Fishways, the Millyard Museum, the art institute, the arena, the baseball park, not to mention the Palace and Old Rex theaters."

Norton laughed, despite the severity of the situation. "Stella, Stella. I can read the names on your list. Now calm down. Let's find a quiet place where we can talk on our phones. We'll call each place on your list, send them the two sketches, and ask whether they have seen our guy. Does that make sense?"

Gillespie was embarrassed. "Looking at the way I just lost it, it's no wonder they never made me a detective."

Norton assured Gillespie that everyone loses it at some point... everyone except KaryTurnell, that is.

The phone calls took the pair a little more than 90 minutes. Unfortunately, not a single one produced a positive response. One woman at the Palace thought she recognized the man in the first sketch. However, when she saw that his head was completely bald, she reneged, saying, "No, Sergeant; the man I saw had a full head of dark hair. I'm sorry."

With the likelihood that the victim had visited one or more of the city's wide range of arts, sports or other cultural venues severely diminished, the team now hoped that Bendix, Kary or Ingolls would have better results.

Chapter 14

When Jack arrived at the headquarters of ARMI, he would have been unrecognizable to Mickey, or anyone else from Manchester he'd encountered previously that day. Instead of the UConn women's basketball cap, he now wore a wig designed to look like the styled haircut of a 50-something-year-old man.

Entering ARMI, he encountered a young woman dressed in faded blue jeans and a dark green Ralph Lauren golf shirt. Looking up from her laptop, she seemed startled by Jack's appearance.

"Oh, excuse me, sir, I didn't see you standing there."

Jack smiled at the woman, whose name, Jayla Cummings, was written on a blue nametag that was attached to her polo shirt.

"Please don't mind me, Ms. Cummings," he replied. "I'm interested in how all of these businesses came to be located here in Manchester. So, I decided to drop by and look around."

Cummings, who usually was situated upstairs in research, was clearly out of her element.

"I, er, wish I could help you, sir. I'm on a coffee break and my boss asked me to sit here until the administrator returns from her break." Pointing to a small upholstered chair near the entrance, she said, "If you'd like to take a seat, I'm sure Janice can answer some of your questions as soon as she returns."

Jack knew that ARMI stood for Advanced Regenerative Manufacturing Institute, whose job was to manufacture engineered tissues, or something similar.

Soon, the hard heels of the administrative assistant's shoes could be heard in the hallway. Cummings turned momentarily to inform her that there was someone who wanted to ask a few questions. However, when she looked over at the chair, Jack had left the building.

※※※※※※

Ingolls' attempts to find witnesses at the airport, rental counter and bus terminal were no more successful than Norton's. She even coordinated with Garrison's MCU people to canvas taxi drivers as well as Uber and Lyft operators. The latter effort took several hours. In the end, no one recognized the man depicted in the sketch.

Instead of relying on the telephone, Bendix decided to visit both the Elliot Hospital and Catholic Medical Center. In each hospital, she was aided in her search by a public relations specialist, who walked Bendix to offices where it was most logical for the victim to have appeared. At CMC, she even took Bendix to interview three EMTs who had been working the previous afternoon and evening. Unfortunately, the results were the same.

Chapter 15

Jack's next stop within the former mill complex was at the offices of DEKA. The company was the brainchild of Dean Kamen, whose life's work was designing innovative, life-changing products. Having already developed numerous medical innovations as well as the Segway device, Kamen's new company was busily perfecting a wheel-chair that would climb and descend stairs.

Jack knew it was getting late, and it would be useless to interact with any of the company's 400 employees. As he entered DEKA's lobby. He spotted a brochure for the company, which he placed in the inside pocket of his blazer, before turning and exiting the building.

While these visits to corporations in the Millyard were not his primary purpose for traveling to Manchester, innovation had always been exciting to him. Being in the vicinity of where inventors like Dean Kamen came to work each day was his equivalent of people who toured the neighborhoods of Hollywood show business stars.

Jack was excited as he entered the hallway outside of FIRST, a program designed to inspire students to help build a better future. Just down the hallway, kindergarten through grade 12 students were being introduced to coding, programming and engineering. Here, they would learn to work collaboratively to solve a yearly robotics challenge.

The temptation to request a tour of the FIRST facilities was great. However, all of that changed when the building custodian walked past him.

"Excuse me, do you have the time," he called.

The custodian, a robust 50 year old who sported a pair of 'sleeves'—

tattoos covering the entire length of his large, muscular arms—ignored him.

Not knowing the closing time of the Manchester Historic Association's museum, Jack had not rushed to arrive there. It suddenly dawned on him that the facility might be closing earlier than he had considered. When he saw that the time on a wall clock read 3:45, Jack's anxiety level increased. In his rush to get to the museum, Jack walked past the building elevator and rushed down a precarious set of steps leading from the main floor of the building to its lowest level. After nearly slipping and falling twice, he finally reached the bottom of the stairs, where a sign indicated that the museum was closing at 4:00 p.m.

Entering the facility, it appeared that the entire staff had gone home early for the day. So, without stopping at the admissions desk, Jack took his own quick tour. Because he had been fully briefed about the location of the one particular display that interested him, Jack bypassed the museum store, the indigenous display, the extensive history of the Amoskeag Mills, and the beautiful pair of antique fire engines. Turning a corner, he stood in front of a wrap-around wall labeled Urban Renewal and New Prosperity. It was then that Jack fully realized the importance of his visit to Manchester.

Chapter 16

Kary was nearly 30 minutes late arriving at the Millyard than he intended. Unfortunately, when he showed the artist's depiction of the victim at ARMI, DEKA and FIRST, no one recognized the man.

By the time he finished talking to the administrator at FIRST, it was nearly 4 p.m. It was then that he saw a sign in the lobby indicating that the museum was housed on the floor immediately below. As the sign directed, Kary entered the building elevator and pushed the button for floor one. Exiting the elevator, he saw a woman docent nearly his age locking the museum door from the inside. Kary peered inside and saw enough of the museum to realize that it definitely would be worth visiting next time he was traveling to Manchester. For the time being, he made no effort to call to the woman who was chatting with a young museum administrator.

As Kary was leaving the Millyard building, he reached for his iPhone and dialed Bendix's number.

"Have you had any luck, Lieutenant?"

"I think the best thing we can say about today is we eliminated a number of possibilities," she replied.

"So, zero hits on medical?"

"Nothing from the hospitals. Norton and Gillespie learned nothing from the tourism sector. And Ingolls struck out with transportation," she replied.

"I got nowhere with the technology side, either. Of course, I've only sampled a very small number of businesses. If my limited math skills are correct, three businesses equals two percent of the 150 that call Manchester home."

"Now what, Commissioner?"

"I'm going to contact Stu Garrison and request that MCU use its personnel to finish canvasing the tech businesses, although, I'm dubious that they'll turn up much."

"So, where does that leave us right now?" she asked.

"There's no doubt that this guy was in town for a specific purpose we haven't discovered yet. Let's not lose sight of the fact that in a dynamic city like Manchester, there are lots of elements to a creative economy."

"I'm afraid you've lost me, Commissioner."

Kary smiled at Bendix's admission. "I didn't think that was possible, Lieutenant. Let's think of Manchester as a ball of yarn. Each element—the arts, commerce, technology, hospitality and transportation—is interrelated. Think about it. Twenty-five years ago, downtown Manchester was a pit. Most of the storefronts were sitting empty. If you passed anyone on the street in the middle of the day, there was a fair chance he'd try to rob you or make a drug deal," he exaggerated for effect. "However, the city has never lacked for innovative people. It also has had a terrific visual and performing arts component. The arts led the way, with new institutions giving hundreds of artists reasons to make repeated trips into town. The next thing you knew, restaurants, shops, hotels, two minor league sports teams and nice apartments followed suit. While not everyone would agree, I've always felt that growth in the arts led the way for technology to adopt Manchester as a home base. That's a reason the city has its wonderful airport, too."

Kary apologized, "All we'll need to do is find the correct strand of that relationship and we'll learn what the vic was doing here and where he went."

"Isn't that a bit like trying to find the proverbial needle in a haystack?" she questioned.

"It may not seem like it now, but we'll find that string; and once we do, the ball will unravel fast," Kary replied.

"Things had better. Because the clock on my Mac is telling me that our 48-hour window closes tomorrow at about this time."

"Then let's see what else we can do to find that first string."

"What do you want me to do?" she asked.

"I'd like you to use that keen research mind of yours. Find as many CCTV cameras as you can in the downtown area and outside the buildings in the Millyard."

"Anything else?"

"Since you asked—yes. You can get in touch with Norton and tell him to work with Gillespie to find out whether any cars bearing out-of-state license plates have been reported stolen in the last 24 hours."

"You think the vic may have driven himself here and had his car stolen?"

"It's certainly a possibility," Kary replied.

"That would amount to one really lousy day... having his car stolen and being murdered, all within a few hours."

Kary grimaced at the possibility, then headed out to the parking lot, before realizing that he had no transportation back to Elm Street.

Chapter 17

Five minutes remained until closing; so, Jack moved through the museum with a sense of purpose. He arrived at a bench where a closed circuit video loop was explaining how a small group of civic leaders saved the Millyard from demolition. Across the way was the display titled Urban Renewal and New Prosperity. This was the reason he had driven three hours from New Haven to Manchester. Everything else he'd done that day was interesting, but this was to be the denouement.

Jack's frustration grew after spending several minutes perusing every bit of the carefully worded and beautifully illustrated display.

"What people told me was correct. I could have saved myself a full day... damn it!"

Jack knew just where to go to vent his irritation. It was the end of the workday, but he hoped the museum's CEO was still in his office. He strode along a re-creation of Elm Street as it appeared years earlier until he arrived at a door with a plaque that read, Executive Director.

Jack remembered the lessons his grandmother had taught him. He could almost hear her say, "You can catch more flies with honey than you can with vinegar." So, he breathed slowly in and out, then knocked on the door.

Chapter 18

Kary began his trek across Bedford and Canal streets, heading toward The Bookery, where he'd arranged to meet Bendix, Norton and Gillespie. As he entered West Merrimack, his iPhone rang. The name on the screen indicated that Bill Harris was FaceTiming from the morgue again. Harris told him that Stu Garrison was also on the line.

Kary couldn't resist an attempt at humor, despite the circumstances. "The three amigos, part dos."

"I realize it's late afternoon, gentlemen. I hope your day has been a productive one," Harris said.

After Garrison muttered something about babysitting Ambrose while the detective sergeant chased his tail, Kary told the others how his team had covered a great deal of territory, but hadn't found anything substantive.

"So, we're pretty much back where we started. Is that right, Kary?"

"I'm not willing to be quite so pessimistic. Let's just say we've eliminated a bunch of possibilities. I'm convinced that, with a couple of breaks, we're closer to solving this than we're aware."

Harris couldn't resist saying, "You've gotta love a glass half full kind of guy."

Garrison said to Harris, "Come on, Bill, let's not dampen my friend's enthusiasm; you must have something for us."

Harris cleared his throat while signaling to his assistant to focus their iPhone on a steel table bearing the body of the victim. Once he was satisfied that the image was clear, he began.

"Your victim is a male, approximately mid-50s to early 60s, who appears to have been in good health. Using that information, we usually are able to pinpoint the time of death by knowing the temperature at the place of death."

Garrison interjected, "Of course, other than knowing that Cat Alley wasn't where this guy died, we have no idea what the temperature was where the murder took place."

"That's true," Harris replied. "However, presuming that he was killed in a building not terribly far from the alley, we can estimate that the temperature was likely in the 70 degree Fahrenheit range, based on models we use."

"That's interesting information, Bill. Now, what exactly does that mean?"

"The typical loss of body temperature in a man of this age who is in relatively good health is 1.5 degrees per hour. So, allowing for the time he spent in the alley, which we've estimated to be about five hours—give or take—we are assuming that the guy was killed sometime between 4 and 5 p.m. yesterday."

Kary couldn't resist saying, "You know what they say about assuming anything, Bill?"

"Yeah, I know, Kary. However, there are other checks that we can make, including putrefaction of the body, insect activity and stomach contents. The guy's last food intake was at around 3 p.m. With the comparative lack of insect activity, the medical examiner feels that his body was stored inside a sealed building until several hours before he was dumped in the alley, at a time of night when insect activity was minimal. So, you now have our best estimate of the time of death, gentlemen."

Anticipating what Kary and Garrison were about to ask, Harris continued.

"As to cause of death, there's no need to guess. We found evidence of extreme pressure being applied at the back of the victim's neck. It's obvious a larger, stronger person surprised him and ultimately smashed his head against a hard object. The force produced intracerebral hemorrhaging, while damaging the supratrochlear nerves. The resulting bleeding produced a situation equivalent to a massive stroke. He would have died within seconds to minutes."

"Gee, thanks for that, Bill," Garrison replied. "How about a translation?"

"The bottom line is we're looking for a cold-blooded murderer," Kary said sternly.

Kary and Garrison were about to sign off when Harris told them, "I'm not quite finished."

Garrison was familiar with Harris' habit of holding back on significant evidence while allowing suspense to build.

"Come on, Harris. Don't be such a drama queen. What else do you know?"

"Do you remember when I told you that we found a strange substance inside the wound on the vic's forehead? Well, we now know what it was. It's something called Rustins Danish Oil… the perfect solution for breaking down dirt and bacteria, while protecting vintage wood," Harris replied.

"Vintage, eh?" Kary asked.

"That's what I said."

"Are you gentlemen thinking what I am?" Kary asked.

"There are all sorts of antique handrails and other woodwork in the Millyard," Garrison offered. "It will take an army of law enforcement people to find the site we're looking for without messing up the murder scene. However, I'll have a group ready to search."

"That will take days, unless we can narrow things down," Kary said, unaware that an important piece of information would soon materialize.

Chapter 19

When no one answered the closed door of the executive director's office, Jack looked around the museum. Only five minutes remained before closing; so, it wasn't surprising that the last patrons already had left the museum. With the CEO nowhere to be found, Jack tried to locate a staff member; however, there was nobody to be found, which annoyed Jack even more.

"Damn it! This is a real pain in the ass. When I see that director, I'm going to give him a piece of my mind."

Jack suddenly felt the urge to use the men's room. He walked to the glass door separating the museum from the rest of the building. Before exiting, Jack decided on impulse to shut off all of the museum's lights, leaving any remaining staff members in the dark. However, in doing so, he also darkened the hallway outside of the museum substantially. There was barely enough light to make his way toward the elevator leading upstairs.

With the museum door closed behind him, Jack began to walk down the nearly darkened hallway toward the building's exit. Before entering the elevator, he stopped briefly to use the urinal in the men's room. He then found his way to the lift, quickly entered, located the button panel, and prepared to push the button for floor number two, where the building's exit was situated. Just as the elevator door was about to close, a large male wearing blue cotton pants and a dark color hoodie slid inside. It was the custodian who he'd encountered minutes earlier.

He was startled, and the fact that the man went and stood in back of him made Jack extremely uncomfortable. As the elevator door was about to open on the main floor of the building, Jack felt the man's large, strong hand grip him from behind. Jack struggled to free himself, but the hold on his neck was too strong.

"It won't do you any good to fight, asshole." The man's voice was deep, with a trace of a French Canadian accent.

"Look, mister, I don't know who you think I am, but my name is..."

"I know exactly who you are. I've been waiting 20 years for this chance. Now, you'll want to be smart. If you are, things will go a lot quicker for you. Struggling or trying to escape isn't going to do you a damned bit of good. And there's no one around to hear you."

Jack began to panic. "Listen to me, will you?! I have nearly $500 in my pocket. Let me go and it's yours."

The big man laughed aloud. "This isn't about money. It's about me taking care of some very old business. Now, here is what you're going to do. You and I will walk out of this elevator, past the doorway to FIRST and out into the foyer. But, you're not going out the front door... don't even think about that. Do you see that set of stairs off to the right?"

When Jack didn't answer right away, the man tightened his grasp on the back of Jack's neck. The grip was so hard that Jack could feel his blood vessels being constricted. It wouldn't take more than a number of seconds before he'd lose consciousness.

At times such as these, they say that a person's life flashes before his eyes. Jack remembered the time, so many years ago, when he was mugged in Boston. After that nightmarish incident, he vowed that nothing like that would ever happen to him again. From then on, he would be prepared to protect against attacks—regardless of their form—on himself or his family's reputation. It was anxiety about his father's legacy that had brought Jack to Manchester that day.

The assailant's voice brought Jack's mind back into focus.

"Do you see that stairway, asshole?" he roared.

With great difficulty, Jack nodded his head.

"That's a good boy. Now, I want you to start climbing. But, be careful; those steps are steep and slippery," he added with a laugh.

"You and I are going to climb until I tell you to stop," Jack was told.

The pain in Jack's neck was intolerable. That's when he hatched a plan. Soon they would have climbed five or six steps, which would make the two of them invisible to anyone entering or exiting the building. Jack hoped his accoster would momentarily loosen the vice-like grip while letting his guard down. In that moment, Jack planned to kick back at the man, hopefully causing him to fall down the stairs hard enough to injure himself.

As Jack began to step up toward number six, he kicked back with all of his might. Unfortunately, he had underestimated the man's considerable strength. Instead of falling backward, the man increased his grip on the back of Jack's neck, then spontaneously shoved Jack forward where his head struck the solid oak bannister with a resounding thud.

Chapter 20

When Kary arrived at The Bookery, he was met by the long faces of his team of three—Bendix, Norton and Gillespie.

"Just look at the three of you. Things aren't that bad."

"That's easy for you to say, Commissioner. You weren't here for that jerk Ambrose's latest tirade," Norton told him.

"For a minute, I thought he was going to attack Sergeant Norton," Gillespie told him.

That possibility, despite the dire circumstances, brought a smile to Kary's face.

"I'll bet you were trembling in your trooper boots, Sergeant."

"You know the answer to that one, Commissioner."

In truth, Bob Norton was highly trained in a number of martial arts disciplines. He was generally regarded as the toughest person—man or woman—in all of New Hampshire law enforcement. Had Ambrose allowed his anger to get the better of his judgment, the outcome would not have been pretty.

"So, what is it that has Ambrose so angry?" Kary asked, although he knew the answer to his question.

Bendix replied, "It seems that the medical examiner's office delayed supplying Ambrose with very pertinent information. Ambrose told us that the delay was two hours; and he blames us."

Gillespie looked particularly upset, a fact that was not lost on Kary.

"I knew about the delay. It didn't seem terribly relevant, because your Detective Sgt. Ambrose couldn't find a loaf of bread in a bakery."

"Well, that's not what he says," Gillespie replied.

Bendix felt it would save time if she explained the last five minutes of Ambrose's meeting with them in The Bookery.

"Ambrose claims that he already solved the case, while we've been busy chasing our tails. He also says he's asked his chief to demand that the governor send us home."

The look on Kary's face remained impassive.

"Is that so?" he asked. "The governor isn't going to do that. And exactly who does the detective think murdered our victim?"

Bendix replied, "He says Manchester PD has a guy in one of their cells who admitted to committing the murder. He's an ex-con named Lucas who says the victim was in his way in Cat Alley. So, as Ambrose tells it, Lucas 'offed him.'"

Kary stood there shaking his head back and forth. "Evidence has been difficult to find so far, but everything we know up until this point contradicts what Ambrose told you."

Now Kary looked each member of his team in their eyes. "I know this murder hasn't provided the obvious clues that all of our other cases did. But, you're all too good at what you do—that includes you, Stella Gillespie—to be anything but confident."

Kary continued, "First, I'm convinced the victim is not some local vagrant. His clothing is way more expensive and well-maintained to belong to a homeless person. His general health was excellent... another factor that convinces me he's not a street person. Early this morning, I'm going to be visiting with Bill Harris at the morgue. I want to have a closer look at the vic's personal effects. I'm convinced that those will help us identify him."

"What would you like us to do, Commissioner," Norton asked.

"Sergeant, you should go home to your family. Meet us at the office at 7:45 sharp tomorrow morning. Lieutenant, how is your list of CCTV installations coming along?"

"I'm nearly finished. Tomorrow morning, I'll have video to look through," she replied.

"Lastly, Stella, do you know what time Ambrose gets off shift?" Kary asked.

"He goes home at five o'clock, almost without fail," she replied.

"That's perfect. I need you to finish that task we haven't completed. Use one of your contacts at Manchester PD to get a list of any cars that have been reported lost or stolen since after midnight on Sunday. Have that information for us in the morning. Meanwhile, our sketches of the victim will have even more time to circulate."

As the three VTF investigators rose to leave The Bookery, Kary called to them. "Remember what I said. You guys are the best at what you do. I promise you we'll find our killer... and we'll find him soon."

Chapter 21

After Kary left the others outside of The Bookery, he arranged to meet Nya in Manchester for dinner. He didn't need to stand outside very long before she pulled up to the curb in her new black Infinity Q50.

"You do have excellent taste in automobiles, my dear," he said after the two shared a quick kiss.

"Speaking of taste; I'm famished. Have you found a place for us to eat?"

"Are you in the mood for pizza? Because, if you are, I've found a hidden treasure less than a half-mile from here. There's only one caveat."

"And what is that?" she asked.

"The neighborhood isn't what it used to be. But, Sergeant Gillespie tells me the Alley Cat's pizza is the best in the city. Beside that, the name has a certain irony, doesn't it?"

Nya's car looked out of place in the less than stellar neighborhood. But the pizza did not disappoint. As they were finishing the last two pieces of a 16-inch pie, Nya asked how his case was going.

"This one has been difficult to figure," he replied. "We can't seem to get an ID for the victim. To make matters worse, the place where we found him wasn't the scene of the crime."

For the next 30 minutes, the pair lingered over their soft drinks, as Kary explained what they had and had not learned to date. The intensity of their conversation reminded Kary of the old days, when Nya had been his investigative partner. There were few, if any, people whose opinion he respected more in such matters.

As they drove back toward Concord, Kary told Nya that he would be leaving early in the morning to visit the morgue at Concord Hospital. Kary explained to her that he wanted a first-hand look at the victim's personal effects before resuming work in the field back in Manchester.

"What do expect to find?" she asked.

"I'm not certain." He recounted for Nya how Garrison and he had viewed the victim's belongings on their cell phones, courtesy of Bill Harris and FaceTime.

As they were preparing for bed, a thought occurred to Nya. "Labels," she told him.

"What do you mean?" Kary asked her.

"You told me the man was found fully dressed and was carrying a small knapsack, right?"

"That's correct."

"It's just possible that his clothes, shoes, socks, or that knapsack was purchased at a store close to where the victim lived."

Nya's idea about labels made very clear sense. "If we can narrow down where he lived, I can have Bendix email those police sketches to news outlets in the general area. Someone is bound to recognize the guy." Embracing Nya, he added, "You are brilliant, my dear."

※※※※※※

Thursday, May 13, 5:10 a.m.

Kary took the elevator to the morgue in Concord Hospital's basement. By agreement, Bill Harris was waiting for him when the elevator door opened. The combination of a low ceiling and dim lights in the hallway gave the place a macabre feeling. Kary shivered involuntarily.

"This place takes some getting used to," Harris admitted to him.

The pair made their way along a corridor until they arrived at a well- lighted room with a large glass door. Inside was a steel table on wheels and two tall stools. Harris encouraged Kary to sit as he pulled the table closer to them.

"Take your time, Kary. I'm interested to learn what you see that we may have missed."

As Kary searched through each of the victim's belongings, the optimism he'd felt the night before began to fade. Item after item either lacked a brand name, or carried a label that was relatively ubiquitous: Gold Toe socks, Fruit of the Loom underpants and undershirt, a Ralph Lauren Oxford shirt, Haggar slacks, and L.L. Bean loafers. Even his knapsack, made by Jack Wolfskin, could have been purchased anyplace from Manchester to LA. Kary let out a disappointed sigh as he reached for the victim's blue blazer.

"What do we have here?!" he suddenly asked aloud.

The label inside the sport coat contained blue writing inside a blue circle with a white background. The name of the store was J.Press, with stores in New Haven, New York, Cambridge, and Washington. Given the craftsmanship of the label and the coat itself, Kary was willing to gamble precious time that the coat had been purchased at a store in one of those four locations, not off the rack at TJMaxx of Marshalls.

Kary was so eager to move forward with this new piece of evidence that he nearly left Harris' office without looking through what remained of the victim's effects.

"Hold on a minute, Bill. What do we have here?"

"It's a man's wig," Harris replied.

"A wig. I thought the guy was bald. What's a wig doing here?"

"It was with his effects. Anyway, you're the investigator. You tell me."

Kary didn't have an answer for Harris. But, an idea suddenly struck him.

"Say, Bill, does that artist nephew still drop by to visit you?"

"As a matter of fact, I expect him here in a few hours," Harris replied. "Is there something else you'd like him to do for you?"

"There is. I need him to draw one more sketch for me. Only this one has to remain confidential," Kary told him.

Harris found Kary's request a bit unorthodox, but in an interesting, devious sort of way. He promised to deliver the finished sketch directly to Kary's cell phone as soon as possible.

Chapter 22

In spite of the success the team had in solving crimes against visitors to New Hampshire, Kary and his two colleagues were still required to borrow a police car loaned to them by the drug task force.

The trip to Manchester reflected a modicum of hope for the first time since the VTF began work on the Cat Alley case. As they pulled away from the parking lot outside their offices on Capital Street in Concord, Bendix said to Kary, "You seemed excited on the phone this morning, Commissioner."

"Yeah," Norton agreed. "So, how about filling us in."

During the next 30 minutes, Kary told the others about the label he'd found inside the victim's sport coat. He asked Bendix to contact each of the four J.Press stores to see if anyone recognized the victim. Then, she was to contact newspapers in each of the four locations to run the two sketches ASAP using their e-newspaper format.

Bendix's encyclopedic mind was already thinking ahead. "So, that will be the *New Haven Register*, the *Washington Post*, the *New York Times*, and the *Boston Globe*. Any others, Commissioner?" Kary instructed Bendix to start with those four papers. Others would be contacted if necessary.

Not that his two colleagues needed reminding, but Kary told them that viewing CCTV coverage needed to be done right away. He also asked Norton to debrief Gillespie about any cars that were reported lost or stolen since after midnight on Monday.

※※※※※※

As the team pulled up to Cat Alley, it was impossible to miss the dramatic change in Stella Gillespie' visage. The sergeant was actually smiling.

"What's up, Stella?" Norton asked. "You look like a cat that's swallowed a canary, if you'll pardon the feline reference. Did Ambrose retire from the force?"

"No, but almost as good."

When Kary approached Gillespie, he noticed that a thin but very fit, dark-haired, young man of about thirty was standing next to her. The man introduced himself as

Mickey Calhoun.

"I've known Sergeant Gillespie for a long time," Calhoun told them. So, when she tells me that I need to speak to a man wearing a fedora, I listen."

Gillespie added, "Mickey recognized our murder victim."

Calhoun told Kary and the others, "I saw the sketches at WMUR online late last night. I headed right to the police station first thing this morning, but some guy named Ambrose treated me like I had two heads. So, I decided to go and find Sergeant Gillespie."

Kary was careful to contain his enthusiasm. Often these tips out of the blue turn out to be without merit.

"What can you tell me, Mr. Calhoun?"

"Please, call me Mickey." Pointing to the interesting vehicle that was parked in the alley, mere feet from where they stood, Calhoun told the team that he had seen the man depicted in the sketches two days earlier.

Kary eyed the vehicle, with the name Peddl stenciled on the back of what looked like a rickshaw. "Was the man in the picture a customer?"

"I prefer the term *client*, but, yes, he was."

"Did he pay you with a credit card?"

"No, I don't take credit cards. My customers pay me cash, at an amount of their choosing. However, one dollar per block is the expected gratuity."

"How did he find you; did he call your cell phone?" Kary asked.

"Some people do call me on my cell phone. When they do, I keep their phone numbers for a short time. Unfortunately, that wasn't true in this case. This guy struck up a conversation, then ended up hiring me to take him down to the Millyard."

Calhoun's responses were less than helpful.

"So, what can you tell me about him?" Kary asked, his enthusiasm beginning to wane.

"His first name is... or rather was... Jack. He appeared to be in his late 50s to early 60s. I'd say he was well-educated, was very interested in the history of Manchester, and must have been a basketball fan. Of course, I'm basing that on the UConn women's basketball hat Jack wore to keep the sun off of his bald head."

An idea suddenly occurred to Kary. "Can you take me on the same route that you took Jack? Is that doable?"

Calhoun agreed to take Kary right away. Before he climbed into the back of the Peddl vehicle, Kary told Bendix, "This is terrific. Let's focus our attention on any CCTV video that shows Jack riding in the Peddl."

"If there's anything to be found, we'll find it very soon."

"How can you be so sure?" Kary asked her.

"Things are much more sophisticated than they were years ago. You couldn't recognize faces at all on the Mayflower, back in your day," she couldn't resist chiding her boss. "But, seriously, these new cameras can be adjusted for pan, tilt, and zoom capabilities."

"If you say so," he replied.

"These modern images are clear; they're also monitored and recorded 24/7."

"Excellent!" Just then, another thought occurred to him.

"How about social media... is it worth checking Instagram or Facebook?"

Bendix thought to herself that she'd created a monster.

Chapter 23

For the next hour, Kary rode in the back of the Peddl, as Mickey Calhoun told interesting stories about the development of Manchester, much as he had done with the now deceased man named Jack.

As he rode in the vehicle, Kary was only half listening to Calhoun's spiel. He couldn't help trying to figure his way through the investigator's holy triumvirate—means, motive and opportunity. It was clear that the murderer, whoever he or she was, had found an opportunity to both kill and dispose of Jack. Based upon Bill Harris' assessment of the body, the means was a combination of the element of surprise and superior strength. Kary felt certain that they were looking for a male who was younger, bigger, and stronger than his victim. But, what was the motivation for murdering someone who—by all appearances—was a stranger to the city of Manchester. The farther the Peddl carried Kary into the Millyard, the more this case bugged him.

※※※※※※

While Kary was in the Millyard with Calhoun, Ambrose made another appearance in Cat Alley. Once again, he was filled with demands. This time, he confronted Gillespie and insisted that the VTF turn over all of the notes from its investigation to him. He quickly admitted that the victim's clothes showed that he wasn't a street person. However, Ambrose was now convinced that the man had been the victim of a robbery gone bad.

"Use your freakin' head, Gillespie," he had told her. "His ID, wallet, and car are missing. That should tell you something."

Norton returned from a brief errand just as Ambrose was getting into his police car. He could see that Gillespie was exasperated. She told Norton what Ambrose had said to her.

Norton smiled and shook his head. "It's interesting how the detective sergeant always appears on the scene and spews his animosity when the commissioner isn't around. So, he's convinced this was a robbery, huh? If that's the case, why was there a wad of bills in the vic's pocket?"

Norton removed his cell phone from a breast pocket and dialed Kary's number. When Norton told him about Ambrose's latest threat, Kary replied, "We're seeing two time-honored principles at work here, Sergeant… the Peter Principle and Hanlon's Razor."

"I'm familiar with the Peter Principle," Norton replied, "and Ambrose sure as heck has reached his level of incompetence. But, don't you mean Occam's Razor, Commissioner?"

Kary smiled as he responded, "Detective Sgt. Ambrose exceeded his level of incompetence long ago, I'm afraid." Kary paused to signal Calhoun that he'd rejoin him in a moment. "Hanlon's Razor applies more closely to Ambrose. It simply states that one should never attribute to malice that which can be adequately explained by stupidity."

Norton laughed at Kary's latest clever turn of phrase. "I'm looking forward to your return from the Millyard. Gillespie and I have some interesting information to share with you."

"That's great. Have you heard anything new from the lieutenant?"

Norton told Kary that Bendix was wrapping up her research on CCTV installations, and would report back as soon as possible.

They agreed to meet at The Bookery at 11 a.m. for some good coffee, delicious pastry and a thorough debriefing.

Chapter 24

With more than 150 diversified industrial establishments located in Manchester, Kary knew that the task of finding any businesses that Jack had visited would take days, if not weeks. The few Millyard firms Kary visited the previous day had turned up no new information. Now, he hoped that the one person known to have spent a meaningful amount of time with Jack could narrow down the search.

When Kary returned to the Peddl, Calhoun told him, "I really didn't talk as much to Jack as some of my clients, but one thing definitely interested him."

"What was that, Mickey?"

"He made two mentions of an urban reuse project he'd read about in *Smithsonian Magazine* some time ago."

"Can you recall what he said about it?"

Calhoun thought for a minute before he replied. "I think he said his father was a really important urban planner sometime in the middle of the last century. Jack told me that there had been a terrible oversight, and he was going to try to find the guy responsible, and convince him to correct it. It didn't sound like their meeting was going to be a friendly one."

Kary thought about what Calhoun had just told him. This made him anxious to pay a visit to the local historic association's Millyard Museum. However, as it was nearly eleven o'clock, he asked Calhoun to bring him back to The Bookery for the meeting with his team.

Chapter 25

When Kary returned to The Bookery, Bendix, Norton, and Gillespie were already seated in the glassed-in meeting room opposite the store's coffee bar. Kary sat in a chair at the head of a long, simple wooden table.

Turning to Bendix, he asked, "So, what have you been able to learn from the CCTV systems in the area?"

"I've learned that there are quite a number of them, that's for certain. The City has cameras all along Elm Street. There are cameras on the Brady Sullivan Plaza Building, the Wall Street Tower and parking structure, and on the outsides of several buildings in the Millyard."

"Good work, Lieutenant. Were you able to find images of Jack on any of them?"

"Using the information that Mickey Calhoun shared with Stella and you, I was able to narrow down the time of my search to between 3:30 and 4:00 on Tuesday. A couple of images show Jack riding in the Peddl. In each case he's seated, wearing his blazer, and there appears to be a dark bag of some sort on the seat next to him."

"That has to be his knapsack," Norton added.

"This is helpful. Anything else?" Kary asked.

"We know from Calhoun that Jack left the Peddl near the entrance to ARMI's headquarters," Bendix told the group. "I've asked one of Captain Garrison's tech specialists to see if Jack shows up on any CCTV images between the Commercial Street area and Elm Street after 4 p.m."

"And…?" Norton asked her.

"So far, there's nothing," she replied.

Kary asked the others whether there is CCTV coverage of Cat Alley.

Gillespie replied, "There's a camera that shows the Elm Street entrance. But, at the time of night when we believe his body was dumped, useful coverage into the alley is about five feet."

"…or just short of where Jack's body was left," Kary added while shaking his head.

Next, Kary turned to Norton and Gillespie. "What were you able to find out about stolen cars?"

Gillespie answered, "Amazingly enough, there were only two car thefts between 1:00 a.m. on Tuesday and noon on Wednesday. That has to be some kind of record for a city this size."

"What about the owners?"

"I'm afraid both have been accounted for, Commissioner," she replied.

"Well, it was a good idea," Kary told the others. "We're going to have to expand that search to include abandoned vehicles, too."

That would need to wait, as Kary needed to update the three about what he'd learned from Calhoun.

"So, it appears that Jack was here to discuss something about the history of this city," Bendix summed what the others were thinking. "That would explain why he went down to the Millyard. Perhaps some member of Jack's family worked there years ago and he wanted to see where."

Information like this reinforced Kary's belief that the time spent getting to know Manchester's dynamics would ultimately pay dividends.

"I'm thinking there was more to his visit than that," Kary added. "Mickey Calhoun had the impression that Jack felt there had been an injustice… a wrong that needed to be made right."

"Is it possible that one of his relatives owned the building where ARMI or one of the other firms is located? Maybe the owner was paid a lot less than the place was worth, and Jack was here to receive his due," Norton conjectured.

"That sounds like an interesting thought, Sergeant. But, why come all the way up here by himself? If we're talking about a large enough sum, it makes sense that he'd hire a big time corporate lawyer to take care of things."

The others agreed that Norton's idea, while thought-provoking, probably didn't have merit. Norton had another thought. "What if his visit was about something greater than money?"

Gillespie laughed, "What's more important than money, Bob?"

"Principle," Kary responded to her question. "What if Jack came to Manchester to correct something that misrepresented either him or a family member?"

Kary's cell phone rang a minute later. The caller was Kary's administrator, Jayne Ingolls. Jayne told Kary that she had just spoken to a gentleman from Connecticut, who saw the two sketches of the mysterious victim in the online issue of the *New Haven Register*.

"His name is Richard O'Neill. Mr. O'Neill told me that he can provide background information about the victim." Ingolls gave Kary O'Neill's cell phone number and said she hoped this was the breakthrough the VTF needed.

Chapter 26

As he punched in the eleven digit number that Ingolls had given him, Kary realized it was the beginning of the lunch hour. When O'Neill answered the phone, Kary apologized if he was calling during an inconvenient time.

O'Neill's gravelly voice betrayed an advanced age. "Don't think anything of it, sir. I am addressing Commissioner Turnell, is that correct?"

Kary replied in the affirmative before beginning his questioning.

"I understand that you've seen the artist's sketches of a man whose demise we're investigating; is that correct?"

"It is, Commissioner. When I saw my younger cousin Jack's image online this morning I was stunned, but not completely surprised, I must say."

O'Neill's reaction disturbed Kary. But first, he wanted to learn Jack's full name.

"Of course, Jack is a nickname... one he's used since elementary school days. His full name is John Jason Hartman. Jack was the only child of the late William Hartman. Perhaps you've heard of him."

Kary admitted that the name William Hartman did not immediately mean anything to him.

"Well, no mind. Please tell me what you need to know," O'Neill replied.

"Let's begin by your opening statement. You were 'stunned, but not completely surprised'. What exactly did you mean?"

"Jack is or, rather was, an exceptional man. He was the progeny of one of the most influential urban planners during the Twentieth Century. My uncle William—his father—became a parent rather late in life. He adored his son, but the boy was convinced that he wasn't living up to the high standard set by William. Ultimately, when William died, Jack felt a huge sense of loss. He also felt that he'd let his father down. So, despite the fact that he became a formidable scholar in his own right, Jack made it his mission in life to protect his father's legacy."

"Was Jack's visit to Manchester related to William's legacy?" Kary asked.

"Indeed it was. Jack went to Manchester with two purposes in mind. He wanted to see a successful example of his father's concept of urban redevelopment."

"So, that was his reason for viewing the former Amoskeag Millyard," Kary replied. "But, why come all the way up here. Surely there were cities closer to New Haven that he could have visited."

O'Neill paused before responding. "True. But this takes us to the reason I was concerned when he decided to drive up there. A family friend had visited the Millyard Museum last week, and came back with a glowing report of the displays there. Naturally, Jack was excited, too. He couldn't wait to hear what they had to say about William Hartman's role in reinventing Manchester after the old mills closed."

"Let me guess," Kary interrupted; "there was no mention of William in the museum's displays."

"That's correct," O'Neill replied.

"But, once again, I'm puzzled. Why wouldn't Jack telephone or email the museum's director? It would have been a lot easier than driving more than three hundred miles round trip," Kary replied.

"Oh, Jack did both of those things," O'Neill told him. "He called and left at least three messages; I lost count of the number of emails. The executive director's name is John Clayton. Apparently, Mr. Clayton didn't choose to respond."

Kary was surprised by this information. "I've known John Clayton for more than 20 years. He was a very highly regarded newsman for years. Besides that, he has a reputation for being both intellectually curious and courteous to a fault. Something isn't right about all of this."

O'Neill replied that the information he just shared came directly from the deceased, Jack Hartman. Kary knew that O'Neill had been offended by his last statement and was concerned the older man would hang up the phone. However, there was information that Kary needed O'Neill to provide before he did.

"By the way, can you tell me what type of car Jack drove, and what his license plate was?"

"He drove a 2012 two-door, dark green Nissan Altima. His license was YNGHART, for younger Hartman. Connecticut plates, of course."

"One additional question, if you'll indulge me, Mr. O'Neill. "I'm still not clear as to why Jack's death didn't shock you."

"I think it's apparent from Jack's actions that he was eccentric; also, he could be impetuous and had a bit of a temper. From his past behavior, I suspect that Jack drove up there, found a place to park, then removed every single item of identification from his person."

"Why would he do something like that?" Kary asked.

"When Jack was a young man he was mugged by some punk while he was visiting his cousin in Boston. The guy took his wallet, watch and a prized Mont Blanc fountain pen. Jack didn't know how to fight back and the bastard gave him a black eye and a bloody lip. When Jack returned home, he refused to report the incident to the police.

He told his parents that he would deal with this his own way. Ever since that day, he's always traveled in big cities without his wallet and other essentials."

"Except cash," Kary added.

"That's correct, Commissioner." O'Neill continued, "When I saw that Jack was dead, it made me ask myself, what if Jack confronted Mr. Clayton and his identification was demanded? What if his failure to identify himself led to some form of altercation?"

Kary was dubious about the scenario painted by O'Neill. However, he was anxious to pump the gentleman for additional information.

"There is one other thing you should know," O'Neill told him. "As crazy as it sounds, Jack was very self-conscious about his hair loss. What little hair he still had on his head was really patchy. So, he shaved his head completely."

O'Neill added, "If you saw Jack outside of his house, he always wore a ball cap."

"What about indoors?" Kary needed to ask.

"Jack carried a toupee with him," O'Neill replied. "He kept it in that half knapsack of his. When he was ready to enter a building, he switched the cap for his wig."

That explained the wig that the medical examiner's assistant, Bill Harris, had shown to Kary and Garrison. It also clarified why Mickey Calhoun and others Jack had met in Manchester only recognized him as a man wearing a ball cap.

Chapter 27

Kary shared what he learned from Richard O'Neill with the others. It was apparent that Jack Hartman had come to New Hampshire because he wanted to confront John Clayton, the history museum's executive director. While there was not yet sufficient proof that the two men had ever met with one another, it cast solid concern about Clayton's role in Hartman's demise.

"With the new information I've received from CCTV footage, there appears to be sufficient evidence to move forward," Bendix told the others. "The CCTV footage between the Millyard and Cat Alley shows no sign that Jack Hartman ever walked out of those buildings."

"I think we've all suspected that was the case," Kary replied.

"So, should we go and arrest Mr. Clayton?" Norton asked.

Gillespie stiffened, starting to object.

Observing her reaction, Kary was quick to say, "Let's not get too hasty. You can see from Stella's response that John Clayton has earned a reputation without peer in this community. We aren't a bunch of Detective Sergeant Ambroses. The VTF doesn't jump to conclusions without sufficient proof."

Kary allowed this to sink in before continuing. "I'd like one more piece of evidence before we go and talk with John Clayton."

"What's that, Commissioner?" Stella asked.

"We had the right idea earlier when you asked about cars that were stolen during the last few days," Kary reminded them.

"That's right. And there weren't any."

"True," Kary continued. "However, I should have told you to ask about cars that were towed because they were abandoned or the parking meters had expired. That was my fault," he added.

Gillespie was very impressed. In all of her years on the police force, she'd never had a boss accept responsibility for a mistake. That error was about to be rectified.

"Sergeant Gillespie, I want you to talk again with your contacts at Manchester PD. Ask them whether a 2012 two-door, dark green Nissan Altima, bearing the license

YNGHART, has been ticketed and impounded. I feel certain that it has."

Ten minutes later, Gillespie returned with the news that Jack Hartman's car was being stored in a nearby impound lot. The lot's owner would meet them there in 15 minutes.

"Oh, by the way, Detective Sergeant Ambrose, Captain Garrison and an old friend of yours from the FBI named Ponds will meet us there."

Standing inside the office of the impoundment lot, the owner informed them that Hartman's car had been towed onto his property at about midnight on Tuesday. Next, thanks to Richard O'Neill's heads up, Norton found Hartman's wallet, identification and credit cards, car keys, as well as his cell phone in a small canvas bag that had been placed in a special hiding cavity beneath the front passenger seat.

By statute, Kary needed to cooperate fully with the other three law enforcement agencies. Garrison and Ponds, both of whom had worked with Kary's team previously, were immediately on board. On the other hand, Ambrose was prepared to head right to the Millyard—sirens and blue lights blazing—to place John Clayton under arrest.

Sensing that Gillespie was about to lose it with Ambrose, Norton signaled her that they should wait outside. Once alone, he didn't beat around the bush.

"Stella, you're way too good of an officer to lose your composure with Ambrose. There are better ways of dealing with people like him."

Gillespie replied, "Yeah, I wish I was able to keep my cool like you."

That comment made Norton laugh out loud. "I'm a big talker, Stella. Before I joined the VTF, my mouth was always getting me in trouble."

"So what changed things?" Gillespie asked him

"Bendix and the Commissioner happened. The lieutenant had put up with some of the same crap you did; so she learned how to keep outwardly calm while channeling that keen mind of hers into out-thinking and out-working all the wise mouths out there. It was a great lesson for me to learn."

"What about the Commissioner?" she asked.

Norton shrugged. "He has our backs, and with his track record, anyone with half a brain avoids challenging us."

"I guess that leaves out Detective Sergeant Ambrose then," she replied with a broad smile on her face.

"Now you're getting it, Stella." As Norton said this, the two shared a very forceful fist bump.

Back inside the office of the impound lot, Kary started to talk with Ambrose but was brought up short.

"I shouldn't need to remind you, Commissioner, that this is my jurisdiction, not yours," Ambrose told him in a threatening tone.

From behind Ambrose came the voice of FBI Agent Ponds. "Actually, Detective, the bureau and MCU have jurisdiction in matters pertaining to murder. And, I for one, am prepared to carry out this investigation the way Commissioner Turnell directs."

Ambrose was furious. However, despite the fact that Ponds' claim of jurisdiction was less than black-and-white, he decided it wouldn't be prudent to mess with one federal and two state law enforcement agencies.

Kary pulled Ambrose aside. "Look at it this way, Detective Sergeant, if you went riding into the Millyard with sirens blazing, and it turns out that Mr. Clayton is innocent, your career would have been toast."

"Oh sure, but it's okay for you to do it, right, mister hot shot commissioner?"

"I won't handle this situation like you suggested... not in any way, shape, or form. Now, be a good boy, and do something about Hartman's parking ticket."

※※※※※※

As a courtesy, Kary called John Clayton on the telephone to inform him that he was a person of interest in an on-going murder investigation. Of course, Clayton sounded stunned, but agreed to meet with the VTF commissioner. He told Kary that he had not been in his office at the museum since before closing time on Tuesday.

"May I ask why not? You have a reputation as a workaholic."

"I'm afraid it's been too well-earned. However, I also have a marriage that I want to sustain. We had a three-day family event, and I promised my wife that I'd leave my cell phone in my brief case. When you called me a little while ago, I'd just turned the bloody thing on. I've missed at least 50 emails and half as many phone calls."

Kary needed Clayton to clarify what he'd had just told him.

"So, you haven't been in the museum since the afternoon on Tuesday?"

"That's correct, Commissioner. Fortunately, I have an excellent assistant and several dedicated docents who are very capable of covering for me."

Now the wheels in Kary's keen mind were turning overtime.

"I have a favor to ask of you, Mr. Clayton. As inconvenient as this may sound, I don't want you to meet with me at the museum. In fact, I don't want you to contact your staff or go near the place until after we've talked."

Clayton was not particularly happy with Kary's request, but reluctantly agreed to honor it. Instead of the museum, they agreed to meet in the lobby of the Doubletree by Hilton, on Elm Street.

"We haven't seen one another in about 20 years, but you'll be able to spot me easily," Kary assured him. "I'll be wearing a brown fedora."

Kary apologized for inconveniencing Clayton, then concluded by saying,

"I'd meet with you sooner, but I'm waiting for an important piece of evidence before we talk."

Chapter 28

When Clayton walked into the lobby of the Doubletree, he immediately spotted the 70ish-year-old man wearing a fedora. While Kary had not seen Clayton in a number of years, he recognized the museum director immediately. His hair had grayed quite a bit, but his appearance was otherwise similar. As was his habit years ago, Clayton's hair was neatly styled; and he wore a navy blue blazer over a checked Oxford shirt that was open at the collar.

Clayton and Kary sat in adjoining plush easy chairs. To break the ice, the two shared a bit of small talk.

"Wearing that fedora is a great way to be recognized in a crowded room," Clayton began. "I see that's still your brand."

Kary removed his hat momentarily, revealing a considerable amount of hair loss. He admitted that the fedora and he had become synonymous; it also kept his balding head shaded on sunny days.

"It seems to me that you dressed similarly when I last met you at a conference up in Concord."

"So, why am I here; and, why couldn't we meet in the museum?" Clayton asked, his voice full of concern.

"Before I answer, let me ask you a question: are you familiar with a man named Jack Hartman?"

The expression on Clayton's face was a quizzical one. "It's strange that you should ask me that," he began. "As I told you earlier, I've been away from the museum for a few days, and that includes avoiding my email and voice mail."

Kary listened intently, all the while he began to shape a picture of what had been taking place.

Clayton continued, "Then, a while ago, after you and I talked on the phone, I started scrolling through my messages. Strangely enough, I had several emails and phone messages from this fellow Hartman. I'd never heard of the man, but he seemed to be insistent on talking to me… he said it was something about his father's reputation."

"Did you do anything about Hartman?" Kary asked.

"Well, first I went through my other messages. I finished doing that about an hour ago. Then, twenty minutes before I left home to meet with you here, I sent Hartman an email, which went unanswered."

Clayton stood for a moment to relieve a crick in his back, before resuming. "I have to confess, Commissioner, that the urgent, frankly angry, tone of his voice mail message played on my mind. So, on the way here, I called him from my car."

"And, of course, there was no answer," Kary completed Clayton's story.

"That's right! But how did you know that?"

"I'm about to explain," Kary replied. "But, before I do, have you watched any state or local news since you left home a few days ago?"

Like Kary, Clayton had a keen mind that was constantly receptive to information, at times processing two sets of news simultaneously.

"The only news I've heard was while my wife and I were in the car. I particularly remember something about an unidentified man whose body was found in Cat Alley, just up the street. Is he the reason we're here?"

Kary nodded. "Yes, he is. However, I can tell you, as of this moment, you are not a suspect in Hartman's death."

"So, Jack Hartman was urgently trying to get in touch with me, and has subsequently been murdered," Clayton stated aloud while shaking his head in dismay.

For the next 30 minutes, Kary told Clayton how a man, subsequently identified as Jack Hartman, was found early Wednesday morning by a passing jogger. Kary proceeded to tell Clayton what the VTF, MCU, and FBI had pieced together during a period of slightly more than 40 hours. Kary explained that the man had no identification on him, which slowed the investigation initially.

"However, we are gaining ground rapidly," Kary told him. "Now, I need to understand exactly what transpired before, during and after the time you left the museum on Tuesday afternoon."

Clayton told Kary his wife called just before 3:30 to remind him about the family reunion dinner that night. Knowing her husband would likely procrastinate about leaving the museum, she had insisted on driving him to work and picking him up behind the museum building.

"I basically flew out of the museum, and barely had time to say anything to Ivan," he told Kary.

"Who is Ivan?" Kary asked.

"Ivan Bergeron is my assistant. Normally, he leaves the building at least a few minutes before I do. So, I had to remind him that it was his responsibility to be certain everyone was out of the museum by 4 p.m. Then he needed to shut off the lights. Once the last staff person leaves, Ed Gagne, the building custodian, checks the front door of the museum before he heads out for the night. I've been known to forget to lock the door. So, Ed's job is to make certain everything is secure."

"So, just to clarify, under normal circumstances, either Ivan or you is supposed to turn off the lights and lock up. Your custodian is responsible for checking that everything has been done properly."

"That's right. On most nights, Ed is the last one out of the building. He has several other offices to clean, and often is alone in the building until 8 p.m."

Kary thanked Clayton for clarifying their standard operating procedure, before adding, "However, it's apparent that everything did not work per usual on Tuesday night. We're estimating that Jack Hartman entered the museum about 10 minutes before closing. We suspect he was murdered shortly after that time. Ordinarily, this would make you a prime suspect. However, since you were with your wife 30 minutes before the museum closed, we will need to focus our attention on Mr. Bergeron and Mr. Gagne. What can you tell me about those two?"

"Ivan looks like the stereotypical intellectual. He's about five foot six, couldn't weight much more than 120 pounds dripping wet, and wears glasses for both near and far vision. He's also extremely mild-mannered."

"So was Clark Kent," Kary couldn't resist saying. "Okay, it sounds like Ivan Bergeron is a long shot to be the murderer. If the crime took place inside your building, as I suspect it did, it would take a very strong guy to move that dead weight a considerable distance."

Kary interrupted their conversation to call Bendix on his cell phone.

"Hello, Lieutenant. Things are progressing here. However, I need Norton and you to do two things for me. First, see what you can learn from CCTV inside the museum building." Before Kary could continue, Clayton was signaling to him.

Pulling a business card from his wallet, he told Kary, "Tell your lieutenant that this is the person at the building management company she needs to reach. There is a camera pointing to the entrance on the lower level, away from where the museum entrance is. There's a second camera on the second level, pointing to the main entrance on the Bedford Street side of the building. Have her tell the management company guy to call me if he has any questions, that I want him to cooperate fully."

Kary nodded his appreciation to Clayton before continuing his conversation with Bendix. "Second, I want you to see what background you can find on two men, Ivan Bergeron and Ed Gagne. This is top priority; so get Stu Garrison's people to help if necessary."

When Kary finished talking with Bendix, he turned to Clayton and said, "Now tell me about Mr. Gagne."

Clayton replied, "I can't tell you very much. He's worked in our building for years. Frankly, he's never exchanged more than two or three words with me at any one time. If I were paranoid, I'd think the man hates me."

This gave Kary pause. He couldn't resist paraphrasing an old Joseph Heller quote for Clayton, "Just because you're paranoid doesn't mean someone isn't out to get you."

Kary's quick repartee initially made Clayton laugh, but suddenly the circumstances didn't seem very funny.

Kary asked Clayton to describe Gagne.

"He's a big guy… not necessarily all that tall… maybe just short of six feet. But, he's powerfully built, like a logger or someone who's used his muscles a lot. I've seen him carry heavy things like concrete and steel stanchions, things I'd barely be able to budge."

Just as Kary was ready to allow Clayton to leave, his phone pinged. It was the message from Harris that he'd been awaiting. Kary looked at the sketch Harris' nephew had produced for him. It depicted Jack Hartman wearing the wig that he habitually wore indoors. The image was startling. Kary enlarged the picture so it filled the screen of his iPhone, then turned it toward Clayton.

"Does this person look familiar?" Kary asked.

"Good grief… is that Jack Hartman?" he exclaimed.

"It is," Kary replied.

"He sure looks a hell of a lot like me!"

Chapter 29

Kary arrived at the museum 15 minutes after he and Clayton parted company. On his way inside, he passed a very strong-looking man of about 50 dressed in a dark green custodial uniform. Kary asked him if the museum was still open. To Kary' surprise, his question was greeted by a very friendly response.

"Yes it is, sir. But, you'd better hurry, because the lights go off and the door is locked at 4 p.m. sharp. You've only got 10 minutes."

Certainly, Ed Gagne's greeting was at odds with the behavior that had been reported by John Clayton.

Kary continued into the museum, where Ivan Bergeron was waiting for him. Kary asked the young assistant to inform Gagne that he would be in a meeting for at least an hour. Bergeron promised Gagne that he would shut off the lights and lock the door himself.

Bergeron seemed nervous, but not overly so. After all, it wasn't every day that a law enforcement commissioner dropped by to interview him. Kary quickly set Bergeron's mind at ease, before asking him to describe—in detail—what had transpired at the museum the previous Tuesday.

"What a terrible afternoon I had," Bergeron began. "Mr. Clayton left the building at 3:30 to attend a family event. Then, about 10 minutes before closing, I suddenly became very sick to my stomach. There was no one in the museum, so I went out into the hallway, heading toward the men's room near the elevator."

"Did you see anyone?"

"Well, I was in quite a hurry. But, I did see Ed, our custodian, standing near the old historic stairway. No one uses those stairs, because they're very steep; besides, he keeps them super polished." Bergeron looked at Kary to see what his reaction was before continuing.

"I needed someone to keep an eye on the museum, because I knew I was going to be sitting on the toilet for quite a while."

"What was your custodian's reaction?" Kary asked.

"He was super understanding. He said there was something he needed to do in the hallway just outside the museum anyway. So, he'd keep an eye on things."

"What happened next?"

"Not a lot," Bergeron replied. "I was sick in there for another half hour or so."

"Did you hear or see anything?"

Bergeron thought for a moment before something occurred to him.

"Yes. It was already past 4 p.m., but someone came into the bathroom, did his business, then left."

"How long was he there?" Kary asked.

"A minute at most. Unfortunately, I wasn't ready to leave right away. So, I never saw whoever it was. It could have been Ed, but he usually uses the custodian's bathroom in another part of the building."

"What time do think it was when you left the bathroom?"

"I'd say it was at least quarter until five. But, that was really strange."

"What do you mean?" Kary asked.

"When I left the bathroom, the hallway was nearly dark. Even stranger, the museum lights were shut off, but the door was still unlocked. Usually, we shut the lights off just before leaving for the night. That way, Ed knows that no one is inside. He then checks to see if the door is locked. So, you see, having the place so dark and the door unlocked is just plain weird."

"Did you hear anything else, either while you were in the bathroom or afterward?" Kary asked.

"Sounds echo in the men's bathroom. So, I heard the doors close and the elevator rising."

Kary thanked Bergeron for his help. To be on the safe side, Kary remained with Bergeron until he had shut off the lights, locked the door, then left the building through the rear exit. As Bergeron reached his car, Kary instructed him not to discuss their conversation with anyone.

Chapter 30

Friday, May 14, 8:10 a.m.

Bendix, Norton, and Kary met with Garrison and FBI Agent Ponds at the Hooksett South rest area. The five occupied a table in a corner of the Hi-Way Diner. Bendix had her computer open and was showing the others what she had found on the two CCTV cameras inside the building at 200 Bedford St., which houses the Millyard Museum. The first set of images was taken from the camera on the lowest level of the building, and showed people entering and exiting from the rear. These images weren't earth-shattering. However, they corroborated what Clayton had told them about leaving the museum at 3:30 p.m. on Tuesday.

It was the images from the camera mounted above the lobby on the second floor of the building that proved interesting. Jack Hartman was seen entering 200 Bedford St. from the front entrance, at about 3:40 that same day.

"So, it's obvious that Hartmann and John Clayton never met that day," Kary said, and the others agreed.

There was very little activity for the next 30 minutes of video. Bendix sped through the images, as people with offices in the building were seen heading to the exits. Finally, at 4:10, there was movement at the very bottom of the frame. In fact, it was so fast that the investigators needed to watch it frame by frame, repeatedly.

In the video, a man who looked like Jack Hartman—wearing his wig—was being forcibly led out of the doorway from the second-floor elevator. The second man, who was considerably larger, was wearing a dark hoodie, so his face wasn't visible. Closer inspection showed that the larger man was holding the smaller man firmly by the back of his neck. A sleeve of tattoos covered the larger man's exposed right arm. The two men soon disappeared up the steep staircase leading to the third floor.

"Wow," Norton exclaimed, "I've tried walking up the stairs in that building. You practically need to be a mountain goat."

"Please explain what you mean," Ponds asked Norton.

"Those are the original stairs from the days of the Amoskeag factory. The individual steps are super narrow; each flight is incredibly steep, and they are kept highly polished to protect the aging wood."

"That sounds like an accident waiting to happen," Bendix said.

"It is," Norton told her. "They're maintained for historic purposes. But signs have been posted and, in some places, there are rope barriers to discourage anyone from entering them." However, the ropes were nowhere to be seen in the video.

"Then, why do you think the large man in the hood is forcing Hartman to go that way?" Ponds asked.

Bendix, who had already spent hours viewing the video, told Ponds, "You'll have your answer in a minute."

Less than 90 seconds later, the man in the hoodie briefly returned from the stairway, and headed back toward the elevator. However, there was no further sign of Hartman. The team looked to Kary for his assessment of what all of them knew.

"It's obvious to all of us what just happened. The larger man, who we suspect to be Ed Gagne, forced Hartman to climb a set of steep steps. I'm certain Gagne is well aware that no one uses them these days." Thinking about the large bruise on the front of Hartman's head and Harris' comment about the furniture polish inside the wound, Kary continued his deduction. "We can presume that Gagne—with or without provocation—slammed Hartman's head against either the railing or a stair with enough force to kill him instantly. The lieutenant can tell you what's next."

"When I reviewed this for the 10th time, I arranged with Captain Garrison for MCU's team to do a blood smear and other DNA testing in the stairwell," she told them.

Kary interjected, "I'm confident we'll get a positive match with Hartman's DNA and blood type. We'll need to get a DNA sample from Gagne as well. And, let's not forget to test for Rustins Danish Oil in the stairway."

"Will that prove anything?" Norton asked. "Gagne can claim that his DNA is all over this building."

"That's true, Sergeant; but, we shouldn't find his DNA on Hartman's neck and the collar of his blazer," Kary replied. As he rose from his chair, Kary added, "I have a little surprise for Mr. Gagne. If it works as I've planned, he'll incriminate himself without needing forensic evidence."

Garrison replied, "I don't suppose you'd care to share your plan with us, Kary."

"Not yet. However, I'd like you, Agent Ponds and Lieutenant Bendix to be parked outside the museum in an unmarked car. Have a few other officers nearby, too."

Norton couldn't resist asking, "Does that mean I get the day off, Commissioner?"

Kary's reply was met with four sets of furrowed brows. "Not at all, Sergeant. I'll want you to be lying down on the job."

Chapter 31

Per Kary's instructions, Ivan Bergeron arrived at the museum just before 9:00 a.m. In his company was an older man who was unrecognizable in his dark hoodie, brown bucket hat, and sunglasses. The two men entered the museum, then soon parted company. Bergeron took his customary place behind the admissions counter at precisely 9:30 a.m., or 15 minutes before Ed Gagne's shift began. Bergeron was finding it difficult to perform his usual tasks due to a long horizontal object situated on the floor near the counter.

At precisely 9:45, Bergeron placed a call to Gagne's phone on the third floor of the building. He told the custodian that there was a small emergency with one of the displays and his help was needed as soon as possible.

Gagne liked Bergeron and was more than happy to help. Moreover, the custodian was feeling especially cheerful that morning. He opened the door to the museum and called, "I'm here, Ivan. What seems to be the problem?"

However, Bergeron was not the one standing behind the counter, as Gagne expected. Instead, John Clayton was there by himself.

"You! No, it's not possible. I dumped your body in the alley. You're dead!"

It didn't take Gagne long to compose himself. "But, if it really is you... no matter... I still have the body bag I used last time."

Having said that, Gagne charged around the corner to the back of the counter. However, when he made it to the other side, he was intercepted by Sergeant Norton, who had been lying on the ground behind the counter.

Gagne was a powerful, dangerous man when angry. Recognizing that he had been deceived, he charged at Norton. The confrontation lasted less than 10 seconds. With one powerful move, Norton threw Gagne down on the ground hard, knocking the wind out of the custodian. Before Gagne could recover, Norton had him lying on his stomach with his wrists cuffed.

Clayton stood back from Gagne, but couldn't resist questioning him.

"Mr. Gagne, why do you hate me so much... what did I ever do to you?"

"You don't remember, do you, Clayton? So, let me remind you. Does the name

Rose Gagne ring any bells?"

Clayton stared at Gagne for a moment. "Rose Gagne is a pretty common name here in Manchester, so…" All at once, Clayton realized who Gagne was talking about.

"I can see it in your eyes. You do remember now, don't ya'!" Gagne's glare revealed pure hatred.

"My sister was barely out of her teens when she was attacked by that miserable psycho, Stevens. The cops knew he was guilty and were going to send him to the slammer for decades. But then, crusading liberal heart John Clayton started investigating. You dug up enough doubt that the jury let Stevens go."

"But…" Clayton's comment was cut off by Gagne.

"When my sister sat in that courtroom and watched Stevens go free, it sucked the will out of her. She never was the same again. When she was lying there dying three years later, I swore to her that I'd get you if it were the last thing I did. This week is the 20th anniversary of Rose's death; and you should be dead, too."

Before being led from the museum, Gagne looked at Clayton. "How can you still be alive? I waited all these years to kill you, and I know you were stone cold dead a couple of days ago."

With Gagne safely in custody, Kary had entered the museum. So, it was the commissioner who responded to Gagne.

"You're right about one thing, Mr. Gagne. You did commit cold-blooded murder here last Tuesday. Unfortunately for your victim, you killed the wrong man."

Hearing that news, Gagne just hung head as he was led away.

Norton said, "You know what, Commissioner, I've been thinking that Gagne would have been smarter to just leave Hartman's body on the stairs. Why go through all of the effort to bag the body and bring it up to Cat Alley?"

Bendix replied, "Even wearing that hoodie, the CCTV video was going to incriminate him. I'm thinking it would have been smarter to find a spot where he could dump Hartman's body into the Merrimack."

Kary's next comment made Bendix and Norton smile. "Think of it this way, if the body in Cat Alley had been investigated solely by Detective Sergeant Ambrose, Gagne would still be walking around as a free man."

Chapter 32

Friday, May 21, 10:00 a.m.

Kary sat alone with John Clayton in his museum office. As a moral human being, Clayton was still feeling guilty about his unwitting role in the death of Jack Hartman.

Clayton explained to Kary, "Stevens really did not attack Gagne's sister, Rose. They never found the guy who did, but it wasn't Stevens. However, it's driving me crazy… what if I hadn't been so determined to write that newspaper column in support of Stevens?"

"I've familiarized myself with the case during the last week, John. And, rather than feel any regret, you should be proud that you helped set an innocent man free. Stevens certainly didn't turn out to be a credit to society, but that's another matter entirely."

Clayton spoke softy, "Thank you, Commissioner. However, it's going to take some time to get over the fact that Jack Hartman was murdered in my stead."

Kary placed his hand on Clayton's shoulder. "Here's my philosophy about deaths like this one, John: life is full of ifs."

"Ifs?" Clayton asked.

"Yes. Just think about it. Unfortunately, fate conspired against Jack. What were the odds of all of these circumstances happening: If this hadn't been the one or two times a year when you're out of touch with social media; if Jack hadn't chosen to leave his ID in the car; if he'd gone straight to the museum, rather than stopping at several other businesses in the Millyard on his way here; if he didn't change from his ball cap into that wig; and, if he hadn't turned off so many lights in the building that Gagne couldn't see him clearly."

Kary continued, "With his wig on and wearing that navy blue blazer, Jack Hartman bore a strong resemblance to you. But, in bright light, there's no way Gagne would have made that mistake. This whole affair has been the result of a bunch of events that easily could have turned out differently. The only thing we can conclude is it was Jack Hartman's time; but fortunately, it was not John Clayton's."

Kary rose as he looked at the time on his cell phone.

"I tell you what, John, I'll leave you to mull all of that over while I spend a couple of hours in this incredible museum of yours."

Epilogue

Following Ed Gagne's arrest, the forensics team found a large vat of Rustins Danish Oil in his supply closet. A hoodie matching the one in the CCTV video was hanging behind the closet door. Also, while it wasn't necessary, Kary received a call from the manager of the New Haven J.Press store. He verified that Jack was a regular customer, and had purchased his blazer there.

The trial of grieving brother and former Millyard custodian, Ed Gagne, lasted a mere two weeks. Gagne was sentenced to life in prison, with a possibility of parole in 2045, at which time he would be 75 years old.

The Visitor Safety Task Force, Major Crimes Unit, and regional office of the Federal Bureau of Investigation all received special citations for their prompt and effective work in solving a thorny case. Sergeant Stella Gillespie also was recognized for her substantial assistance in bringing Gagne to justice.

Following an emergency meeting called by the Manchester Police Commission, Paul Ambrose was demoted from his rank as a detective sergeant.

It was the commission's finding that Ambrose was negligent and showed very poor judgment in the performance of his duties. As of this writing, he has been assigned to the department's traffic desk, where he served until his retirement at the end of 2020.

To replace Ambrose in the Manchester Police Department's detective bureau, Sergeant Gillespie has been assigned on an interim basis. It is presumed that the assignment will be made permanent once she has satisfactorily completed LEAA-mandated coursework.

※※※※※※

Kary's team, working in close conjunction with the state's Major Crimes Unit and the FBI, had solved its fourth case since the VTF's inception. This time, the brunt of the investigation had taken less than 50 hours. Paul Ambrose's antics aside, the governor and general public were pleased to learn how well several law enforcement agencies could work together.

Kary's constant reference to the ball of yarn concept, and its significance in being able to solve the case, had been borne out in the end. Spearheading Manchester's recent growth, there was a symbiosis among tourism, technology, health services, arts and culture, and transportation. Once the team found where the victim's presence intersected with that complex array of characteristics, the case was quickly solved.

The Remorseful Pawn

A Commissioner Kary Turnell Murder Mystery

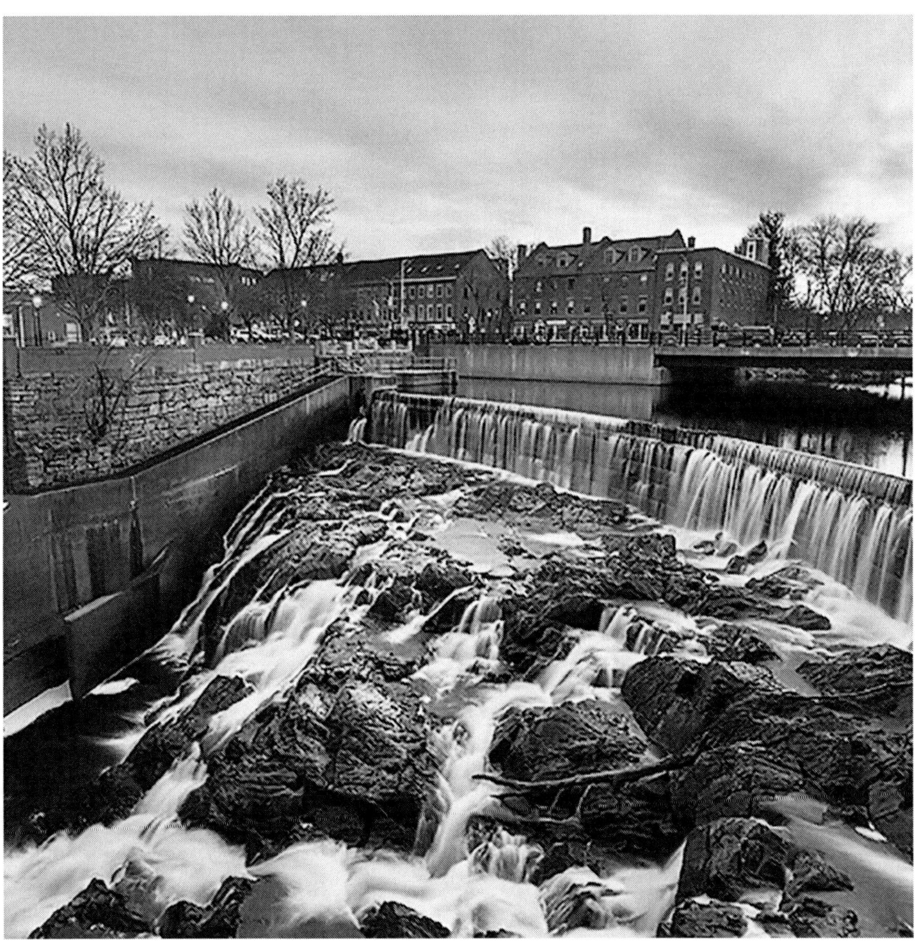

Mark Okrant

Prologue

Decades after graduating from the state university in Durham, the slightly balding 50-something year old still looked forward to annual visits to Dover, a historic mill town situated seven miles from his alma mater.

During college days, he would ride from campus with his roommate, heading up Route 108, then north on Route 16. His companion towed a fiberglass canoe on a wooden trailer behind a 1970 Ford pickup. They would make their way up Sixth Street and Watson Road, then launch in the Cochecho River. Perry Stockton was filled with memories of those paddling experiences along that river, whose waters ranged from extremely peaceful to potentially deadly.

While Stockton hadn't called New Hampshire home in several decades, his nostalgia for Dover remained with him throughout the years. So, when it came time for his annual visit to the old brick manufacturing city, he was determined to use the occasion to get a weight off his chest, permanently.

After grabbing a flight on Southwest Airlines from Philadelphia to Boston, Stockton then hopped on a C&J Trailways bus at Logan Airport. Less than an hour later, he was in Dover. There was no thought of purchasing a round-trip bus ticket, as he was certain one of his old buddies would be happy to give him a ride back to Logan, but first there was a long overdue issue to finally put to rest.

He couldn't escape a feeling of trepidation about possibly meeting one particular guy from his college days, someone he hadn't seen in decades. Were the pair to meet, there was no way to be sure how Stockton's reception would go, as there was an equal possibility of earnest reminiscing or full-on aggression.

A chill ran up Stockton's spine as he remembered the one who was the real instigator of what happened all those years earlier. He had absolutely no desire to see this particular former classmate, but avoiding him might be out of the question. As his bus came closer to Dover, Stockton admonished himself for a lack of courage—now and several decades earlier.

"If only I had a set of balls, things would have turned out differently."

That mood continued as the bus pulled up to the terminal at 23 Indian Brook

Road. Stockton's growing feeling of foreboding proved prophetic and lasted until the moment his body plunged into the Cochecho River.

Chapter 1

Perry Stockton was excited to be meeting with several old buddies from back in his UNH days. While it had been exactly a year since he visited the campus in Durham, the decades-old memories flooded back to him. Some of them made him smile; however, on the whole, they filled him with guilt and apprehension. The Eighties was a difficult time to negotiate, particularly if you felt the "man" was out to get you and everyone else.

The first person he was going to see hadn't been embroiled in the same craziness that swallowed up what remained of Stockton's innocence. Joey Swift was something of a "crunchy granola." Swift only attended classes because he knew how difficult it was for his parents to send him to school. Both his mother and father worked two jobs to afford tuition. So, even though he was bored out of his mind most of the time, Swift owed it to them to stay in school and get his degree.

Nor was Joey Swift a party guy. His idea of a good time was being out in the woods or floating down one of the area's many tree-lined streams, preferably by himself. It was Swift who read a need in Stockton's contemplative, oft gloomy personality. Swift saw that his roommate needed an escape from whatever surreptitious circumstances were weighing upon him.

The two were roommates in Christensen Hall during freshman year. After much cajoling, Swift finally convinced Stockton to come with him on one of his canoeing trips down the nearby Cochecho River. Stockton barely spoke a word during their entire trip, thus convincing Swift that he'd made a mistake inviting his roommate. However, he received a surprise at breakfast the next morning when Stockton asked him when they could go canoeing again.

While the two young men never roomed together again after that first year on campus, a strong, easy bond developed between the two. Swift received a second pleasant surprise at the beginning of their sophomore year when Stockton returned to campus from summer vacation and announced that he'd purchased a canoe of his own. Swift was more than happy to store Stockton's canoe in an empty rack on his trailer. For the next three years, whenever their class schedules allowed, the pair would head out on trips along the Cochecho and other streams in the area.

On graduation day, Stockton told Swift that he wanted to give him the canoe. Swift protested, but Stockton insisted that there was no room for the canoe, either in his parents' apartment building or in his life. Indeed, Stockton never paddled a canoe again. However, circumstances were quite different for Joey Swift, who never left the outdoor recreation field. For two decades he served as the director of Dover's recreation department, taking particular pride in overseeing the popular canoe launch located right on the Cochecho in Henry Law Park.

Chapter 2

On the way to meet Swift, Perry Stockton walked briskly from where his Lyft driver had dropped him near the corner of Washington Street and Henry Law Avenue. As he entered the grass-lined path that formed Dover's beautiful river walk, Stockton finally found himself almost relaxing, until he spotted a tall, broad-shoulder guy wearing a black raincoat, standing in a crowd about 200 yards from him.

"No, it can't be. Shit!" he blurted out loud.

Without a second glance, Stockton turned on his heels and ran down the path toward the canoe launch facility, moving as fast as his out-of-shape body would carry him. He prayed that Joey Swift would be there to meet him, as they had arranged.

When Stockton arrived at the canoe rental platform, Swift noticed that his friend was decidedly out of breath and looked positively petrified.

"What's up, man? You look like you've seen a freaking ghost," Swift asked with genuine concern.

"It was worse than that," Stockton told him. Only then did he dare look back at the crowd of people he'd seen a minute earlier. However, whoever had spooked Stockton was no longer there… if, indeed, he ever was.

As a long-time friend, Swift knew that Stockton and some of his so-called friends were not on the best of terms during their last month at UNH.

"But, what the hell, dude, that was more than three decades ago. Most of your so-called friends from the Students for Complete Change are probably dead, for all you know." Realizing that his friend's mental state was still in the danger zone, Swift asked, "Do you want to talk about it, Perry?" placing his arm around Stockton's shoulders.

Stockton now was feeling more foolish than scared. After all, with his 20/400 vision, he couldn't really be sure whom he saw, especially not in a crowd, and from a distance of at least a football field away.

"Never mind; I don't want to talk about it. I'm okay. I tell you what, let's just take a walk along the river. I need to meet my old pal Monica in about an hour."

Monica was Monica Waters. The two briefly were a couple at the university. Even after Stockton realized that romance wasn't in the cards for the two of them, they remained very dear friends. Not even time and geographic separation changed that.

"Monica's still working for the Children's Museum. She wants me to show up before 3 p.m."

"And what Monica wants, Monica gets," Swift chided his friend, trying unsuccessfully to disguise his disappointment about the short amount of time Stockton and he would spend together until later that evening.

The Butterfield building, which housed the Children's Museum, was just around the bend on the river walk. As they sauntered along the path, Swift could tell that his old friend had not really dismissed whatever or whomever he had seen earlier. In fact, Stockton's surreptitious effort to see if someone was following them had not gone unnoticed.

When they reached the museum's set of tinted double-glass doors, Stockton stared appreciatively at the three impressive arched windows whose granite facing adorned a former brick factory. After a reluctant goodbye, Swift returned to his canoe rental platform and Stockton entered the museum, but not before scanning the crowd of people who were enjoying the riverwalk on a perfect partly cloudy day.

The bookish looking 50-year-old woman who staffed the museum's semi-circular admissions desk barely acknowledged him, but once Stockton told her that he had an appointment to see Monica Waters, her expression brightened considerably.

"You must be Mr. Stockton," she said. "Monica has been looking forward to seeing you."

Five minutes later, Waters, a wafer thin former elementary education teacher who still dressed and looked the part, came down a hallway from the left side of the entry desk. Waters had long since moved away from the field of public education, but never lost her love for working with children. Her position at the Children's Museum as events planner gave her opportunities to interact daily with excited kids and their overwhelmed but happy parents.

Waters took Stockton on a tour of the museum, which allowed the pair some time to reminisce about the old days. Stockton seemed disengaged, barely taking notice as they passed by the numerous colorful and interesting exhibits. Waters knew him well enough to sense that something was troubling Stockton.

"What's going on inside that handsome head of yours, Perry?" she asked. "You're not still ruminating about all that stuff that went on during senior year, are you? You really got yourself tied up with some crazy characters back then."

Her friend's response told Waters all she needed to know. His facial expression was more than one of regret. No, it was something else... it was fear she was seeing on the face of Perry Stockton.

Trying to change the subject, Waters asked him whether he'd been in touch with any of his real friends from campus.

"If you mean, am I in contact with the old SCC people, then the answer is no, absolutely no. But I do keep in touch with Joey Swift and Dominic Riccio. In fact, I just spent an hour with Joey, and I'm meeting Dom at his restaurant for an early dinner." After a few seconds, he asked Waters whether she was in touch with anyone.

The truth was, Waters would have married Stockton in a minute back in their UNH days. Unfortunately for her, he only had eyes for that girl in the anarchist student group.

"Are you trying to find out if I'm seeing any guys from those days? Well, the answer is no. However, I'm still good buddies with Portia DeLisle. You remember her, don't you?" she added with a smile. "We were supposed to meet for dinner tonight, but she backed out for some reason."

In point of fact, revisiting memories of Portia DeLisle did nothing to help Stockton's frame of mind.

Chapter 3

The shouting was reaching decibel levels that threatened to expose what the group was plotting on that cold February afternoon in 1987. As usual, it was Tyler McCann doing his best to bully Perry Stockton into agreeing with his point of view. The three co-eds, Honor Pemberton, Iris Mayhew, and Sabrina Valentine, were all sitting with their heads bowed out of embarrassment about the vile language the two men—mostly McCann—were using. Stockton was near desperation. As he looked over at the three women, he asked himself why he continually exposed himself to McCann's crazy tirades. He especially questioned why Sabrina was in the room. She wasn't a believer in their cause like the others. Rather, her presence was at the pleasure of Titan, the group's leader, guru, and chief instigator.

It was something of a miracle that the six of them had made it to senior year. Their zealous effort to undermine the university administration was no secret. Everyone from Dr. Morris, the university president, to the wet-behind-the-ears campus police rookies knew about the group and their intentions. However, knowing about the organization calling itself Students for Complete Change, or SCC, and catching the wrong-doers were two different things.

The six students in the room organized the political action group, the SCC, during their first year on campus. The members had been aghast that the school failed to take a stronger stance against indifference by the administration in Washington, D.C. While calling itself a bastion for liberal thinking and the sustainability of world cultures, the UNH president and deans had turned a blind eye to what SCC deemed atrocities against immigrant groups.

The fact that the six people in the room were still on campus was no mean feat. First, as group organizers, demands on their time rivaled that of a scholarship athlete. Meetings, recruitment of dozens of other members, and designing brochures and other media packages took an enormous amount of effort. Even more essential was the ability to "cover their asses" in the event something went wrong during a protest. Somehow, these six students were able to run the gauntlet while keeping their grades above the Mendoza Line.

Stockton and McCann began their membership as reluctant allies. However, as Titan demanded more of them, and each coveted the position of first-lieutenant to their leader, things changed. McCann began by working behind the scenes to undermine Titan's faith in Stockton. However, as the smarter of the two men, Stockton more than held his own with McCann during the many heated planning sessions throughout their final two years at the university.

It was during the planning and execution of one last big expression of disdain for the administration that things went terribly wrong. With fewer than two weeks remaining in their senior year, a final SCC protest, designed to gain universal media coverage for their cause, produced disastrous results, and cost a dedicated young university administrator her life.

Chapter 4

There was one more old university friend whom Stockton planned to visit. Dominic Riccio, who taught Stockton how to make the perfect spaghetti sauce during their days at the university, was now owner of the Dover Brickhouse in the downtown area. Stockton arrived a few minutes late to 2 Orchard St. and found that the restaurant already was crowded with locals and university students.

Riccio greeted his old friend with a big hug and a wet kiss on the cheek. When Stockton reached up to dry his face, Riccio admonished him.

"Don't you wipe that off, *cazzo*. After all, who used to keep that big jerk McCann from pounding you back in the old days, eh?"

Stockton's mood quickly darkened. He admitted to Riccio that he spent his final term at school afraid that McCann, that big wild boar of a man, was going to kill him.

"I never understood why you put up with McCann's shit, Perry," Riccio told him. "That guy was freakin' crazy... him and that black trench coat... what was with that anyway?"

Stockton replied as he touched his friend on the shoulder. "I sometimes think that the only reason he didn't kill me back then was because he knew you'd make him pay big time."

Riccio laughed. "Down in the Bronx, we ate dudes like that for breakfast. McCann knew better than to give me shit." Riccio always wondered what Stockton and his SCC friends really were doing during their college days. There had been rumors; however, Riccio was like most of the students on campus... he didn't know how to separate truth from fiction. But now, with his friend sitting across from him, he was determined to learn what he could.

"So, come on, Perry, give already. What went on back then?"

Stockton stared across the table at his old friend. Before answering, he looked around the restaurant, just in case Tyler McCann had materialized somehow. So focused was he on assurances that his six-foot-two rival from the SCC days was nowhere to be seen, he failed to notice that a pretty middle-age brunette sitting at a neighboring table was eavesdropping on their conversation. Unfortunately for Stockton, the resonant quality of his voice made him easy to hear, even above the din of the dinner crowd.

"You and everyone else on campus knew as much about the SCC as we wanted you to," he began.

"Yeah sure. Students for Complete Change. You guys were rabble-rousers, sort of like the SDS back in the Sixties… only less destructive," Riccio added.

"We weren't quite as tame as you might have thought, Dom," Stockton replied.

"Really! What do you mean? I'm sure you weren't the ones responsible for the explosion that killed that lady dean…?"

After a slight, imperceptible hesitation, Stockton said with a wan smile, "My lips are sealed, Dom; we were all sworn to secrecy about any and all SCC activities."

"Come on, Perry. This is me—Dom—besides that, it's been 30 years. Surely you guys are home free after all of this time."

Stockton shook his head. "I'm not so sure about that."

"I get it, *compagno*. After all, you and McCann were the heads of the SCC. So you'd probably still be in deep shit. I guess ya gotta be careful."

Stockton looked directly at Riccio. As he did, he shook his head back and forth. "I won't talk about the explosion. But one thing I will tell you is that McCann and me weren't in charge of crap."

"Whatdya mean?" Riccio asked, perhaps a bit too loud. "Your names were in the school newspaper for three years, mostly for small shit. Are you telling me that was fake news?"

"I'm afraid so. McCann and I ran the meetings, placed ads, and talked to the media. But we were actually lieutenants in the organization. The real decision maker was another student whom we called Titan. The crazy thing is, McCann and I were two of the few who knew Titan's true identity."

As the two talked, Stockton devoured his meal, a burger topped with hand-cut fries. Under the stressful circumstances, he washed his meal down with three 16-ounce glasses of Howlet, a locally crafted pale wheat ale.

Riccio couldn't believe what he was hearing, and was desperate to learn more. "So, you guys weren't the real decision makers. It was this dude Titan?"

Stockton couldn't resist teasing his old friend. "Who said Titan was a dude?"

"You mean the SCC was run by a chick?" Riccio blurted out loud.

"I didn't say that either," Stockton laughed. "The only thing I'll tell you about Titan is that he or she was a student at the U, just like us."

"In the same class?" Riccio questioned.

Stockton nodded.

"Holy crap! Did I know this Titan?"

"That's all I'll tell you for now," Stockton replied. "Except to say that McCann and I would have done almost anything to please Titan back in those days. Both of us wanted to be the sole second in command. But, I found out the hard way that there was one big difference between us."

"What was that?" Riccio asked.

"There were limits to how far I was willing to go."

"But that wasn't true of McCann?" Riccio questioned.

As Stockton stared across the table at Riccio, he simply shook his head back and forth.

Stockton managed to part company from his old college friend without elaborating about the terrible accident that shook everyone on campus to the core years earlier. He also held tight to the identity of Titan.

As he left the Dover Brickhouse, the woman who had been listening to their reminiscences reached into her pocketbook and pulled out her cell phone.

Chapter 5

With daylight starting to fade and the three beers doing their job, Stockton left the restaurant and began walking unsteadily toward a meeting with Joey Swift. As he headed northeast from the corner of Central Avenue and Orchard Street, Stockton had an inexplicable urge to visit the fish ladder, a stretch of five interconnected concrete pools that allow alewives, herring, and other fish species to bypass the Cochecho Falls during spring. Perhaps he was enticed by the symbolism of overcoming seemingly insurmountable barriers—something Stockton was hoping to do the next morning.

A combination of the alcohol he'd consumed and a good deal of deep thought caused Stockton to drop his guard. Unaware that a black, late model Infinity QX80 with tinted windows had pulled into the parking lot near the fish ladder, he failed to notice when a tall man dressed in a long, black trench coat, exited the car.

The man quietly closed the space between them. Passing the falls, which were surprisingly strong for early summer, Stockton stopped and, momentarily mesmerized, looked down to watch the water flowing through the rocks at their base.

The man in black moved deliberately. Looking in all directions to be certain he wasn't being watched, he moved right beside an unaware Stockton. In one fluid motion, he grabbed Stockton by the neck, thrust a long, sharp instrument into a particularly lethal spot, then shoved the helpless victim over a railing onto the fish ladder. At the same moment when Stockton's body was seen by a passer-by, the tall man was heading back to his waiting car.

When Perry Stockton failed to arrive at their appointed meeting time, Swift called Stockton's cell phone, then dialed a second and a third time. Now, he suspected trouble. In all of the years Swift had known him, Stockton was never late for anything. He even was born prematurely. As Swift sat on a wall overlooking the Cochecho, he remembered how his friend had looked absolutely terrified a few hours earlier, when he thought Tyler McCann might have been tailing him.

Swift reached for his cell phone and immediately called the two others whom Stockton had traveled to Dover to see. Monica Waters answered on the first ring, as was her habit.

Seeing Swift's name on caller ID, she answered with a cheerful, "Hi, Joey. Are you and Perry having fun?"

"Perry hasn't come back to meet me. That's why I'm calling. I was wondering if he was with you? After all, you're much prettier than I am."

Waters' brow furrowed. "No, I wasn't expecting to see him until tomorrow. I promised to give him a ride up to campus in the morning, then to Logan so he could catch his plane home. I'm 0 for 2; I was supposed to be meeting Portia DeLisle for dinner tonight, but she canceled."

Her annoyance at being stood up by DeLisle was immediately replaced by concern about Stockton. "Promise me you'll have Perry call once he shows up."

Swift promised he would, then immediately dialed the cell phone of Dom Riccio, Stockton's earlier dinner partner.

"Hey, Joey. How've you been, man? Look, it's really busy here. So, I can't talk long. What's up?" Hearing that Swift was looking for their mutual friend Perry, Riccio replied, "We had a great meal together. Although he seemed really troubled about something."

Swift agreed that he'd noticed the same thing, but his chief concern was why Stockton hadn't met him as planned.

"That sure as hell isn't like Perry," Riccio agreed with his friend's assessment. Then, hearing a lot of noise and confusion coming from the front of the restaurant, he asked Swift to give him a couple of minutes to investigate.

However, Riccio was gone for more than 10 minutes. When he returned, Riccio sounded totally distressed. His tone of voice alarmed Swift.

"Dom, what the hell is going on?" he shouted.

"They just found a body on the fish ladder, no more than a block from here. And, from the guy's description, it sounds like Perry!"

Swift broke the connection on their phone call. But, when he rang Stockton's cell phone again, there still was no answer.

Chapter 6

Mildred Thomas loved to end her day by walking across the Central Avenue Bridge by the falls on her way home from her shop each evening. On this one night, she decided to stop and look down into the impressive rocky gorge beneath the cascade. It was a view she would never be able to forget. There, barely visible on the fish ladder below, was the body of Perry Stockton. Thomas' shrill screams filled the evening silence and did not stop until another passerby called 911.

Within five minutes, the local police and fire departments were on the scene. It would take another hour before a member of the state's Major Crimes Unit arrived. Once it was determined that the victim was from out of state, Sgt. Bob Norton from the New Hampshire Task Force for Visitor Safety, or VTF, received orders to head to the scene.

The fact that Bob Norton was still a member of the VTF both pleased and surprised Kary Turnell, the agency's commissioner. Several years earlier, the governor-elect learned the importance of out-of-state visitors to New Hampshire's economy. He had heard from the governor of a southern state how a violent crime spree directed at a family of tourists had negative ramifications that proved very costly to the reputation of that state's travel industry.

Armed with this information, the governor-elect was determined to be proactive and appoint a commissioner to oversee the welfare of visitors to New Hampshire. What began as a public relations demonstration turned out to be one of the governor's most successful actions. He struck gold when he appointed Kary Turnell, a highly regarded criminologist, as the task force's first commissioner.

During the last three years, Turnell, the no-nonsense tough-as-nails Norton, and Lt. Mary Bendix, a cerebral computer whiz, had solved four murder cases involving out-of-state victims. While the governor had been anxious to establish the task force, Turnell soon learned that there was almost no funding for the new agency. All he received was a two-room office in downtown Concord and an administrative assistant. Fortunately, due to the generosity of Bill Williams, the director of New Hampshire's drug task force, Kary was assigned Bendix and Norton—two excellent career investigators—and very fortunate when both elected to remain on Turnell's investigative team.

During each investigation, Turnell and his team exhibited excellent fact-finding skills, while working seamlessly with local, state, and federal law enforcement agencies. Moreover, Turnell's willingness to share credit with his law enforcement counterparts made the task force extremely popular from the State House to Main Street.

By the time local EMTs had removed Stockton's body from the fish ladder, Dover police Detective Sgt. Luna Hill was waiting for the arrival of county coroner, Isaac Pratt. Pratt smiled when he saw that Hill was the detective on duty.

"I might have known that you'd show up here, Detective Sergeant," he said mirthlessly.

"Now, you know very well that there's no one else you'd want here, Dr. Pratt," she chided him.

"Before you ask… and I know you're going to… I have no idea what the cause of death is. I've barely had a peek at the body." As Pratt said this, he handed Hill a plastic evidence bag containing a wallet, stubs from both airplane and bus tickets, and very little else. Before long, Sergeant Norton arrived on the scene.

Chapter 7

Old feelings surged through Monica Waters' mind after Perry Stockton left the Children's Museum. Back during their college days, Monica had pursued Stockton, albeit unsuccessfully. She lacked the aggressiveness of some of the other girls in her dorm. So, she continued to develop a close friendship with Stockton, while secretly hoping that he would think more of her than just "a bright girl and a really good shit, to boot."

Stockton was one of the few men Monica met who had the intellectual chops that she expected of a boyfriend. By the time they were sophomores, she was already beginning to suspect that Stockton had pursuits that were far more secretive, and well outside her world. That year, Monica professed her love for Stockton to her roommate and best friend, Portia DeLisle.

In truth, Stockton was far more physically attracted to DeLisle than Waters. DeLisle was a tall, curvaceous brunette who wore her black hair in a braid that extended down her back all the way to her waist. Unbeknownst to Waters, the man of her dreams had tentatively pursued DeLisle, even asking her to join him on a trip to Portsmouth for the day. Not wanting to offend her best friend, DeLisle politely refused that invitation, telling Stockton she was spending the weekend with her boyfriend. In truth, she spent the weekend at home with her family. Meanwhile, DeLisle had designs on another classmate, a fit, self-assured, well-dressed sophomore named Richardson Wilcox. Unfortunately for DeLisle, her chances with Wilcox were no better than Stockton's with her. But, that didn't stop her from pursuing him.

※※※※※※

During the second semester of their first year at school, Stockton and McCann assumed co-leadership of the SCC. At least, that's what the other 25 members of the organization were led to believe. The actual leader of the SCC was a fellow member of their class who was known simply as Titan. By design, Titan remained in the background, giving marching orders to his two co-lieutenants—Stockton and McCann.

The relationship between the two figureheads worked well enough for three years.

Each seemed satisfied to share both responsibilities and glory with the other. McCann was clearly the more aggressive of the two, while Stockton proved to be an ingenious planner. Largely owing to Stockton, the members of SCC were able to execute disruptive activities like sit-ins and frequent graffiti that gained them a good deal of attention from both the administration and the media. Most important: law enforcement and the university's administration always seemed to be one step behind them.

As their junior year was nearing a conclusion, the relationship between the two men changed dramatically. Truth be known, the impetus behind their schism was none other than Titan. He told his two lieutenants that he expected one of them to assume a larger role within the organization during their senior year. Titan told the pair that he would base his decision upon scrutiny of their performance by the end of the school year.

It soon became apparent that both men coveted the opportunity for increased leadership. The difference was that there were limits to how far Stockton was willing to go to impress Titan. McCann had no such scruples. As his counterpart began to present more and more confrontational ideas to Titan, Stockton called for a more measured approach. With Titan refusing to intervene, McCann became more and more aggressive in his behavior toward Stockton. While there was no doubt about his superior intellect, Stockton was no physical match for McCann, a heavily muscled six-foot-two mesomorph. Gradually, over the course of a month, McCann began to bully Stockton, at one point threatening to "kick his pathetic ass."

While the bullying tactic, on its own, didn't impact Titan's choice of a successor, it affected the final act of the SCC, and contributed to the onset of Stockton's PTSD.

Chapter 8

Hill and Norton stood on the walkway looking to where Stockton's body had been found. The white nylon tent shielded curious passersby from the work Pratt was meticulously conducting 10 yards away. While the short, slim Hill and the compact, muscular Norton had met one another at law enforcement meetings during the past several years, they didn't know one another well.

It was Hill who broke the ice.

"My friend Stella Gillespie had a lot of good things to say about you, Sergeant."

Her reference to the sergeant who assisted the VTF in Manchester made Norton smile.

"You know Stella?!" he smiled. "How is she doing? I hope those guys in Manchester were smart enough to make her a permanent detective," he asked.

"Yah, she's a fulltime detective now and absolutely loves her job. I'll tell her you said hello," she added.

Before the pair could discuss what was going on just below them, they heard the familiar voice of Capt. Stu Garrison, Kary Turnell's friend and counterpart with the state's Major Crimes Unit. Garrison was already on the scene directing the actions of two of his men.

"We definitely have to stop meeting like this, Sergeant Norton."

Norton saluted the MCU captain and introduced Garrison to Hill.

"I assume the man in the fedora will be here soon," Garrison inquired.

"That's a Roger, Captain. You know how this works. I show up first, do all of the real work, and then Commissioner Turnell and Lieutenant Bendix arrive and receive all the credit," he said with a smile.

"I suppose we'll have other company before too long." Garrison was referring to FBI agent Ponds who had worked with the MCU and VTF on numerous occasions.

Garrison then turned to Hill and requested, "Bring me up to speed, Detective Sergeant."

Hill removed the case notebook from the breast pocket of her uniform. Flipping through a few pages, she began to tell both men what was known about the incident.

"The vic's name is Perry Stockton, male, age 54. He resided in Philadelphia. Based upon the contents of the evidence bag, he took a plane from Philly, then boarded a bus at Logan and arrived in Dover early this afternoon."

"Does anyone know what he was doing here?" Norton asked.

"Not yet," Hill replied. "But, we have a woman and a gentleman waiting to talk to us. The woman says she arrived at the scene right after the vic fell. Also, the man is a local restaurateur who was having dinner with Mr. Stockton until about 30 minutes ago."

"That's good work, Sergeant," Garrison told her. "We'll need to have a talk with them, but it makes sense to wait for Commissioner Turnell to arrive."

"Did I hear someone taking my name in vain?" came a familiar voice from behind Garrison.

The three officers turned to see two people approaching. The senior citizen wearing a brown fedora was unmistakably Commissioner Kary Turnell, a man whose reputation as an investigator was without peer. Standing next to Kary was Lt. Mary Bendix, a serious, no-nonsense woman in full dress uniform, carrying her ever-present laptop computer.

Kary and Garrison exchanged a firm handshake. While Kary had never met Hill, Bendix and Hill were well acquainted, as they both were active in the women's law enforcement organization. The two exchanged warm handshakes before Hill told Bendix, "Based on your reputation as an Internet surfer, I have a feeling we'll need that geek-box of yours before very long."

"I'll be ready," Bendix replied with a smile.

※※※※※※

After Hill and Norton canvassed the scene, they walked over to the female eyewitness, who identified herself as Mrs. Thomas. She was understandably upset by what she had witnessed. A woman police officer stood by to offer comfort.

The officers introduced themselves to Mrs. Thomas. Once they were certain she was up to being questioned, Norton asked her what she had seen.

"I saw that man down there," she paused to point near the coroner's tent. "I didn't actually see him fall, but I think it must have happened a few seconds earlier."

"What makes you say that, Mrs. Thomas?" Hill asked.

"Because I'm almost certain he moved his arm before he collapsed and just lay there."

"Moved his arm?"

"Yes, it looked like he was pointing toward the south bank of the river."

"And did you see anything over there?" Norton asked.

"My attention was focused on him, but thinking back, I remember seeing a tall man. I'm pretty sure he had on a long black coat."

"What was he doing?"

"He was walking away from the river," she replied. "Don't you think that was odd?"

"What do you mean?"

"Well, if you had just seen what I saw and heard me screaming at the top of my lungs, wouldn't you be concerned about the man lying down there?" she asked as she scanned their faces.

※※※※※※

The source of Monica Waters' consternation was her former UNH roommate, Portia DeLisle. Beautiful Portia hated the aggressive attention she received from men back during the university years. She preferred to act like a woman of mystery who flirted when she felt like it, but remained elusive in the end. As the two women became closer friends, Waters suspected that DeLisle secretly had her eye set on someone at the school, but it proved to be unrequited.

The same evening as Stockton's visit to Dover, Waters and DeLisle were scheduled to have dinner together at a downtown restaurant. They had discussed these plans for weeks. DeLisle had even called Waters several days earlier to be certain that their girls' night out was still on. Then something strange happened.

While the two women were talking on the telephone at breakfast, Waters told DeLisle that Perry Stockton was coming to town, and would be heading up to the university in the morning. Suddenly, DeLisle claimed that there was an electrician at her door. Before hanging up, DeLisle promised to call Waters right back. However, no telephone call was forthcoming. Instead, when Waters arrived at her office in the morning of her meeting with Stockton, there was a telephone message slip on the desk. It read, "So sorry. Something has come up. Will need to reschedule. Kisses, P."

Chapter 9

Unbeknownst to the investigative team, Mrs. Thomas was not the only person standing within view of the fish ladder. Fifty yards away, with a perfect angle of the scene below, was a tall, dark-haired woman.

As she stood silently waiting for the flap of the coroner's tent to be pulled open, the woman's thin cigarette dangled loosely from her lips. Only when the EMTs began the arduous process of removing the gurney holding Stockton's body did the woman drop her cigarette. As she extinguished the butt with the point of her Christian Louboutin shoe, she reached inside the pocket of her Burberry jacket and hit a button on a cell phone.

"Perry Stockton is dead," she said quietly, then listened for 30 seconds before disconnecting without saying goodbye.

※※※※※※

Having heard there was a body lying on the fish ladder, Dominic Riccio instructed one of his employees to take over at the bar in the Dover Brickhouse. A feeling of dread came over Riccio, as he ran out of the restaurant toward the river. He arrived just as the first officers were beginning to apply yellow crime scene tape to the area. Riccio's worst fears became a reality. The bright yellow jacket worn by the victim was unmistakably that of his old friend Perry Stockton.

Riccio had a very good relationship with members of the Dover police department, who frequently visited his restaurant after shifts. So, when Detective Sergeant Hill first arrived at the scene, he immediately approached her.

"What's up, Dom? You're going to need to move away from here," she told him.

Riccio was obviously shaken. "No… you don't understand, detective… the guy lying down there is one of my best friends."

Hearing that, Hill told Riccio to stand back away from the gorge and wait for someone to interview him. So, despite having left his busy restaurant, he waited patiently for the investigative team to talk with him.

Hill walked over to Riccio, with Sergeant Norton accompanying her. After brief introductions, they asked Riccio to tell them when he last saw the victim alive.

Riccio had lost all track of time. Looking at his watch, he told them, "It's been about an hour. Perry and I just had dinner together at the Brickhouse." Hill and Norton could see that Riccio was shaken by the experience, but they needed to press forward.

"Was anyone else at dinner with you, Dom?" Hill asked him.

"No; it was just the two of us."

Now Norton interjected, "We know Mr. Stockton was living in Philadelphia. Do you know what he was doing up here?"

"Yeah, sure. Or, at least I thought I did."

"You need to explain what you mean, Dom," Hill told him.

"Perry has remained very close to three of us from our UNH days. Besides me, there's Joey Swift and Monica Walters. He tries to come up and see us every year."

Norton looked at Hill. "Do you know those people, Detective Sergeant?"

"Yeah, I do. Joey's our city recreation director and Monica directs events at the children's museum. They both work within a few blocks of here."

Norton made a note in his field notebook before asking Riccio, "Is it possible one or both of them had a falling out with Mr. Stockton?"

"Nah… no way, Sergeant. You're barking up the wrong tree. Them two loved Perry like a brother. But, you should ask them yourself."

At that point, Riccio excused himself, citing the need to get back and run his restaurant. Before he left, Hill told him that he should remain available for questioning. As Riccio neared the entryway to the Dover Brickhouse, there was something—or someone—that was bothering him. He knew it would come to him later.

Chapter 10

During the last three years they spent at the university, each member of the leadership of the SCC remained monogamous. Titan had insisted, saying that the smaller number of people who knew their personal business the better.

"One less person to provide state's evidence," Titan had told Stockton and McCann," then laughed ferociously at his own joke.

Therefore, while Stockton initially had a strong interest in dating Portia DeLisle and had fended off the interest of Monica Waters, he dated Sabrina Valentine exclusively once he rose to the rank of SCC lieutenant. Stockton enjoyed his time with Valentine, especially during covert visits to her dorm room, but both knew their relationship was strictly a college affair. Sadly, owing to overuse of antidepressants while at the Durham campus, Valentine developed early onset dementia and was institutionalized before her 25th birthday.

McCann's choice of a girlfriend placed him surprisingly ahead of his time. Honor Pemberton was a brilliant, beautiful African American woman. Pemberton's problem was that she had a conscience. As a consequence, following the terrible explosion on campus during the group's senior year, Pemberton did a complete about face. Needing to escape the constant reminder of what the SCC had done, she joined the U.S. Army. Sadly, she was among the first soldiers killed during Desert Storm—ironically the victim of an IED that detonated under her jeep.

Titan's relationship to Iris Mayhew was known only to the couple itself, plus Stockton and Mayhew. The liaison nearly did not happen at all. During the couple's third date, Titan looked up from his five-feet six-inch height and informed the taller, leggy blond that he intended to sleep with her soon and often, but she must never tell anyone about their connection. Mayhew was spooked initially; but, ultimately, his mysterious, self-assured demeanor won her over.

Mayhew's relationship with Titan ended on graduation day. During July of that year, she began a relationship with an older man. Less than a year later, Mayhew contracted AIDS and died at the age of 23.

Chapter 11

Norton and Hill were interviewing Mrs. Thomas and Dominic Riccio. Meanwhile Kary, Garrison, and Bendix waited patiently for the coroner, Dr. Isaac Pratt, to complete his initial examination of Perry Stockton's body inside the tent nearby.

Once the body was removed to the parking lot, Pratt instructed his assistant to leave the tent in place for the time being. Next, he removed his gown, mask, and gloves and placed them in a large plastic zip lock bag. He then headed to the three investigators who were waiting to talk with him.

Garrison and Pratt had worked together on a number of cases, so no introduction was necessary. However, this was the first time Kary and Pratt were meeting. Pratt wasted no time breaking the ice.

"The man in the fedora, I presume? Dr. Turnell, your reputation proceeds you, sir. I'm Isaac Pratt, Strafford County Coroner."

"It's a pleasure. I've heard excellent things about your work as well," Kary replied. Next turning toward Bendix, he continued, "And this is my smarter right arm, Lt. Mary Bendix. The lieutenant has been with the task force since its inception."

"Ah, yes, the Visitor Safety Task Force, or VTF, as we have come to regard it with affection in the law enforcement community. I've already met your Sergeant Norton. I'm guessing he can be a handful for criminals to deal with."

Garrison replied before Kary could, "You wouldn't want any part of that young man, Isaac. Let's leave it at that." Then addressing the subject at hand, Garrison added, "So what can you tell us about the circumstances surrounding Mr. Stockton's demise?"

"Actually, I can tell you quite a bit," Pratt replied. "Stockton's body was badly bruised from his fall onto the fish ladder," he said.

"So, the fall is what killed him?" Garrison questioned.

"Yes and no," Pratt offered with a wry smile. "In all likelihood, he wouldn't have survived his fall."

"But…?"

Garrison held both arms out with his palms extended as a way to encourage Pratt to cut to the chase.

"I'm getting there, Captain." Now Pratt couldn't resist a toothy grin at the investigators. "Of course, the autopsy will tell us the whole story. However, I can tell you with a reasonable amount of certainty that it was not the fall that caused Mr. Stockton's demise."

Pratt was enjoying himself a bit too much for Garrison's liking.

"While you're stringing us along, Doc, a killer is running around loose!"

Pratt realized he had overplayed his hand. "While I was examining the body, I looked for obvious wounds. At first, I figured the contusions on his skull and spine told me all I needed to know. That's before I saw a puncture wound on his neck. My best guess is that Stockton was stabbed in the vertebral artery… probably with a long needle, an awl or an icepick."

"Which artery did you say?" Bendix asked while wincing.

"The vertebral artery," Pratt repeated, "although it's mere conjecture at this point. The vertebral artery is situated deep in the bony canal. It would take either a great deal of skill—or luck—to accomplish that. The victim would die almost instantaneously due to cerebellar and brainstem infarction."

"I have no idea what you're talking about," Garrison told him. "So, tell me this, if you're correct about this vertebral artery, what does it tell us about the killer?"

"Your killer is either medically trained or a contract killer… or both."

"I presume you didn't find much blood on the victim," Kary offered.

"No, there isn't a lot of water in the fish ladder, but enough to wash away whatever was on his body. Also, finding any DNA evidence where Stockton was grabbed is unlikely."

Garrison replied, "A professional would know not to leave evidence behind."

Chapter 12

At Kary's request, Riccio arranged for an assistant manager to take his place in the restaurant. Kary, Garrison and Bendix accepted Riccio's offer to meet in a small event space that was not being used that evening. A few minutes later, they were joined by Monica Waters and Joey Swift.

Riccio greeted his old university friends with an apologetic expression on his face. "Sorry to drag you into this, guys. But, Commissioner Turnell, Captain Garrison, and Lieutenant Bendix asked me who else Perry came to see in town."

Swift shrugged, an indication that he wasn't troubled to be called. Waters simply gave Riccio a light pat on the hand.

Kary started the interview with a disclaimer. "The fact that we're talking to all of you at the same time should be a clear indication that none of you is suspected of contributing to Mr. Stockton's demise."

At Kary's mention of Stockton, tears began to flow down Waters' cheeks.

"Can you tell us why you're crying, Ms. Waters?" Bendix asked.

"Please call me Monica," Waters sniffed. "Perry and I were dear friends—both at college and until now," she told them. "I always wished for more; but Perry just saw me as a good friend. I suppose I accepted that 30 years ago. But, you can't blame a girl for hoping."

"Did you see Mr. Stockton while he was in town?" Garrison started to ask her, but was cut off by Swift.

"We all saw Perry. But, I suppose we should tell you about his visit in chronological order," he added.

Kary thought Swift's suggestion was excellent, and encouraged him to lead off.

Swift explained that Stockton was a close friend of all of them, dating back to their UNH student days. Whenever he had business in the area, or simply wanted to see his friends, he sent the three a text message, informing them about the date and time of his arrival. Naturally, each of them changed other plans to accommodate Stockton's visits.

"Did he meet with all of you at the same time?" Kary asked.

"Not usually," Riccio responded.

"Why not?" Kary asked.

"Because we were all very close to Perry, but not one another."

Kary asked for an explanation.

"We all know and like one another, but we move in different social circles. There's nothing more to it than that," Waters answered for the others.

Kary asked each to describe what seeing Stockton on this occasion was like. When he heard Swift's response, his attention was piqued.

"Perry seemed out of sorts to me," Swift began. "When he showed up at our meeting place along the river, the guy looked like he'd seen a ghost."

"More like a McCann," Waters corrected.

"What's a McCann?" Bendix asked. All the while, she was typing furiously on her Mac notebook.

Riccio replied first, "Tyler McCann... that asshole." Both Swift and Waters nodded in support of Riccio's statement.

"Perry felt certain that he spotted McCann standing down the path in Henry Law Park. But when he looked back... and he kept turning around... McCann was nowhere to be seen," Swift told them.

"Did he say what this person looked like?" Garrison asked.

"Not really. McCann is a big, tall dude. Perry said the guy he saw was tall and wearing a black trench coat. McCann always wore a black trench coat," Swift told them.

"Sort of like a certain someone who wears a fedora," Garrison couldn't resist kidding Kary.

Swift continued, "But, when I questioned Perry, he said he didn't want to talk about it. So I dropped the subject."

"He was still nervous about something when he came to see me 15 minutes later," Waters told the investigators. "One thing I can tell you, McCann has stayed in Perry's head all of these years," her eyes teared as she said this.

Asked to explain more about Stockton's relationship with McCann, the three proceeded to tell the investigators how Stockton and McCann were co-leaders of a student protest group during their time at UNH.

"They were a non-violent protest group, the SCC..." Waters began.

"At least that's how things started out," Riccio interrupted. "One of their so-called non-violent protests ended up causing the death of a UNH administrator. Privately, each blamed the other for the incident."

Hearing this, Kary looked over at Bendix who knew instinctively that he was going to ask her to look into the group and the incident Waters and Riccio had just described. Kary was certain that Bendix would soon know more about the SCC than its own members.

Once Waters and Riccio had completed their descriptions of visiting with Stockton, Kary had the three tell the investigators everything they knew about Perry Stockton's relationship to Tyler McCann.

"One last thing," Kary asked. "Are any other members of your graduating class at UNH living here in Dover?"

Kary looked at the three as he said this. Swift and Riccio immediately shook their heads back and forth. Waters appeared to be considering the question a bit longer. However, she didn't say anything, a fact that wasn't lost on the man with the fedora.

After the three had left the room, Kary, Garrison and Bendix remained seated at a table to discuss what they now knew.

"As usual, the MCU and the VTF are left with a mess to clean up in a hurry," Garrison offered. "The news media will be all over this. I'm sure the governor will be pushing us as soon as he hears."

"So what's next, Commissioner?" Bendix asked.

"I want to know everything there is about the SCC back in Stockton's day. Who were the members? What actions did they take? And, most important, who was killed in that SCC incident and how did it happen?" Next, Garrison chimed in, "I'll be on the horn to the FBI; and we'll put out an all points bulletin to find Tyler McCann."

"That all sounds great," Kary replied. "Let's rendezvous with Norton and Hill to see if anything we've heard is contradictory. Also, I think we will have more to learn from one of the three people we just interviewed."

Chapter 13

Using her superior Internet research skills, it didn't take Lieutenant Bendix very long to learn about Perry Stockton. During his student days at UNH, Stockton had been a Social Studies Education major. By making a few telephone calls, Bendix soon learned that Stockton's academic advisor, Dr. Jerry Levin, was still a member of the faculty. She wasted no time contacting him.

When Levin answered his office phone, he was surprised to hear the voice of a police lieutenant on the line.

"I have to admit that the last person I'd expect to contact me is a police officer. What can I do for you, Lieutenant Bendix?"

Bendix explained to the professor that she was looking for information about an alumnus named Perry Stockton.

Levin informed Bendix that he not only remembered Stockton very well, but the two had remained in touch throughout the years. He remembered Stockton as a bright, albeit erratic student who blossomed after leaving the university. He was living outside of Philadelphia since his graduation. Beginning in 2000, Stockton was employed as a community planner, working mostly in towns situated in eastern Pennsylvania.

After Bendix explained to Levin the motivation for her call—Perry Stockton's untimely death—she could tell that the professor was in a state of disbelief.

"That's insane!" he blurted into the phone. "Perry just contacted me a few days ago. He said I'd be receiving a visit from him either today or tomorrow."

"Did he indicate the purpose of his visit?" Bendix asked.

"As a matter of fact he did." Levin told Bendix how Stockton had been involved with a group called Students for Complete Change. "He was one of the leaders of the group... unfortunately."

"What do you mean by 'unfortunately'?" Bendix asked him.

"If you go back through the old newspapers, you'll learn that there was an explosion inside Thompson Hall, our administration building, back in 1987. One of our deans, Dr. Bell, was killed in the blast. Bell was barely in her thirties, about my age at the time. She had two young children. It was rumored that the explosion was the work of the SCC, but nothing was ever proven. I think the administration wanted the bad publicity to just go away. The state police and the FBI investigated for a while, but nothing ever came of it."

"So, you think the purpose of Mr. Stockton's visit was to learn more about the explosion?" Bendix questioned.

"Not exactly, Perry was coming up here to meet with school officials and the police so he could confess."

Bendix's keen mind quickly processed what she had just heard.

"So, he was willing to open up a major can of worms just like that?"

Levin replied, "It wasn't a sudden impulse on his part. He told me that Dr. Bell's death has weighed on his conscience for a long time. Perry had been very ill a few months ago. I think that episode convinced him he needed to come clean about his role in the explosion."

Bendix asked, "Do you think Stockton was acting alone? It would have taken a good deal of planning to do something like that."

"I'm certain he wasn't. Back in those days, Perry and another student named Tyler McCann were the co-leaders of the SCC... or, that's what the rest of the school believed."

"I don't follow," Bendix replied.

"Since Perry's graduation, things he's said have led me to believe that there was a third person—a guy he called Titan—who was the real head of the SCC. For whatever the reason, Titan remained in the shadows. Whenever the SCC publicized an event or received media coverage, you never heard a thing about Titan. It was always Perry and McCann who received the credit or scorn."

"Is it possible that this Titan was a figment of Stockton and McCann's imagination?" Bendix asked.

"I doubt it," Levin replied. "Also, from what I've heard about Mr. McCann, he was a nasty piece of work back then. Perry was fearful about everything concerning the SCC."

"Then why would he stay involved with them?" Bendix asked.

"I'd have to say that Perry believed in the cause, even if he didn't like some of the messengers." Levin thought for a minute before adding, "Even decades after they graduated, I could never convince Perry to level with me about Titan. And now, with Perry dead, I suppose you'll have to ask Tyler McCann those questions."

Chapter 14

The years had been kind to Portia DeLisle in more ways than one. Now in her mid-50s, DeLisle hadn't lost much of the physical allure that initially attracted Perry Stockton to her. Even at a short distance, DeLisle appeared tall and attractive. Her black hair now came from scheduled appointments with the Dover Hair Salon; and the long single braid that once extended well down her back had been replaced by a short, layered style that complemented her rich dark eyes.

Back during her days at the university, Stockton's involvement in the SCC was the only thing about him that intrigued Portia DeLisle, but it was never enough of a reason to date him. While Stockton soon dismissed her as a passing fantasy, DeLisle never lacked for attention from other males on campus. However, she rejected all of them, while holding out hope for the handsome, but aloof, Richardson Wilcox.

DeLisle was able to attract Wilcox's attention for a few weeks. However, her brief fantasy about being Mrs. Richardson Wilcox ended hurtfully one night at a college mixer, when she saw how Wilcox looked and acted when in the presence of a pretty, long-haired redhead who soon became his one and only.

Years after graduation, DeLisle spotted Wilcox at an alumni event and quickly re-introduced herself. To her surprise and joy, Richardson returned her evident interest. His motivation was mainly physical, and though DeLisle wanted more, she had to be satisfied with time spent at one of their apartments. Not even DeLisle's closest friend, Monica Waters, knew of the relationship between the self-important Wilcox and the ever-hopeful DeLisle.

Chapter 15

Norton and Hill arranged with Dom Riccio to meet again in the Dover Brickhouse's small event room. At Kary's specification, there were two discussions. The first was a review of evidence attended by Kary and his team, plus Garrison and Hill.

"Okay, everyone; so what do we know?" Kary asked.

First, Norton and Hill described how Stockton had arrived from Philadelphia to visit with old friends.

"Apparently, he made an annual pilgrimage to Dover to see those three," Hill told the group.

"He also went up to Durham during those visits," Bendix added.

When Kary asked Bendix the purpose of those trips to Durham, Bendix replied, "He went to visit his former academic advisor. But I'll save that for my turn to talk."

Norton continued summarizing what Hill and he had uncovered.

"An eyewitness, Mrs. Thomas, told us that Stockton appeared to die about a minute after his fall."

"But not before pointing toward the parking lot by the river," Hill added.

"Mrs. Thomas told us that she looked in the direction where Stockton was pointing," Norton told them. "And when she did, she saw a tall man wearing a long black trench coat. He was walking away slowly."

"Mrs. Thomas also said the man never turned back, even when she was screaming at the top of her lungs," Hill reported.

Next, Garrison reported that Dr. Pratt, the coroner, told them that he'd found a deep puncture wound in Stockton's neck.

"It appears that Stockton was stabbed by an assassin who knew exactly where to make his thrust," Kary added. "This was no random killing."

Garrison chimed in, "Let's not forget that Joey Swift said Stockton seemed very nervous about something. Wasn't there mention of a person named Tyler McCann? I believe they were in a protest organization at the university back in the 80s."

"That's right," Bendix replied. "And Monica Waters said Stockton had been nervous during his time with her, too."

"This is all good intel, people," Kary told them. "But, for the present, we have no solid proof that this McCann person was even in Dover at the time of death." At that point, Kary turned to Bendix and said, "See if you can work some more of that CCTV magic, Lieutenant."

Next, returning his attention to the others around the table, Kary remembered something that bothered him at the end of their first meeting with Stockton's three friends.

"Do you all recall when we asked Swift, Waters and Riccio whether anyone else from their UNH days is living in Dover?" he asked.

The others nodded.

"Swift and Riccio said no, but..."

"Monica Waters never answered your question," Hill offered enthusiastically.

"That is correct, Sergeant," Kary smiled at Hill. "My sense tells me that is a line of questioning we need to pursue."

Next, Bendix reported what she learned during her meeting with Professor Levin, Stockton's old academic advisor.

"My conversation with Dr. Levin was eye opening," Bendix began. "The reason that Perry Stockton planned a visit to UNH was to confess about his role in the explosion that killed a college administrator back in 1987."

Following various expressions of astonishment, Bendix told the others how Stockton had recovered from a prolonged, nearly fatal illness. Afterward, he was determined to set the record straight.

"This is excellent work, Lieutenant," Kary said. He looked at his watch and realized that it was past time for their meeting with Stockton's three friends. "Let's continue our visit with the three friends. Afterward, I'd like to hear your thoughts on where this is leading."

Chapter 16

Tyler McCann never wanted to be a university student. He grew up in a navy family that lived in coastal communities all over the United States. Constantly the "new kid" in school, he developed a hard edge against his classmates, teachers, and especially the coaches he encountered. As he passed puberty, his body began to fill out impressively. By 15, he stood six-feet two-inches, and was an athletic, heavily muscled 200 pounds.

Most boys would have given anything to share his circumstance. Every coach wanted McCann on his team; every athlete and cheerleader pursued him. While he was more than happy to accommodate the cheerleaders, McCann derived a bizarre sense of pleasure out of disappointing the jock element.

Invariably, coach after coach and team captain after captain would receive the same message, "I'm not interested; don't ask again." It wasn't that McCann hated sports. Away from school, he played them frequently and with passion. His refusal to play was founded on something deeper… he knew it caused others anguish.

McCann never considered attending any school after high school, much less a prestigious eastern university in New England. He figured that his career path would lead to work as a policeman or firefighter. However, two events changed his thinking.

At his mother's insistence, McCann took the National Merit Scholarship examination. While McCann was reasonably intelligent, he'd been an underachiever in high school. When his mother told Tyler she had signed him up for the exam, he only agreed with the intention of showing her how foolish the idea was. When his results were posted, McCann soon found himself fielding letters from college admissions programs situated nationwide. The letters sat in a stack on his bureau until a second fateful event changed his life forever.

McCann liked to spend his free time hanging around the local fire station. Given his father's frequent absences during lengthy military deployments, McCann adopted the local fire chief as a surrogate parent. In truth, the young McCann idolized the chief. That was until one late afternoon when a young firefighter rebelliously failed to follow a direct order from the chief. Instead of attempting to reason with the much younger man, the chief grabbed him

by the front of his uniform and pummeled him. When McCann attempted to intercede, the chief quickly lashed out with the back of his hand, bloodying Tyler's nose and mouth in the process.

While the chief quickly realized the terrible mistake he'd made and apologized for losing his temper, the damage was done. From that time forward, McCann not only avoided the fire station, but carried a deep-seeded resentment toward authority figures.

Mrs. McCann was a surprised person when, several days later, her son told her that he was through with the idea of being a firefighter. Instead, he would be accepting one of the college scholarship offers he'd received. When his mother asked McCann which school he planned to attend, he replied, "I'm thinking about it."

In truth, he hadn't given any of his college mail a second glance. So, when his mother asked him again where he intended to go to school, McCann went up to his room and simply reached into the pile of letters, retrieving the one from the University of New Hampshire. That is how Tyler McCann came to be a student at Durham.

Chapter 17

With their private meeting completed, the investigators remained in the back of the Dover Brickhouse, as Riccio, Waters, and Swift joined them. Kary made a quick assessment of the expressions on their faces and determined that Waters appeared the most reticent to talk with them. So, of course, he quickly focused his attention on her.

"The last time we were together, I asked you all whether there is anyone from your undergraduate days at UNH presently living in Dover. Mr. Riccio and Mr. Swift both indicated that they didn't know of anyone else who lives here. But, you, Ms. Waters, never answered my question. Will you please do so right now?"

Waters' face turned scarlet. It was apparent to everyone else in the room that she was holding back.

"I don't understand how that is relevant," she replied, while avoiding Kary's gaze.

"You'll have to allow me to judge that," Kary replied. As he said this, Kary adjusted the crown on his fedora, which was sitting on the table in front of him. Norton and Bendix had seen this gesture before; and they knew that their boss was losing patience with Waters. Bendix decided that having another woman question Waters might gain her trust. She slyly got Kary's attention, then touched herself on the shoulder. It was a signal that she should take over questioning Waters. Kary almost imperceptibly nodded his approval.

"Ms. Waters… may I call you Monica?" Bendix began. Waters indicated her approval, so Bendix continued. "I'm certain it's more than a little intimidating being questioned by so many law enforcement officials all at once. Let me assure you that you're not in any trouble. However, we need to move fast to collect information so Mr. Stockton's killer can be apprehended. You want that, too, don't you?"

Waters began to dab at her eyes with a tissue. "Of course, I… all of us do."

"I'm certain that's true," Bendix continued. "So, we're asking you about others from UNH because someone else may know more than the three of you do. You won't be getting anyone in trouble by giving us a name. We just need to talk with them."

"Portia lives here," Water's response was barely above a whisper. However, Riccio heard what she said clearly.

"I'm so stupid… I should have known," he bellowed.

Now attention was shifted from the tearful Waters toward the incredulous restaurant owner.

"Please explain, Mr. Riccio," Kary requested.

"Last night, when me and Perry were having dinner together, I did what I always do—I scanned the room. It's an old restaurateur's habit. I do that for two reasons. It helps me understand who's eating here, and who isn't."

Even though he knew the answer to his question, Norton couldn't resist asking, "What's the other reason?"

Riccio laughed as he answered, "I see if there are any good-looking women… you know, any dating material."

"So, what did you see?" Bendix asked him.

"There was a very good-looking dark-haired woman sitting at the next table. I can't prove nothing, but she seemed to be eavesdropping on us. At the time, I thought she was interested in me and figured I'd talk with her when she paid the check."

"And did you do that?"

"No. Because she went outside to make a phone call, then left about the same time Perry did." Riccio continued, "There was something very familiar about her. She reminded me of a co-ed I tried to hit-on back in the day. As it turns out, that was Portia DeLisle, all right. I had no idea she was living here in Dover."

Swift chimed in, "It's like we told you before, Commissioner, we all travel in different social circles here."

Now Bendix's attention returned to Monica Waters.

"How well do you know this Portia DeLisle, Monica?"

"Very well. We were roommates and besties at UNH. We've remained very close since both of us moved here."

"Are you still roommates?" Norton asked.

"No, but we spend a lot of time together. In fact…" she started to say.

"In fact, what?" Bendix asked.

"We were supposed to have dinner together, but she cancelled out on me. She made an excuse about an electrician coming to the house. I didn't say anything, but I knew that was bogus."

"Why is that?" Hill asked her.

"Because, she lives in a pricey apartment building. Nothing ever goes wrong in that place; unlike where I live."

"But, something could have broken down," Norton protested.

"I'm not sure I can explain this, because you don't know Portia. Nothing short of a national emergency keeps Portia from girls night out… with one exception."

"Let me guess," Bendix offered. "Her emergency must have been a man."

"You're good, Lieutenant. I'm certain that she stood me up to be with a certain someone. She's been seeing a guy lately who is making her very happy. Normally, Portia can be on the snarky side… it's one of the things I've always enjoyed about her."

"But, not lately?" Bendix questioned.

"No. She's been so bubbly and mysterious that I hardly recognize her."

The word mysterious attracted Kary's notice. "What do you mean by mysterious?" he asked her. "And do you know who her love interest is?

"I don't know who he is, Commissioner. The one thing she let slip is he's someone from our UNH days. As to the mystery…" Waters shrugged. "All I can tell you is she's acting like some film noir femme fatale whose on a dangerous mission."

"And you don't know what that could be?" Kary questioned her.

"No; and you have no idea how much I'd like to know what Portia has gotten herself into," she replied.

"I can tell you one thing," Kary told her, "before very long, I fully intend to know what Ms. DeLisle has gotten involved in, because something tells me it has a great deal of impact on your friend Mr. Stockton's death."

"I have one last question for all of you," Kary told the three. "Did any of you know that Perry Stockton was going to visit UNH and what the purpose of that visit was?"

"I did," Swift replied, as Waters nodded in agreement.

"And, did you mention this to anyone else?" he asked.

Swift shook his head, no, at the same time that Waters answered, "I told Portia about it."

"This, ladies and gentlemen, may be a game-changer," Kary said sternly. Then, looking at Garrison and Bendix, he added, "Let's have that APB put out on Tyler McCann and another on Portia DeLisle. We also need to see any CCTV coverage of the area outside of Mr. Riccio's restaurant around the time of Stockton's death. And, let's see if there's footage in Henry Law Park, and at the river bank near the fish ladder. There's no time to waste."

Chapter 18

When Tyler McCann arrived in Durham for his first year of college, he carried a large chip on his shoulder. Long distrustful of his contemporaries, he also had a deep-seated distrust of authority. Therefore, when he spotted a poster promoting the Students for Complete Change on the bulletin board in Jessie Doe, his freshman dormitory, McCann was intrigued.

Arriving for his first meeting with the SCC group, he was surprised to learn that the organization, if one could call it that, was brand new. With no one there to run the meeting, the 20 students in attendance simply began to talk, or rather complain, about conditions on the campus and the nation, in general. When it was his turn to talk, McCann stood up and, relying on his size to create the proper atmosphere, told others in attendance, "If this is going to be nothing but a bitch session, count me out."

After several minutes, McCann noticed that two attendees, both first-year student s according to their name badges, expressed the greatest understanding of the likely mission of the fledgling organization. One of them, a nerdy-looking guy who said his name was Perry something-or-other, offered to take names and dorm numbers and arrange the next meeting.

As the meeting was breaking up, the student named Perry stood in the doorway talking with the other guy McCann had singled out. When McCann approached the exit, the second student asked him to stay behind for a few minutes. It was then that McCann learned the identities of the two students who were to become his co-conspirators, during good times and bad, throughout the next four years.

By reading nametags, McCann learned that the nerdy guy was named Perry Stockton. It became immediately apparent that Stockton's innocent-looking appearance made him the perfect front man for an organization that might be taking questionable actions to promote change on campus.

When McCann read the second guy's nametag he was surprised to see that it simply read, "Titan," without any mention of a surname. Never one to avoid a challenge, McCann immediately entered Titan's personal space. To his surprise, Titan did not retreat from McCann's threatened confrontation. Instead, he actually moved closer to

McCann and drew Stockton toward them.

"What the hell does Titan mean?" McCann asked the smaller, but athletic- looking man.

Placing his right hand on the chest of his sport coat, Titan replied, "I'm Titan, and that's all you need to know for right now. And, what's with you and the black trench coat?" he chided the larger man. "You going to a funeral or something?"

"Nah, it's just my thing," McCann replied.

Titan quickly returned to the subject at hand—the new organization. "It's obvious that the three of us are going to need to assume leadership of the SCC if it's going to accomplish anything meaningful. I've got an unlimited number of ideas on how to proceed, but I don't want 'The Man' to ever know who I am."

"By 'The Man' I take it you mean the administration," Stockton said.

"The president, the deans, the cops, the press, or anyone else," Titan replied. "You two will help lead the SCC. I'll be working side-by-side with you, but you'll be the public faces of the organization."

What Titan did not tell the pair was that they would be leading an organization that constantly butted heads with authority, while attracting considerable media attention, as well as both admiration and scorn on the part of other college students. Stockton would later admonish himself for lacking the guile to question Titan's long-term motivation. And, by the time Stockton realized what he'd let himself in for, both McCann and he were too deeply committed to turn back.

For the first three years of working together, the three men got along reasonably well. Titan trusted Stockton's reliability and attention to detail. McCann could be unreliable, but his unbridled passion was an important component of the fledgling campus protest movement. Much time was spent together planning, then spending casual time with their girlfriends. The six of them joked that they were the only ones who shared two secrets: Titan's real name and the technique of avoiding attention before each unruly SCC event was about to take place.

Relationships among the three men deteriorated measurably toward the end of their senior year. Titan was encouraging the others to take steps to cement the SCC's legacy permanently. His solution for doing this was a gradual escalation of vandalism that called attention to their cause. While McCann was completely supportive of the idea of acting as a modern day Robin Hood, as he labeled it, Stockton was concerned about innocents being injured or worse. Always one step ahead of his two lieutenants, Titan began to leverage the situation as a test of their loyalty—to him. Soon, the more aggressive McCann was using his physical advantage to humiliate Stockton in the presence of Titan and the three girlfriends. Were he more mature, Stockton would have seen this as the appropriate opportunity to leave the SCC. Instead, he decided to impress Titan by escalating the nature of the organization's next big protest. It was a decision he would regret for the rest of his life.

Chapter 19

Tyler McCann was sitting in his office overlooking Boston's iconic Faneuil Hall when his cell phone rang. The caller was someone he recognized, but hadn't thought about for decades. McCann wasn't overjoyed to hear the voice on the other end.

"You want me to meet you in Dover later today? That's not a hell of a lot of notice."

But the caller had been persistent, promising to make it worth McCann's while if he showed up.

So, McCann packed an overnight bag and, on the same day that Perry Stockton took a bus into Dover, the big man headed north in his vintage Lincoln Continental.

※※※※※※

When Joey Swift returned to his apartment following the meeting with the investigators, he flopped onto his second-hand leather Lazy Boy. As he sat there sipping an alcohol-free beer, Swift began to review what had transpired since Perry Stockton's arrival.

He recalled the look on Stockton's face as he approached their meeting place at the canoe launch. Stockton's cheeks were red and there was fear in his expression and body language. Following a brief embrace, Stockton had continuously looked up and down the pathway in Henry Law Park.

When Swift questioned Stockton about what was troubling him, his friend had not really answered. However, it hadn't taken a genius to comprehend who put such a fright in his old friend. Clearly, Stockton believed he'd seen Tyler McCann, his personal nemesis from their university days.

While pretending that he was looking for a canoe rental patron, Swift had carefully scanned the park in search of McCann. He might have gotten a brief glimpse of a tall man dressed in a long black trench coat, but couldn't swear to it. Beside that, when Swift looked again, the man had disappeared into the crowd along the riverbank.

Chapter 20

On the evening of Perry Stockton's death, Tyler McCann was in a rush to leave Dover. Driving south along the Spaulding Turnpike, McCann was distraught that he'd failed to have a civil discussion with Stockton.

"If only that wuss had given me a chance to talk," he lamented. Now, there was only one thing to do; and that necessitated this trip to downtown Portsmouth.

McCann loved nearly everything about Portsmouth—its working seaport, locally owned specialty shops and restaurants, engaging outdoor activities, vibrant nightlife, fascinating cultural history, and local character.

He arranged to stay overnight at a friend's small hotel located within walking distance of the historic downtown area. But, with the earlier frustration in Dover still on his mind, McCann wasn't ready to settle in for the night. Leaving his car in the Spare Spott parking area, he walked up Chapel Street, and crossed Bow Street before entering a favorite watering hole, the Old Ferry Landing. McCann smiled as he saw the familiar dark brown, staggered cedar shake shingles offset by the bar's matching red door and awning. He loved the atmosphere of the place, beginning with the sign on the roof showing a full mug of beer.

McCann entered and walked past the long, narrow pine bar, heading to one of the outdoor seats facing the Piscataqua River's Old Harbour. A cute waitress, young enough to be McCann's daughter, took his order of a Seadog Blueberry Wheat on tap with a bag of pretzels. He sat looking at the view of two bridges connecting Portsmouth to the neighboring town of Kittery, Maine, and was beginning to relax when he heard his cell phone ring.

"Someone wants to meet with you," the now familiar female voice was barely audible over the din of the bar crowd. "You'll get another phone call."

There was no mistaking who the caller was and whose message she was delivering. Now too agitated to remain on the outside deck, McCann walked to his car and headed directly to the hotel room.

After spending a sleepless night, he arose, showered, and went looking for a good cup of coffee and a copy of the *Portsmouth Herald*. Leaving his car in the hotel parking lot, McCann walked the six blocks to a place called the Book and Bar on Pleasant Street. Entering the granite-faced building, he stopped at the bar where he purchased a cup of black Sumatran coffee, before sitting in a comfortable-looking captain's chair at a small round table. With the smell of the strong coffee brew tantalizing his nostrils, McCann began to scan the front page of the newspaper. His expression changed immediately when he read the headline: "Former UNH student found murdered in Downtown Dover."

McCann continued to sip his coffee as he read the entire two-page description of what transpired the previous evening. He was showing remarkable constraint until he saw a place in the article that read, "Police have an all-points bulletin for two other UNH alumni, Portia DeLisle of Dover and Tyler McCann of Boston." Having read this, McCann stood up slowly, so as not to attract attention, and walked toward the door without donning his black trench coat.

Chapter 21

Immediately after breakfast, Lieutenant Bendix sat in the back room of the Dover Brickhouse with her ever-present laptop on the table in front of her. Dominic Riccio had given the investigative team permission to use the room in his restaurant as investigation-central for the case.

"Perry was my good friend; he was one in a million. So, anything I can do, just let me know," Riccio had told Kary.

Soon joining Bendix were Kary, Norton, Garrison and two of Stockton's UNH friends—Monica Waters and Joey Swift. Bendix had obtained copies of some CCTV footage from the previous afternoon and evening and, with Riccio's permission, the video was projected onto a 70-inch television monitor in the back room.

Kary had requested the presence of Waters and Swift, hoping that one or both of them could recognize people depicted in the video. The first video they examined was taken from a camera mounted above Henry Law Park and pointing south along the bank of the Cochecho River. Just as Perry Stockton appeared in the video, Swift called to Bendix and asked her to freeze the frame.

With the video stopped, Swift left his chair and walked toward the television screen.

"That's Perry; I'm sure it's him." Asked to corroborate, Waters responded tearfully, "Yes, that's Perry."

At Kary's instruction, Bendix reversed the video for a full minute, then ran it forward at a slower speed. Soon, Kary stood up and pointed toward the screen.

"Look... right there... see how Stockton keeps looking over his shoulder. Now he's picked up his pace. Someone has him really spooked."

Everyone in the room had reached the same conclusion. Now Kary asked Bendix, "Is there some way to see whom he may have been looking at?"

"Unfortunately, there isn't a clear view, Commissioner. I've even checked to see if there were other CCTV units in the area. I'm afraid this is the only one."

As they slowly reversed the video, Swift leaped from his chair.

"There... right there, Lieutenant," he cried out to Bendix. With the image frozen and made as clear as possible, a tall man wearing a dark trench coat was barely visible at the top left corner of the screen. Within two seconds, the man turned on his heels and speedily walked away. His body language suggested he was frustrated or disappointed.

"It seems something annoyed him," Kary said to the others, "because he sure left the area in a hurry."

"He does look a lot like my memories of Tyler McCann," Swift told them. "He's certainly tall enough; and McCann always wore that trench coat, even on sunny days."

"But, you can't be absolutely sure, can you?" Kary asked him.

Swift felt about 70 percent sure, but that wasn't enough.

"This creates a dilemma," Kary looked broodingly at the others. "Without better visual proof, we have no solid evidence that McCann was even in Dover yesterday, much less in a position to murder Perry Stockton."

"I wish the news were better, Commissioner," Bendix told him. "However, I do have two other videos that could help us a lot."

Minutes later, Bendix had loaded the CCTV coverage taken by a camera mounted on the roof of Lexie's Restaurant, directly across the river from where Stockton was murdered.

"Unfortunately, there's good news and bad news here," she told the others.

"Of course there is," Norton—ever the skeptic—replied.

"It seems really well-positioned," Kary said to Bendix. "What's the bad news?"

"The camera rotates one hundred and eighty degrees. So, we don't have everything we would have, had the camera remained focused on the area where Stockton was killed. Here, I'll show you what I mean," she continued.

The group watched as they saw Stockton walking from west to east along the south bank where the river meanders.

Swift pointed, "It looks like he was heading to meet me near the canoe launch. Now I see why he never made it."

That comment made Waters' tears start to flow all over again.

The group watched as a tall man wearing a dark broad-brimmed hat and a long black trench coat slowly approached Stockton from behind. Unfortunately, just as he appeared ready to grab Stockton, the camera rotated, leaving the two men out of view. By the time the camera returned to its original orientation, Stockton lay face up on the fish ladder, and his assailant was walking at a surprisingly slow pace south toward a nearby parking lot.

"This certainly corroborates Mrs. Thomas' testimony," Kary told the others.

However, something about Stockton's attacker left Kary uncomfortable.

Bendix had seen that expression before. Kary had powers of observation and deduction that few others shared, and she learned to trust them.

"What's going on in that head of yours, Commissioner?" she asked him.

"It may be nothing," he replied; "but there's something about the two images of the guy in the trench coat that we've looked at," he replied. "Perhaps I'm just grasping at straws."

Neither Garrison nor Norton was convinced; but Bendix, who possessed a mind that rivaled Kary's wasn't about to dismiss the commissioner's concerns.

Needing to move on, Kary asked Bendix if there was other CCTV footage to examine.

"As a matter of fact, I think you'll find this next segment very interesting," she replied.

As the video continued, they could see a woman standing near a crosswalk where she had an excellent view of the murder that just transpired. She may have been witness to the entire incident, yet exhibited none of the hysterics Mrs. Thomas had shown. At one point, she dropped a lit cigarette onto the ground. Next, she snuffed it out with the toe of a high-heeled dress shoe, then called someone on her cell phone. With that accomplished, she turned away from Central Avenue and walked toward the Dover Brickhouse.

"What's the time on this video?" Kary asked Bendix.

"It's 7 p.m., Commissioner."

"Are you thinking what I am, Lieutenant?" Kary asked her.

"I'm way ahead of you, sir. There's a CCTV camera mounted on the roof of Mr. Riccio's restaurant. I figured she might have headed this way, so I just downloaded the footage from last evening."

"Pure genius, Lieutenant," Kary told her. "You're going to spoil me."

A few minutes later, Bendix played the footage from the video camera mounted on the Dover Brickhouse's roof. Very soon, a woman dressed exactly like the person in the previous video appeared on camera. The woman's pointed dress shoes were visible before her face came into the light.

"Oh, no!" Monica Waters cried out. "It can't be." Before anyone could question her outburst, Waters blurted, "That's Portia DeLisle!"

Chapter 22

McCann left the Book and Bar, turned right and began walking as fast as his legs would carry him down Pleasant Street. He turned right when he reached the corner of Court Street. His intended destination was the main office of the Black Heritage Trail of New Hampshire at 222 Court St.

Because of McCann's love and respect for his late girlfriend, Honor Pemberton, he had kept abreast of the organization's attempt to tell the story of how African-Americans contribute to the nation's culture, in the face of efforts to subvert their acceptance. He had promised himself to visit with the woman who might have become his mother-in-law—if only things had been different.

Arriving out of breath, McCann paused a minute before entering the green two-story clapboard building.

"What the hell am I doing here?" he admonished himself. "Her mother probably won't even speak to me."

The 'she' to whom McCann referred was Helen Pemberton, mother of McCann's late UNH girlfriend, Honor Pemberton. Back in the days when McCann and Honor were dating, Mrs. Pemberton had exhibited mixed feelings toward him. At the top of her list of concerns was the fact that McCann was a big white guy who presented a considerable contrast to Honor's rich brown skin tone. Secondly, McCann appeared to carry a great deal of angst. He had what Mrs. Pemberton called a chip the size of a melon on his shoulder. Finally, there was the issue of the Students for Complete Change. Mrs. Pemberton feared what that association might do to her daughter's delicate psyche, a concern that proved to be on target.

McCann entered the building through a large, brown-stained wooden door. He was greeted in the lobby by a gray-haired African American woman wearing a nametag that read, 'Tasha'. Tasha, a woman about McCann's age, flashed a friendly smile at the tall white visitor and asked if she could help him.

"I hope so, but possibly not," he replied hesitantly. "I'm here looking for a woman who used to work here. Her name is Helen Pemberton."

"Oh she still works here, all right. We're gonna have to haul her out of here on a stretcher, because that woman isn't ever gonna retire."

Tasha told McCann to remain by the front desk while she looked for Mrs. Pemberton. After a few minutes, Tasha returned to the lobby in the company of an elegant woman who appeared far younger than the age McCann suspected she was.

"How can I help you, sir?" she asked while staring at him for some kind of recognition. Within less than a minute, McCann's face registered with her.

"Tyler? Is that you?"

McCann could barely speak, such were the emotions he was feeling. "Yes, Mrs. Pemberton, it's me. I've come to ask for your forgiveness."

The elderly woman could have sent McCann on his way, but that would have gone against every lesson she'd learned while growing up in rural Virginia. Instead, she led him to a back room, so the two of them could have some privacy. Once McCann had entered, Mrs. Pemberton closed the door quietly and directed him to a faded leather loveseat across from her desk.

"I expected you to visit, Tyler, but that was 30 years ago. When you didn't come, I wondered whether you really cared about my little girl."

McCann's eyes immediately began to tear.

"Care? Yes, I cared. In fact, I never loved anyone before I met Honor and haven't since. I know people refer to someone as the love of their life; but she really was."

"So, you're not married?"

McCann shook his head no.

"And you never have been?"

His response was the same.

"Then, why didn't you visit Honor's sisters and me?"

McCann's eyes continued to tear. That was the last thing he wanted to do in front of the elderly woman. "I didn't come because I'm a coward."

"I don't believe that for an instant, Tyler. Honor didn't talk much about the university and that protest group you both belonged to; but I know she was proud that you were such a strong leader."

"I was an asshole with a big mouth," he replied too quickly, then apologized for the language he'd used. "The truth is, when I heard that Honor had died in Iraq, I cried like a baby for a month or more… non-stop. Then, when I finally stopped crying, I became a stinking drunk. I lost everything: my job, my apartment, my car. Hell, I even lost the respect of my mother, may her soul rest in peace. It took almost 10 years before I started leading a stable existence. The truth is, I'm still not in great shape."

"I'm sorry you've gone through all that," she told him. Then Mrs. Pemberton fixed her gaze on McCann. "But, now that you're here, there are answers to questions I've been waiting to hear."

McCann could feel a tightening in his stomach; his breathing felt forced. His instinct was to flee, but he knew that Mrs. Pemberton deserved those answers.

"When my Honor finished her education at UNH, she should have been the happiest woman on the planet. After all, she was the first in our family to receive a college degree. But, the daughter who returned home from college was not the same person I sent there. She walked through my door with a distant look on her face. At first, I thought the two of you had a falling out, and she was suffering from a breakup."

"If only that were true," McCann said. "I'd never want to lose Honor; but that would have been far better than what happened to both of us." Even after 30 years, McCann was oozing guilt and despair through every pore.

Chapter 23

Portia DeLisle sat alone in a room at the Sheraton Portsmouth Harborside Hotel that was registered to Richardson Wilcox. She stepped out onto the room's private deck, allowing her eyes to take in the panoramic view. To the left, she could see the working harbor. Straight ahead she viewed the beautiful brick buildings on Market Street and the formidable steeple of North Church. It was a gorgeous late afternoon; however, despite the presence of numerous colorful watercraft, from tugboats to pleasure yachts, DeLisle's mind was elsewhere.

There was plenty to think about. On the positive side, DeLisle was in the company of Richie, a man whose attention she had coveted for years. And what better time to be with him? If things worked out as he intended, his life—and hers—would be changed forever.

Unfortunately, things weren't that simple. She had lied to her best friend, Monica Waters. Even worse, DeLisle had spied on a former UNH guy, Perry Stockton. Back in the day, Stockton had tried to date her but DeLisle knew her friend Monica was super attracted to him. No matter; Stockton never was interesting enough for her. Her taste ran toward mysterious and powerful men. The others need not apply.

That morning's newspaper confirmed what she already knew— Perry Stockton was dead. So, while that story wasn't a surprise, the notice in dark black lettering certainly was: she and Tyler McCann were people of interest; and both were being sought by law enforcement officials. Pairing her with McCann was almost more than she could stand. Back before he met Honor Pemberton, McCann had pursued her aggressively... too aggressively. He was drinking heavily at a college mixer, at which time he'd reached up her skirt. DeLisle still got a cold chill when she remembered the unwanted invasion and the hard slap that was her response.

Not surprisingly, DeLisle hated McCann from that moment on, even though he never showed the slightest interest in her again. That didn't matter; once Portia DeLisle developed a grudge, she hung onto it forever. So, when DeLisle was asked to make a surreptitious phone call to lure McCann up to Dover, she did so without questioning the potential consequences.

It was while sitting alone in Wilcox's room that DeLisle made a costly mistake: she ordered room service.

Chapter 24

As his meeting with Mrs. Pemberton continued, McCann experienced a wave of emotions. His mood went from sad to irritated, before finally arriving at a sense of calm he hadn't felt in decades. However, not until McCann bared his soul to the elderly woman.

"Tyler, I've been waiting a long time to learn the circumstances surrounding my beautiful Honor's complete change during the last months of her life. What was so terrible that it caused my daughter to wear a military uniform, something she never considered doing."

McCann had no desire to discuss something that was so terribly painful to him. Nevertheless, he owed it to this beautiful human being to tell her the truth.

"Everything happened because we were so wrapped up in that damned group," he began.

"You're talking about the Students for Complete Change that Honor and you joined?" she questioned him.

"We did more than join, Mrs. Pemberton. Six of us ran the SCC."

"Six of you? Are you talking about Perry Stockton and his friends?"

"That's right. Three of us guys and our girlfriends were the leaders. Stockton and I were the public faces of the SCC, but it was really another student named Titan who ran the whole show."

"Just who was this man Titan? My Honor mentioned him once in my presence, but when I asked her about him, she went mum. I might as well have been talking to the Statue of Liberty."

Just as her daughter had done decades earlier, McCann avoided the topic of Titan's identity. It was an agreement he, Stockton, and the three college women had promised to keep. However, he began to set out the circumstances of that horrible afternoon during the final month of their senior year at UNH.

"Titan was sort of like UNH's Napoleon Bonaparte," McCann told her.

"I don't understand."

"He was a little guy... half a foot shorter than Stockton and eight inches less than my height," McCann told her. "But, he was full of confidence; he had a kind of swagger. And Stockton and I looked up to him." He paused, then said, "I'll tell you something I never told anyone else."

"What's that?" she asked.

"I was kind of afraid of Titan. He obviously came from a wealthy family, wore really nice clothes, and always had money, lots of money."

"Money for what?"

"Two weeks before we graduated, Titan told his girlfriend Iris to have us meet him in a courtyard outside the student union. None of us ever refused Titan; so we were all there."

"What was so special about that meeting?" Mrs. Pemberton asked.

"Titan took a photocopy from the small leather briefcase he always carried. I couldn't believe what he was showing us."

"Why… what was it?"

"It was a picture of a small bomb he had someone make. He told us that the bomb needed to be planted in Thompson Hall the following Sunday. He said there was nothing to worry about; it would be ready to detonate. All we'd need to do is flip a small red switch, then get the hell out of there."

"And you agreed to do that?" she was astounded. "Oh, Tyler!"

"Titan was a really smart guy. He could have been a psychologist. Looking back, he was playing Stockton and me off one another. It must have all been part of his master plan."

"I don't follow; what do you mean?" Mrs. Pemberton asked him.

"It was like this. Stockton and I wanted to be the number one guy in Titan's eyes. So, each of us, in our own way, tried to make himself look like the better man, even if it meant tearing the other one down."

"So then, what did all of this have to do with the bomb?"

"Titan told Stockton and me that we needed to place the bomb in Thompson Hall together. He didn't trust anyone else. And, he said that our girlfriends should be there to serve as lookouts."

"That son of a bitch!" Mrs. Pemberton cursed aloud. Then catching herself, she added, "I'm sorry, Tyler; I haven't sworn like that since Honor's funeral."

Tyler barely noticed her outburst. He was transformed to a time when he was considerably younger, and susceptible to the will of another college senior.

"Things might have been different if it weren't for that chicken, Stockton."

"Do you mean the explosion wouldn't have happened?" Pemberton asked.

"No. What I mean is Honor wouldn't have been anywhere near the building. I was planning to make her go back to the dorm with Sabrina, Stockton's girlfriend. I just needed Stockton to keep an eye on the entrance to the building and warn me if anyone was coming."

"Are you saying that he didn't do that?"

"That's right. At the last minute he couldn't go through with it. He said this was way beyond anything he'd signed up for. Before I could convince him, he and Sabrina left the building. To my dying day, I'll hate myself for insisting that Honor stay with me until the bomb was activated."

Mrs. Pemberton told McCann that she remembered the reports on the explosion. "It was a Sunday, correct? Wasn't the building usually empty on the Lord's day?"

"Usually, yes. But Dr. Bell, one of the deans, decided to go in to be certain our senior class grades were in order. Her office was right below where we'd planted the bomb. The explosion broke free a giant chunk of concrete. When the debris fell, it killed her instantly."

"And you all escaped arrest somehow, didn't you?"

"That's right. The cops didn't know anything about Titan and Iris. Stockton told the rest of us that Dr. Bell probably saw Sabrina and him leaving the building. But, they just kept walking."

"And neither of them thought to warn Honor and you that Dr. Bell was entering the building?"

"There was no way to do that," McCann replied. "None of us had cell phones back then. After we learned about the explosion and Dr. Bell's death, Honor absolutely freaked. She refused to talk to me again."

Mrs. Pemberton thought a minute. "I suppose you can't blame her for that. I doubt I could have lived with that on my conscience."

McCann agreed.

"Now Tyler, you need to tell someone about this. You owe it to Dr. Bell's family and to Honor to set the record straight," she told him.

Mrs. Pemberton excused herself briefly and went out to the lobby. When she returned it was with a copy of that day's newspaper in her hands.

"I presume you've seen today's newspaper?" she asked him.

"Yes I have, but..."

"Tyler, think about it. The police are looking for you and this woman, Portia DeLisle. They think you killed Perry Stockton."

"I swear to you, Mrs. Pemberton, I didn't touch Stockton. I received a phone call saying he was going up to UNH to tell authorities about what we did during senior year. So, I went up to Dover looking for him. But, I could never get him alone. Even though it frustrated the hell out of me, I decided to wait and consider my options."

"Well, it's obvious someone got him alone. Could his death have anything to do with the story you just told me?"

McCann thought about her question. "Maybe; but there's not many people around who even know this whole story. Honor and Iris are dead; Sabrina is in a sanitarium. Now Perry's gone, too. If the police find Portia DeLisle, she may know something."

By the time he rose to leave, McCann looked completely wrung out. It appeared to Mrs. Pemberton as though he hadn't been sleeping at night. He waited for the elderly woman to come from around from the other side of the desk. A small woman, she rested her head on his breastbone as the two hugged. Before leaving, McCann reached into the inside breast pocket of his black trench coat and removed a business size envelope.

"I'd like you to do something for me, please. Put this envelope where no one else can find it, and please don't open it yourself. In case anything happens to me, please see that it gets into the hands of the state's major crimes unit or the FBI. Then someone who thinks he's invincible is going to have a nasty surprise.

It was then, as McCann walked back toward his hotel room, that he received a text message: "Meet me at the wharf near Ceres Street, tomorrow, 6 a.m."

While McCann was uneasy about what this encounter would mean, he was curious in light of Perry Stockton's death. It was time to find out why,

after all these years, he was being pursued—and by whom.

Chapter 25

The call came to Stu Garrison's cell phone. As Sergeant Norton was walking passed him, Garrison grabbed Norton's shoulder and signaled for him to wait before rejoining the investigators' meeting.

Once Garrison hung up his phone, he stood there absorbing what the caller had just told him.

"What's going on, Captain?" Norton asked.

"That was the Portsmouth PD. They just fished Tyler McCann's body out of the Harbor."

"Holy shit! That really adds another dimension to this investigation," Norton told him.

"It certainly reroutes things," Garrison replied.

Once Kary and Bendix were apprised of the new development, the group agreed to head down to Portsmouth immediately. Garrison told Kary that he'd be contacting the FBI on the way south.

Upon arrival at Ceres Street, the investigators received a surprise. The Rockingham County coroner was on vacation. So he'd asked Isaac Pratt to fill in for him until the following week. That proved to be a break for Kary and the others, as Pratt was familiar with the events in Dover.

As Kary and Garrison approached, Pratt couldn't resist his typical patter.

"Gentlemen. If you wanted to meet again so soon, we could have met at Popovers, or one of the other great coffee joints in the city. There was no need for anything this rash," he said while pointing to the investigation tent that was set up along the wharf. A row of multi-story brick buildings loomed behind them, giving the setting an ominous feel.

Garrison was all business. "I'm presuming that this isn't a drowning, or you wouldn't have called us down here in the middle of the Dover investigation."

"You're correct, Captain," Pratt replied. "There are several things we learned right away." Signaling a local detective to hand Garrison the evidence bag, he continued. 'First, of all, we have confirmed that the victim's name is Tyler McCann, a 55-year-old man from Boston."

"There was no cell phone in the evidence bag. However, there was a receipt from the Hotel Portsmouth, a small lodging on Court Street."

"I'll have Lieutenant Bendix head over to the hotel in a few minutes, to see if she can recover McCann's phone, Stu," Kary told Garrison. "Can you grease the skids for her, so we don't have to go after a search warrant?"

Now, Pratt was ready to continue. "I'm estimating the time of death to be 6 a.m. And this was not a drowning incident."

"And you know this because…" Garrison began to question.

"As best I can tell without a full autopsy, there is no water in the victim's lungs. Therefore, he was dead before his body entered the harbor."

"Were there any witnesses?" Kary asked Pratt and a Portsmouth detective who was listening to the conversation.

They learned that there were no witnesses, owing to the early time in the morning when the incident occurred. However, CCTV had provided an interesting development.

Before heading over to the Hotel Portsmouth, Bendix opened her laptop. After instructions from the local detective, she was able to download the CCTV video. As Kary, Garrison and Bendix watched, they saw a tall man wearing a dark trench coat walking briskly toward the wharf near Ceres Street. As they were about to comment, the detective said, "I've seen this already. Please keep watching, Commissioner."

Within moments, a second tall man, also dressed in a dark trench coat, followed the first toward the wharf. Several minutes later, one of the men—and only one—walked away from the meeting spot.

"I knew it!" Kary exclaimed while lightly punching Garrison in the arm. "There were two men wearing trench coats up in Dover. Now the question is, 'why'?"

※※※※※※

The video supported a feeling Kary had all along. Now he couldn't resist hypothesizing about the means of death. "I suppose the next thing you're going to tell us is you found a puncture wound in his neck."

"You're every bit as smart as everyone has told me, Commissioner. Just like Perry Stockton, it appears Mr. McCann was stabbed in the vertebral artery, also with a long needle, an awl or icepick."

"So, once again, we are looking for either a person who is medically trained or a contract killer," Garrison said to the others.

"As we discussed earlier, I can't be absolutely sure without a full autopsy report. However, I can tell you that the ME's office in Concord confirmed that I was correct about Mr. Stockton's cause of death. And there's more," Pratt continued.

"More?" the other investigators asked in tandem.

"Yes, judging by the location of Perry Stockton's stab wound and the angle of thrust, I'd say his assailant was right handed and at least six feet tall."

"That would fit the description of our Mr. McCann over there," Garrison said. "Only, McCann certainly didn't kill himself."

"Also, he didn't meet the profile of a person with surgical skills," Kary added before turning to ask Pratt, "Can you tell us anything about the killer's height based on what you've seen here, Isaac?"

Pratt consulted his notes for a moment before responding. "Looking at the angle of thrust, I'd say Mr. McCann's killer was his height or nearly so. Of course, you realize that this is educated conjecture at this point."

"That's just great!" Garrison exclaimed with a wan smile. "So, we have some tall but skilled dude going around killing other tall people in their 50s who are visiting the state."

Kary smiled at Garrison's sarcastic comment.

"Well, we're not completely out at sea on this case, Stu. These two guys were about the same age; they knew one another; they attended UNH during the 1980s. And let's not forget that they were both involved somehow with a protest group called Students for Complete Change."

"It does make sense that the deaths are tied somehow to that student organization," Garrison replied.

"I'm convinced that the SCC, as they called themselves, is the common denominator in these murders. Unfortunately, with Stockton and McCann both dead, we're running out of people who can help us close the loop."

The loop was about to be squeezed a bit, however, when Garrison's cell phone rang. The conversation ended abruptly.

"Portia DeLisle has been found."

Chapter 26

Kary and Bendix rode over to the Sheraton Portsmouth Harborside Hotel in Garrison's state police car. For three decades, the Sheraton had been Portsmouth's premiere large-event property. Its four stories contained 180 guest rooms and more than 13,000 square feet of event space. As a result, the hotel served as a venue for everything from weddings, to tourism conferences, to political confabs. On the day that the investigative team arrived at the Sheraton, the statewide Republican party caucus was meeting to select its nominees for the U.S. Senate and House of Representatives.

Garrison pulled through the main entranceway and parked his car next to the one Sergeant Norton had been driving. As they entered the lobby, the three investigators walked past the registration desk and spotted Norton standing half way up a set of stairs leading to the hotel's large mezzanine.

"So, where is Ms. DeLisle, Sergeant?" Garrison asked.

"I'm not sure, but this gentleman knows," Norton replied while pointing to a thin, balding man dressed in kitchen whites, who stood nearby. "This is Jonathan Burke. He delivers room service to the third and fourth floors."

So as not to overwhelm Burke, Kary, and Garrison interviewed him alone. Burke told them that he had received a call late in the afternoon the previous day. His boss in the kitchen told him he had a delivery for Room 448. Jonathan liked making deliveries to that room because it was the largest suite in the hotel, the one frequently reserved for celebrities and political candidates. This was much more than a hotel room; it was more like a fancy condominium with a full kitchen and a master bedroom on its second floor.

"Are you certain that it was Ms. DeLisle whom you saw?" Garrison asked.

"Well, I wasn't at first, sir," Burke replied. "Something about her looked familiar. I've always had a good head for faces; and hers is a particularly pretty one. It wasn't until I got home last night and looked again at the front page of the *Portsmouth Herald*... that's when I was sure it was her. So, first thing this morning, I called the number listed in the paper."

"Have you seen her since?" Kary asked him.

"Oh no, sir. I wouldn't see her again unless she ordered more room service. And, she didn't do that while I was on duty."

Kary and Garrison took the elevator up to the fourth floor and waited in the hallway outside of room 448 for Bendix and Norton to arrive. When all four were together, Garrison knocked on the room door. There was no answer.

"This is the state police, Ms. DeLisle. Please open this door, or we'll be forced to use a passkey to enter."

The door to the room opened and the investigators found themselves face-to-face with a large man wearing kitchen whites who was pushing a service cart. As an experienced police officer, Norton quickly felt around the cart to determine whether a body was being smuggled away. He touched something solid, but too small to be a human being. So, the kitchen worker was allowed to pass.

A moment later, a fit-looking man in his fifties, dressed in an expensive suit, approached them from inside the room.

"Can I help you officers?" he asked.

"We're looking for Portia DeLisle," Garrison told the man. "May we speak to her?"

"I'm afraid you've missed Ms. DeLisle. She spent the night here, but left earlier this morning."

From behind Kary came the voice of Sergeant Norton. "I'm certain you wouldn't mind if we search for ourselves, would you?"

"As a matter of fact, I do mind. You don't know who I am, do you, Sergeant?" Before Norton could answer, the man replied, "My name is Richardson Wilcox, and I'm going to be your next U.S. Senator. However, right now I'm busy preparing to give a speech. So, unless you have a search warrant, I'm going to have to ask you to vacate the premises."

As the door closed, Norton had a sudden revelation. Without a word to the others, he ran toward the stairwell and disappeared through the doorway.

Chapter 27

What ensued was a race against time. Norton realized that the waiter had a two-minute head start. He hoped that the combination of his own police conditioning and pure grit, plus a large dose of luck, would enable him to catch the man.

Norton tore down the stairs, at times leaping the last several steps in hopes of saving valuable seconds. Ahead of Norton, the waiter had taken a leisurely trip with the cart down a guest elevator. As instructed in case he was being followed, he exited the elevator on the second floor, then switched to the nearby service elevator, with the intention of riding it directly to street level. Once there, he was to dispose of his cargo in one of the huge dumpsters near the loading dock behind the hotel. Unfortunately for the waiter, one of the line cooks had called the elevator, thereby causing it to stop briefly beside the main kitchen on the first floor.

When Norton exited the stairwell, he was running full steam. A compact, powerful man, a collision with a hotel patron would have been truly unfortunate for all concerned. Fortunately, most of the guests were sequestered in meeting rooms, so Norton continued until he spotted a state trooper standing next to the exit door. Norton recognized the trooper from a case the pair had worked on together.

Without excusing himself for interrupting the trooper's conversation, he called out, "Harry, please come with me… right now."

Tossing the trooper his car keys, Norton asked the man to drive him somewhere quickly. The trooper immediately sensed that this was an emergency. So, without a word, he ran ahead of Norton and the pair jumped into Norton's waiting police car.

"Where to, Bob?" he asked Norton.

"Just drive me around to the loading dock. Take a right turn out of the driveway and head down Russell Street about 50 yards. I'm going to need to jump out of the vehicle as soon as we get there."

The two officers arrived at the loading dock just as the waiter was preparing to empty his load into a tall dumpster. On instinct, the other officer let out a single blast of the siren, freezing the man in the process.

As Norton jogged up the wide driveway, the waiter attempted to create an escape route by pushing the cart into Norton. In a single nimble move, Norton jumped out of the way and forcefully laid the man face-down in the service driveway.

As Norton was handcuffing the waiter, he spoke into the man's ear.

"Now, suppose you tell me who you are and what you were removing so urgently from the room upstairs."

The waiter explained to Norton that the occupant of room 448, a Mr. Wilcox, had instructed him to come up to his suite and wait in the entry while his lady friend, the pretty woman with the black hair, placed something into the cart.

"So, you definitely saw a woman in the suite with the man who came to the door?" Norton questioned him.

The waiter indicated that there was a woman in the room.

"Did you ever see what you were removing from the suite?" Norton asked him.

"No, I promise, Sergeant. I was told that everything was wrapped up and I was to leave it that way. My instructions were to throw everything away... coverings and all... without looking at them."

"And that's exactly what you did." Norton made no effort to hide the scorn he was feeling.

"Yes, sir. The guy offered me a $100 tip. That's a lot of money for a working stiff with four kids. Besides that, I could tell once I started wheeling the cart that there wasn't no body or nothing inside. It wasn't heavy enough. So, I figured, what the hell..."

Leaving the waiter in the hands of the other officer, Norton removed a sheet that was covering the contents in the cart. He slowly removed the towels that covered each item. As he worked, Norton used his cell phone to photograph each item. When he finished, Norton turned toward the other officer and did a fist pump as he exclaimed, "Yes!"

Norton couldn't wait to share what he'd learned with Kary and the others.

"This next conversation with Mr. Richardson Wilcox should be a gem," Kary replied.

Chapter 28

When Richardson Wilcox answered the knock on the door of room 448, he received quite a surprise. Instead of four law enforcement personnel standing outside in the hallway, there were seven.

Garrison did the introductions of Kary, Bendix, Norton, Sergeant Hill from Dover, the police detective who assisted them on the wharf in Portsmouth, and—saving the best for last—Agent Ponds from the FBI.

Wilcox was incredulous. "What the hell is the meaning of this?" he demanded. "This is an important day for me, and I simply won't be interrupted. As I told you earlier, unless you have a warrant, I'm not going to let you inside this room."

Kary, removing his fedora, stepped to the front of the group.

"You may want to rethink that stance, Mr. Wilcox. We have evidence that you and your house guest, Ms. DeLisle, have committed two felonies within the past 48 hours," he began.

Wilcox attempted to close the door in Kary's face, but his effort was blocked, courtesy of Sergeant Norton's right boot.

"Now, as I was saying before you rudely interrupted me," Kary continued, "either you admit us to your room or we will be obliged to arrest you and notify your fellow party members about the circumstances. That certainly won't do much to help your senatorial aspirations, sir."

"This is blackmail. I'll have all of your badges for this," Wilcox blustered.

"I'm willing to chance that," Kary replied. "Also, I must advise you that a warrant to enter these premises has been petitioned. And, I can assure you that we won't be going anywhere until it arrives. So, why don't you play nice and allow us to enter? And, in the meantime, how about inviting Ms. DeLisle to join us."

Wilcox made no effort to hand over DeLisle, so Kary told Bendix and Hill, the only two women in the group, to please locate and interview her separately.

※※※※※※

After a careful search of Wilcox's suite, Bendix and Hill found evidence of DeLisle's presence in the form of clothing and makeup. However, she was nowhere to be seen inside the condo. At Bendix's direction, Hill went out onto the deck and was about to admit defeat when she noticed a large cabinet for storing food and other incidentals during private outdoor events. She signaled to Bendix and the two women simultaneously yanked open the two doors as DeLisle spilled out onto the deck.

"I just love a game of hide and seek, don't you, Lieutenant?" Hill couldn't resist.

"I certainly do, Detective Sergeant," Bendix responded with a wry grin on her face. "The only thing is, Ms. DeLisle, you just lost the game."

While the five male officers interviewed Wilcox, Bendix and Hill demanded DeLisle provide them with answers.

※※※※※※

Kary took the lead interrogating Richardson Wilcox.

"Stand up for a minute, Mr. Wilcox."

Wilcox complied, but not before correcting Kary. "It's Doctor Wilcox, Commissioner."

"My apology, Dr. Wilcox. What kind of doctor are you?"

"I'm the head of vascular surgery at Dartmouth-Hitchcock Hospital," Wilcox replied.

The five officers shared a knowing look; however, Kary was just getting warmed up.

"I'd estimate your height at about five feet, eight inches, is that correct?" Kary deliberately overestimated the man's height.

Wilcox couldn't suppress his innate arrogance. "I hope that isn't the best you can do, Commissioner. I'm five feet six inches in my stocking feet."

"It must be tough being a shrub among the trees," Garrison couldn't resist.

"Not at all," Wilcox replied. "I'm about average height, and I stay very fit." Wilcox immediately regretted being baited into the last statement.

Now, Kary was ready to lower the boom. Removing a pair of men's shoes with six-to-eight inch heels and soles from the bag, he set them on the ground near the chair where Wilcox was now sitting.

"Then, perhaps you can tell me why you've ordered these shoes," Kary continued. All the while, he fixed a stern look at Wilcox.

Wilcox started to object, but Norton was having none of that.

"Those are yours all right, Wilcox. And the waiter you hired to dispose of them is in police custody," Norton attacked.

"That man must be lying. Those are not my shoes," he insisted.

"Please, Mr. Wilcox. Don't insult me. Perhaps you'd like to try them on for us," Kary continued. "In fact, the shoes are only part of your special outfit, aren't they?"

As Kary said this, he removed a long, black trench coat from the same evidence bag. "Here's the rest of your costume," he continued. "Now do you recognize everything?"

"I certainly do not. And this is an outrage. I want my lawyer brought here right now!"

"You don't get to see a lawyer unless we arrest you, Wilcox," Norton told him. "Why don't you just confess, and we'll ask your lawyer to join us."

Chapter 29

Things were going a bit more smoothly out on the deck, where Bendix and Hill were interviewing Portia DeLisle. Unlike the haughty front that Wilcox was presenting, DeLisle was clearly frightened by Bendix's suggestion that she might be tried as an accessory for first-degree murder.

"Murder? Oh, no. I'm no murderer," DeLisle cried.

"You didn't kill anyone yourself, but we suspect that you helped the murderer in the other room do his dirty work."

Bendix then asked DeLisle to give them her phone. "I have a feeling we're going to find all of the evidence we need to link you to the deaths of Perry Stockton and Tyler McCann."

"Tyler McCann is dead?!" DeLisle appeared genuinely shocked by that news. "Look, I hated Tyler back in our UNH days. He sexually assaulted me, and acted like it was his right to do so. I've loathed him since then, but we hadn't been anywhere near one another for decades."

Bendix remained cool and focused. "We'll see what your telephone records have to say about that. Also, for your information, we've already had a look at Tyler McCann's phone."

Suddenly, DeLisle burst into tears, sobbing uncontrollably. After several minutes passed, she admitted to Bendix and Hill that she had been caught in something that was too big for her to handle. "I'll tell you everything I know," she promised the two officers.

"This whole thing began a couple of days ago when my friend called me on the telephone to make dinner arrangements."

"You're talking about Monica Walters," Hill interrupted. "We've been interviewing her."

Bendix shot Hill a look that clearly indicated she should not interrupt DeLisle again.

DeLisle blew her nose into a handkerchief before continuing. "While Monica and I were talking, she told me that Perry Stockton was coming to visit Monica and a couple of other UNH friends, then was going to head up north to Durham the next day. She told me he was planning to talk to some people about the group that Tyler and he led back in the 80s."

This time it was Bendix who interrupted DeLisle. "The Students for Complete Change. Did Monica Waters tell you Stockton was going up to Durham to confess?" Bendix asked her.

Now DeLisle's voice was barely above a murmur. "Yes, she did."

"So, tell us what you did next."

"My boyfriend, Richie Wilcox, was a student at UNH back in those days. I figured he'd be interested in what Perry was planning to do. So, I called him."

"And was he interested?"

"It's always hard to tell what's going through Richie's mind. He plays his cards close to the vest, if you know what I mean. He didn't say anything for almost a minute. But then, he asked me to do the strangest thing."

"What was that?"

"He asked me to call Tyler McCann and tell him what Perry was planning to do. He said Tyler would have a personal interest in Perry's visit to our alma mater."

"How did you react?"

"I protested, of course. I told Richie that he knew full well how much I hate Tyler. But Richie insisted. He told me to call Tyler without identifying myself. I was to say I was passing along a message from Richardson Wilcox. Then I was to tell him that Perry Stockton was coming to Dover, would be spending the night, then heading over to UNH to talk with authorities in the morning. I was told to say that Richardson Wilcox says Tyler should come to Dover and persuade Perry not to go up to campus."

"Why call McCann at all?" Bendix asked.

"Because Perry was afraid of Tyler. So, Richie thought Tyler could dissuade Perry from going up to campus," DeLisle replied.

Having finished this part of the story, she asked Bendix and Hill if she was finished.

"Only if there aren't any other phone calls or actions on your part that we'll be interested in learning about," Bendix replied.

"Look, Lieutenant. I love Richie Wilcox. I met him at UNH but had to wait decades for him to show an interest in me. So, when Richie called and told me that I needed to follow Perry, I figured it must be important to his campaign or something."

Bendix was dubious about DeLisle's explanation, but allowed her to continue.

"I was to wait until Perry finished visiting Monica at the Children's Museum and tail him. So, when he went to the Dover Brickhouse, I went inside and was able to get a table next to where Perry and Dominic Riccio, the owner, were sitting. I'm sure neither of them recognized me. I may still look pretty good for my age, but it's been 30 years. I heard them talking about the old days at UNH and figured I should call

Richie right away and let him know."

DeLisle hung her head. "I guess I figured Richie would tell Tyler what was going on and let him know where to find Perry."

"What did you do next?"

"I went outside and smoked a cigarette, waiting for Perry to leave. I followed him toward the river, then stayed back near central Avenue. I was still standing there when Tyler grabbed Perry from behind and pushed him down into the fish ladder."

Given DeLisle's role in luring McCann to Dover, it was understandable that she felt certain that the big man had killed Stockton. Bendix wasn't so sure.

"If you were so sure it was McCann who killed Stockton, why didn't you call the police?"

"Because I felt responsible for both Perry and Tyler being there. All I wanted to do was get the hell away. So I called Richie. His phone rang for a long time. When he answered, I told him that Perry was dead. He told me where I should wait, then came and picked me up and we drove right down here to Portsmouth."

"Was that the last phone call?" Bendix asked.

"No, Richie was worried that Tyler was going to get us all into trouble. So, he asked me to call Tyler and tell him to be on the wharf near Ceres Street early in the morning."

"And, did you make that call?"

Again, DeLisle burst into tears. "Yes, I did. But, I swear to you on my mother's life, I had no idea that anything was going to happen to Tyler."

As DeLisle stood up to go back inside of the suite, a thought occurred to Bendix.

"I have one other question, Ms. DeLisle. Tell me again how long you have known Mr. Wilcox."

"More than 30 years. I dated him briefly at UNH back in the 1980s."

Now Bendix's keen mind was in overdrive. "Were you a member of the Students for Complete Change back then? Is that how you knew Perry Stockton and Tyler McCann?"

DeLisle's tears started to flow again. But she steeled herself. "No, I had nothing to do with the SCC; but, like most people at the school, I knew they existed."

Chapter 30

Kary made a phone call that he had been dreading. When the governor was on the line, Kary informed him of the investigative team's suspicions about Richardson Wilcox.

"Let me get this straight, Kary. You're telling me that a man who is favored to be the next Republican nominee for U.S. Senate is a cold-blooded murderer. How certain are you?"

"I'd say 90 percent at this juncture, sir. We're looking for one more significant piece of evidence before we're ready to charge him."

"So, what are you looking for from me?"

"Well, sir, this is a political hot potato. If we arrest him and he's exonerated, the embarrassment would be immeasurable. However, if we leave him alone and he's formally charged, that won't look good either."

The governor sighed and said nothing for a full minute. "I hired you because I believe in your instincts, Kary. To date, you haven't let me down. So, what does that gut of yours tell you?"

"I have an unusual solution, Governor. It's one that covers all of our asses, including Mr. Wilcox and the political party."

That evening, to the surprise of Garrison and the other investigators, Richard Wilcox was permitted to appear before throngs of admirers and accept the nomination of the Republican caucus as its next candidate for U.S. Senate. After a 10-minute speech and a short round with well wishers, he told those assembled that he was not feeling well and needed to go upstairs to his suite. As Wilcox walked to the exit of the convention facility, he was immediately joined by two security personnel. Only, the two men who were escorting him were Capt. Stu Garrison and Sgt. Bob Norton.

※※※※※※

With Wilcox and DeLisle now ensconced in separate rooms on the third floor of the Sheraton Harborside, the investigative team moved into a small meeting room on the first floor of the property.

As was his modus operandi, Kary walked up to a white board at the front of the room. With the help of the others, he outlined the investigation:

1. Perry Stockton visits 3 friends in Dover; told them he plans a visit to UNH to confess to authorities
2. of girlfriends dead; 1 mentally incapacitated
3. During afternoon, tall man in black trench coat seen in vicinity of Stockton
4. Stockton is killed that evening along Cochecho River à witness says tall man in black trench coat seen leaving the area (was it McCann??)
5. Riccio felt certain that DeLisle was in his restaurant eavesdropping
6. McCann leaves for Portsmouth à purpose of visit there remains uncertain
7. Wilcox and DeLisle go to Sheraton Harborside for conference
8. DeLisle calls McCannà tells him to meet on Portsmouth wharf
9. 2nd tall man in dark trench coat follows McCann onto wharf
10. McCann's body found that a.m. floating in harbor
11. Same MO used to kill both Stockton and McCann
12. DeLisle admits to making phone calls at behest of Wilcox. Claims ignorance of their real purpose
13. Wilcox in possession of elevator shoes and long black trench coat
14. Wilcox is a vascular surgeon… definitely has necessary skill set
15. Is this enough to charge Wilcox with murder—*must find motivation*

The investigators were proceeding to argue the pros and cons of charging Wilcox, and possibly DeLisle, with murder in the first degree. Norton and Garrison were convinced that there was not enough solid evidence. Kary, with support from Bendix, reminded the others that there were two men in black trench coats.

"I'm thinking that Tyler McCann was set up. I think he was lured up to Dover, then purposely placed in a position where he'd be seen on CCTV. I believe that the real murderer intended all along to be seen on CCTV posing as McCann."

Norton still wasn't convinced. "I just don't think we have enough evidence to get a conviction on Wilcox. Why on earth would a candidate for U.S. Senate do that?"

"I agree that there's a problem finding a motive for Wilcox," Garrison added. "Although, he did have the elevator shoes and the trench coat."

"He can always claim that he was dressing up for a costume party," Norton argued.

This brought a groan from everyone in the room. "Then, why go through all the cloak and dagger to get rid of it?" Bendix reminded the others. "No, I think the shoes and coat are our strongest link between Wilcox and the murders."

"What about Portia DeLisle?" Norton asked.

"I tend to think Ms. DeLisle is a middle-age woman who was looking for love after a life of bad choices, but got played in the process," Kary told him.

Bendix squeezed Kary's shoulder in appreciation.

"I also think that Ms. DeLisle truly believed that it was Tyler McCann who murdered Perry Stockton," Kary continued. "DeLisle must have been wracked with guilt for having lured Stockton to his death."

Garrison was about to ask how the mysterious Titan fit into things, when his cell phone rang. He listened intently before instructing the caller to send someone to the meeting room.

When the door opened, an attractive 70-plus-year-old African-American woman entered. She explained that she was the mother of Tyler McCann's former girlfriend, Honor Pemberton. She told the team that Tyler McCann had visited her recently and left a sealed envelope. He made her promise to hang onto it unless something happened to him.

"I saw in this morning's *Herald* that Tyler's body was found in the harbor. As soon as I read that, I knew I had to find someone to give this to. That's why I'm here."

Garrison took the envelope from Mrs. Pemberton and thanked her. He opened it, and placed a single handwritten sheet on the table between Kary and him. The note described how Perry Stockton and Tyler McCann had been members of Students for Complete Change at UNH back during the 1980s. While they were the public face of the organization, the real leader of the group was a student calling himself, 'Titan.' It was Titan who orchestrated the bombing of Thompson Hall, which resulted in the death of a young administrator. Two days earlier, it was revealed to McCann that Stockton planned to inform the authorities about the organization. Only six people knew the identity of Titan—and the three women were no longer a threat to him. That left only Titan himself, plus Stockton and McCann.

"But, why after all of this time would this guy Titan care?" Norton asked.

By this time, Garrison had scanned the letter all the way to the bottom, and knew what McCann was telling them. He replied, "Remember that this is an election year."

"I get that; but why not just let sleeping dogs lie?" Norton asked.

It was left to Kary to fill in the final blank. "Richardson Wilcox was Titan. Wilcox's identity as Titan needed to remain buried if he was to become our next U.S. Senator; and, he was this close to being nominated. So, can you imagine what the news of his involvement in one of the state university's most infamous episodes would do to his political aspirations?"

Kary continued, "Monica Waters was going to drive Stockton up to UNH to confess about the bombing. After she told her best friend, Portia DeLisle, about the intended visit, we know that Ms. DeLisle innocently told her boyfriend, Wilcox, about the visit. Wilcox couldn't allow that to happen. I think he hoped that McCann could scare Stockton out of testifying. But, just in case, Wilcox was prepared to take matters into his own hands."

"You're talking about his disguise as a tall man in a black trench coat," Norton offered.

"That's right. Everyone who knew McCann was aware of his penchant for wearing a black trench coat... including the reticent leader of the SCC, Titan. But, fortunately for us, Wilcox had a hell of a time walking in those elevator shoes."

"Which is what made you suspicious that there were two men in black trench coats," Garrison commended Kary.

"But, why kill McCann?" Norton asked.

"Wilcox was a desperate man, Sergeant. He couldn't chance that McCann would keep his mouth shut once he learned that Stockton had been murdered," Kary replied.

"What's interesting is that Stockton might have taken the blame alone, without giving up the others' names," Norton offered.

Bendix waded in, "Also, we may well have charged McCann with killing Stockton. And Wilcox might have gotten off scot-free."

Suddenly, Kary broke out in a big grin. "I'll be certain to remind Titan about that the next time I talk with him. He needs a large dose of humility."

※※※※※※

Instead of spending the next six years as a lawmaker at the U.S. Capitol in Washington, Richardson Wilcox, AKA Titan, received a sentence of 25 years to life at the federal prison in Berlin, N.H. The district attorney was more lenient with Portia DeLisle. She pled guilty to the dual charge of fleeing from justice and aiding and abetting Wilcox to carry out two felonious acts. However, because she did not cross a state boundary and the judge felt that she was acting in ignorance, her sentence was reduced to 10 years in the N.H. Correctional Facility for Women.